P9-DGM-231

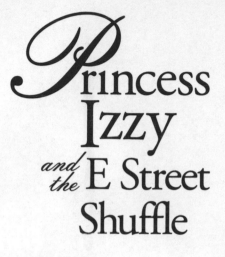

Princess Izzy *and* *the* E Street Shuffle

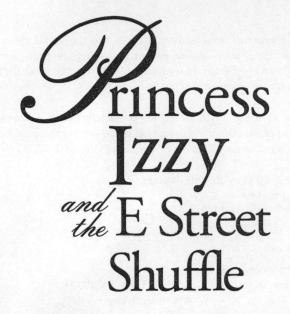

Princess Izzy and the E Street Shuffle

The Unlikely True Story of Isabella, Her Secret Adviser, Her Jealous Husband, and How It All Affected Me

BEVERLY BARTLETT

NEW YORK   BOSTON

5 Spot

Warner Books

Time Warner Book Group
1271 Avenue of the Americas, New York, NY 10020
Visit our Web site at www.twbookmark.com.

Printed in the United States of America

First Edition: March 2006
10 9 8 7 6 5 4 3 2 1

Library of Congress Cataloging-in-Publication Data
 Bartlett, Beverly.
   Princess Izzy and the E Street shuffle / Beverly Bartlett. — 1st ed.
      p. cm.
   ISBN 0-446-69559-9
   1. Young women—Fiction. 2. Automobile mechanics—Fiction.
3. Springsteen, Bruce—Influence—Fiction. I. Title.
   PS3602.A8394P75 2005
   813' .6—dc22
                                                    2005005035

Book design and text composition by Ellen Gleeson
Cover design: Brigid Pearson
Cover photo: Herman Estevez

To Jim and Simon

*A*cknowledgments

I first want to acknowledge the lifetime of encouragement and support that my parents, John and Ann Bartlett, have provided to me and my writing. From editing my earliest childhood efforts to giving me a laptop so I could write at the coffee shop, they have helped make it possible for me to pursue a dream.

My husband, Jim, not only encouraged me to write but practically insisted on it. He was brave enough to tell me what was horrible, and kind enough to say some things were good.

Katy and Jeff Yocom, Graham Shelby, Rebecca Barnes, Glenn Ow, and Elizabeth Bevarly also gave me valuable advice and feedback. Fran Ellers, Cynthia Eagles, and Kirsten Tagami spent countless hours of their otherwise well-spent youth helping me hone my royal punditry skills.

Finally, I want to thank my agent, Scott Hoffman, and my editor, Beth de Guzman, both of whom made this a much better book.

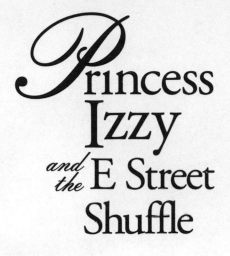

Princess Izzy and the E Street Shuffle

$\mathscr{P}$rologue

$\mathscr{T}$he press always hated it when she wore brown. It wasn't that it didn't look smashing on her. It did. Oh, it did. Brown captured the hazel tint in her eyes, gave a glow to her skin, made her hair look slightly brighter, fresher, more alive. "But how are we supposed to write about it?" Ethelbald Candeloro would often say, speaking for all the reporters on the royalty beat. "We can write a smart sentence about a princess in an electric-blue suit with platinum buttons. And we can write a sweet story about a princess in a sea-green ball gown with pearl detailing. And we can go gaga about a princess in red. But what the hell are we supposed to write about a princess in *brown*?"

That's how bronze became a chic fashion term during the height of her celebrity. But that is another story for another venue. I have not prepared a discussion on the princess's influence on hemlines or hats or any other aspect of haute couture. I raise the subject now only because I want to start the story of Isabella Cordage on the unseasonably cool October day, all those years ago, when she agreed to become Her Royal Highness the Princess of Gallagher.

From that day forward, the world would always note what Isabella wore. So it seems I should mention what she wore that day, before it mattered so, before she had professional advisers and complaining photographers and the biting commentary of a nation of so-called journalists.

On that day, she wore a brown wool sweater with a bright pink turtleneck that provided just a bit of color around her face. A wool skirt, also brown, barely reached her knees, and below that she wore brown tights. It was a simple, unexceptional outfit that she wore an awful lot back then. It was comfortable and versatile, and her mother had told her the color looked great on her. So that was what she wore the morning she went for a walk in the gardens of Glassidy Castle with His Royal Highness the Prince of Gallagher, who was commonly known as Prince Raphael and whom she had called Rafie ever since they were quite young.

And he asked her to marry him. And she said yes.

She never wore that outfit again. For several years, in fact, she didn't wear brown at all. People forget that. Her insistence on brown now, the press's disdain for it—these have become part of her legend. In researching this book, I discovered that after the day of her engagement, there was not a documented case of her wearing brown until five years into her marriage, on that infamous stormy morning . . . But now I'm getting hung up on fashion again. I apologize. I had merely wanted to mention that brown outfit she loved so much, the one she never wore again after accepting the proposal. Some people would read a lot into that. But not me. At least not yet. I never editorialize until the end. When you've seen all that I've seen and come to know the princess the way I've come to know her, you realize that things are not always the way they seem with her. Wait and see. That's been my motto. Wait and see.

Chapter 1

$\mathscr{A}$s far as he was concerned, the great tragedy in the otherwise comfortable life of His Royal Highness the Prince of Gallagher was that he knew from the time he was twelve that he could not, would not, *should* not even dream of marrying for love. His mother and father had made that clear. On the rare occasions when the royal family dined alone, they would always go on and on about the troubles that had recently plagued their British cousins in the House of Windsor. The scandals, the divorces, the unending criticisms of the royal family.

"But that," King Philippe would proclaim, "is what happens when heirs to the throne do not marry wisely."

So Raphael began to settle into the notion that he must marry sensibly. He couldn't be bothered with what he might personally find attractive or interesting; he was to think solely about the good of the country and of his family. He had to find a woman who was handsome enough to represent a good-looking country, but not one who was too caught up in looks and fashion and all of that. Such interests, he observed, brought nothing but trouble.

In fact, it would be preferable if the woman in question had no interests at all. The ability to *feign* interest—that was the important quality in a princess. A princess—or prince, for that matter—who is genuinely interested in things is bound to start thinking that the clinic she's touring might need money more than it needs royal visitors, or that the Saudi government's desire to dress her in black garb on state visits is inexcusable, or that, *my word,* Prince Andrew really is an old bore and must they invite him to the wedding, third cousin or not?

Far from the popular notion of a princess being privileged and spoiled, a good princess is the most undemanding of creatures. She smiles at anything placed before her. She is impressed by anything people attempt to impress her with. ("Well now, look at how the children used macaroni to spell out 'Welcome Your Highness'! I must say, I've never seen its equal!") Above all, she must be absolutely uninterested in her own feelings, which are the hallmark conversation topic of common women. Such nonsense, Prince Raphael had noted, tended to annoy even his professors at school, educated but common men, all of them. So for a crowned prince like himself, well, it would just be . . . unbearable.

No, his parents were quite right. He should not marry for love.

At least that was his thinking as a boy, and as I said, he later considered it one of the great tragedies of his life. But if you assume, therefore, that the prince did not love Isabella

Cordage, then you are assuming a bit much. For the truth is, despite all that talk of duty and family loyalty and the good of the country and other such sensible nonsense, when it came time for Raphael to marry, he paid no more attention to his parents than most young men do. He married exactly whom he wanted to. He just didn't admit to doing so.

And the fact that she had some noble ties and was very presentable and could feign interest at even the most dreadful exhibit of mid-twentieth-century household tools was so much the better. The truth was, he adored her. He just didn't realize it.

He had known Isabella, of course, since he was a small child. Her father was of minor but storied nobility, having inherited the title "Earl of Cordage" from the legendary man-child who had, six centuries earlier, played such a critical role in the War of the Hundred Hills. But there is no need to get bogged down in that sort of familiar history. The point is that her minor nobility was just enough to make Isabella Cordage a suitable playmate for the little future king. So she was among about two dozen children, all about the prince's age, who were regularly summoned to the castle—via elegant hand-painted invitations, of course—for small circuses and large birthday parties.

At first they played together with the unself-conscious abandon of all small children, unconcerned with their differences in gender or the degree of their nobility. But as the years wore on, the relationships became more strained. The boys and girls resented the adult expectations (which, by puberty, hung in the air like the stifling humidity of the worst summers along the Bisbanian Sea) that they would, out of all the world, date and marry only within this small circle.

Furthermore, the boys resented that they were so obviously a mere consolation prize compared to one particular classmate. The girls, meanwhile, were annoyed that in the whole melodrama of their young and difficult lives, the only story anyone cared about was which of them would marry Rafie.

Isabella, being among the least noble of the children, perhaps resented the whole thing more than most. In her teenage years, she developed—in addition to a small acne problem and the fine, flyaway hair that she battled through life—a tart tongue and smart attitude with His Highness, once famously going so far as to tell him that any modern woman would consider a man with a crown about as desirable as a man with a sexually transmitted disease.

"If she wants money, there are plenty of men who have that," she said, loudly enough to be overheard by guests at the largest ball of Bisbania's summer racing season. "And if she wants fame, a good rock star will do nicely. What does marrying a king get you except endless grief, tawdry speculation about your reproductive system, and a steady stream of editorials saying you're too formal and frumpy or else asking why you don't carry yourself with more grace and poise? A princess can't win, can she? If I were you, I'd worry about whether anyone would have me."

Not even a flicker of reaction passed over the prince's face as he replied simply: "How interesting."

And he walked away.

Isabella was unreasonably flustered by his even, royal response. The prince, despite his decorum, was hurt and strangely intrigued. There were a hundred women at the ball, and he thought only of her: *Why doesn't she like me?*

But do not misunderstand. This is not one of those predictable romantic comedies in which the man and the woman spit fire at each other for dozens of episodes before falling completely in love. It is true that Isabella and Raphael were often curt, sour, or standoffish with each other. But it wasn't so bad as all that. They were just children, after all. They sparred at times, but they also quite enjoyed each other. The tabloids reported the "sexually transmitted disease" comment many times over the years, but they mostly never bothered with what happened a few days later, when Raphael and Isabella saw each other at the races and Isabella, who had managed to find a way to pull her problem hair into an attractive bun, tried to smooth things over. "Oh, Rafie," she said, "I'm afraid I was dreadful the other night. I was trying to start a philosophical discussion about the unreasonable expectations of royal women, but I fear it came out like some sort of disrespectful rebuke."

She smiled here in what she hoped was a winsome way and pinched his arm in a friendly guy-chum manner. "I'm sure you'll find a woman who is quite up to the job," she said. "Someone who will not only appreciate you for your own sweet nature but will think of all the good she will someday do as queen."

Raphael brushed off the incident as though he barely remembered it. "Oh, of course, I knew quite what you were getting at. If I appeared put off, I was just rather distracted by the visiting grand duchess. She does take quite a lot of attention."

Then they smiled weakly and cheered the horses, and Isabella cashed a very nice ticket by correctly putting a little money on a long shot named Apology Accepted.

(I assure you that truly was the horse's name. For all my faults, I'm not so silly and pedestrian as to make up farfetched but insignificant details like that. Not that a name is ever completely insignificant. You can tell so much about people by what they chose to be called. And people do choose for themselves, ultimately. Your mother might call you Araminta, but you can introduce yourself as Minty or Ara or Tiny or—why not?—Scooter. You have a choice, and the choice you make reveals much about you. But a horse, of course, has no choice at all, and the name he is given does not, to the dismay of amateur bettors anywhere, have any impact on his racing ability. So the name Apology Accepted was, as I said, completely insignificant.)

After Isabella's apology, everything went on much the same as before. If anything, her friendship with Raphael warmed a bit. Isabella was always the prince's first choice when he needed a partner in a card game. And it was always a sweet relief to be seated next to her at state dinners, which would often happen if there was no visiting royalty who needed tending. Isabella was the only woman Raphael knew who didn't start looking around the room in a distracted way when he shared his thoughts on the ethics of using drug therapy for lisping problems in children. (The mechanics of speech were an interest of his.) And she had a wonderful little wiggle in her waltz that he admired on the dance floor. At the racetrack, she shouted and yelped in a lusty manner when her horse was headed toward the finish, so unlike most of Bisbania's noblewomen, who would merely clap their hands in a patty-cake fashion: fingers pointed straight upward and palms tapping together in an unenthusiastic, robotic motion. Once he believed that he even heard Isabella call out, "Move it, nag face," as her horse headed down the stretch. But when he asked her to repeat herself, she claimed to have been clearing her throat. "I have a bit of a cold," she said.

Isabella was a delight.

So no one should be surprised that Raphael found himself smitten when Isabella returned home after studying at Yale, an American school where she picked up some appalling Americanisms as well as a master's degree in art history and a preference for lower-cut blouses. Gone was any teenage brittleness, and they quickly fell into a routine of riding and tennis and conversations that lasted a bit longer than average in receiving lines at holiday banquets.

Then one day Raphael's valet, Vreeland, mentioned while selecting the prince's wardrobe that Edwina, the crowned princess of the Selbar Isles, was growing into quite a young woman, and the prince suddenly realized what had happened.

It was all over. Without so much as a kiss or any event that you could call a date, without consulting his parents or Vreeland or any of the assorted advisers who had chosen his school and his major and even his hobbies, Raphael had chosen a wife. And she was not Edwina, the crowned princess of the Selbar Isles. She was Isabella.

Raphael acted upon this decision with all of his characteristic impulsiveness and insensitivity, failing to appear for a snorkeling date with Edwina the very next morning by explaining that he was busy selecting mushy poetry to send to Isabella. Obviously, this not only crushed Edwina's fragile ego but also angered her father, King of the Selbar Isles and Beaches, and thus caused endless grief for King Philippe. In fact, the missed snorkeling date is the *real* reason behind that year's devastating Bisbania–Selbar Isles waterway dispute, the one that stranded fishing boats, tourist ferries, and, rather famously, a certain former U.S. president in the company of an attractive young woman (not his wife).

But none of that mattered to Raphael, who argued to his father that if Edwina was going to be as sensitive as all that, she would have made a horrible Bisbanian queen anyway. Isabella, he suggested, would have handled a canceled date with far more panache, though he did not plan on testing the matter. For Raphael did not even once stand Isabella up, though their relationship did have the usual peaks and valleys.

There are some biographies out there that will get into all the nitty-gritty of the courtship, that will tell you about their first kiss and their first argument. These biographies will tell you exactly how many times Isabella considered moving back to America and how many times Raphael thought that Bisbania was perhaps ready for a bachelor king.

But I don't want to tell that story, and you don't want to hear it. They were just two young kids dating. They had, in the parlance of the time, "issues." Who cares? If you want that story, you can get plenty of it at your local junior college. Just go sit in the cafeteria and ask some woman how her boyfriend is. You'll hear enough, and it will be no different from this.

Here is all you need to know: They dated for two years. He hinted at his intentions. She expressed reservations. He persevered. His parents were concerned because Isabella could be a bit of a handful, but they could hardly complain, given that they had included her in the circle of suitable young women since the beginning. ("She was supposed to be the one who made the others look good," Queen Regina hissed to her husband when they recognized what was going on.)

Finally, they went for that walk in the gardens of Glassidy Castle, and Raphael put his question to Isabella in a simple, straightforward way. "Please, Isabella," he started. Then, in a calculated attempt to use less formal language, he finished with "Won't you marry me?" Isabella said yes. They held a press conference. And when some silly young reporter asked her if she was ready for the royal family, she threw back her head, laughed, and said, "Maybe the question is: 'Are they ready for me?'"

The media would play that bit a million times over the years, and it became a standard piece of her story. But that only goes to show you the power people have when they're the ones editing your video. You could point to that remark and say it meant something, but you just as easily could point to the moment earlier, when someone asked how she felt and she said: "Humbled, really. All I want is to be a good wife and someday a good queen."

Did either comment really mean anything?

We'll see. As I said, I don't editorialize until the end.

The announcement was a big hit and got a good deal

of world attention. Ever since the troubles in the House of Windsor, the world rejoices when a seemingly mature, suitable woman becomes engaged to a prince. (Even if it's just the Prince of Gallagher, the heir to a mere slip of a throne, the kingship of a tiny city-nation so snugly nestled between the Bisbanian Sea and the southernmost Alps that, for many centuries, it could be reached only by foolhardy climbers and expert seamen.)

To help with the wedding preparations, the castle immediately assigned Isabella a maidservant, a middle-aged woman named Secrest who had recently inherited the job from her mother. (The famously lucrative royal pension plan meant that castle positions were often handed from one generation to another, assuming the family had the appropriate work ethic and skill at keeping secrets.)

Isabella, in a meaningless burst of egalitarianism, insisted that Secrest's job title be changed from maidservant to "royal associate." The formal proclamation, signed by the princess in what now seems a youthful, carefree hand, incorrectly lists Secrest's name as Secresta.

But neither the name nor the title made much difference to Secrest, who did not get a raise or even a noticeable increase in respect with the "promotion." The change did, however, make the appropriate splash in the tabloids—and the more serious media. Conventional wisdom suggested that using nonservile titles like "royal associate" demonstrated Isabella's thoroughly modern spirit. "I'll associate with this royal any day," Ethelbald Candeloro wrote in the gushing style typical of the media during the engagement.

So the world celebrated. Stamps were issued. Plates were created. Oh, you remember the whole thing, I'm sure. And if you're not old enough to remember—which, silly me, I guess most of you aren't (it's been so long ago!)—then just think about one of the other recent weddings, and you've got the idea. They're all the same, really.

Isabella wore white, of course. But she made a bit of a splash by having some color woven into the silk gown. The neckline was embroidered with a royal blue pattern of tulips, a tribute to some Dutch blood on her mother's side. Around the wrists and hem, the tulips were red.

It was stunning. You forget now how stunning and bold and beautiful it was. It was copied so much later that it became sort of cliché. Another great idea spoiled by mass production. But isn't that always the way?

Having a Yalie step into line to the throne especially thrilled people in the Americas, who were always up for a good royal wedding. Reporters came from both sides of the Atlantic and the Far East as well. The ceremony was conducted in Bisbania's ugly, guttural official language, which had long ago been abandoned for English by everyone other than the royal family and even by the royals in all non-ceremonial occasions. Isabella—it can now be told—had some trouble with a few of the words, because of the slight American accent she had picked up. But luckily, Raphael, with his interest in speech disorders and defects, was able to work with her beforehand. In the weeks leading up to the wedding, the young couple practiced into the scandalously wee hours of the morning.

But no one other than the royal family cared about the words. The world's favorite moment came when the young couple stepped out of the church doors and a burst of sunlight broke through the cloud cover and shone on them like a spotlight. They were glancing upward and laughing. They looked absolutely blessed.

That picture must have been reprinted a million times. When I look at it, I always study the prince's happy face and try to figure out what he was thinking. Was he thinking: *Ah, the people love her and she is sensible and sane and pleasant company and I've done my duty by selecting an able queen?* That was, more or less, the line he gave his parents, and so we cannot, without accusing him of lying, think he did not believe it. But I wonder, as I look at that smile, if maybe he wasn't feeling a bit mischievous. If he didn't, on some level, know what he'd let himself in for. If he didn't think he'd gone and done it, pulled a fast one on everyone.

And her eyes? Have you ever really looked at her eyes in that picture? Her face betrays only rapture, but there is something frail about her eyes.

Later, when the tabloids turned on her and all the biographies were written, much was made of how Her Royal Highness reportedly wept into her pillow the night before her wedding. So maybe it is only tiredness I see.

But I think far too much was made of the weeping. For neither the tears nor the nightmares—she reported later that she dreamed that night of flashbulbs, thousands of blinding flashbulbs—meant that she did not want to marry the prince.

She did want to marry him. He was a good and gentle man. He was handsome and he made her laugh. They did so love to spend time together. They thought it was great fun to whisper wildly inappropriate remarks at solemnly formal occasions. They both loved to read and liked to talk about their favorite authors. Watching a movie together while cuddled on the sofa during the rare Friday night that didn't involve state functions was just . . . heaven.

The prince made her happy.

But that was only a fortunate happenstance, a fringe benefit. It was what Isabella's American classmates would sometimes refer to as "gravy," a vulgar phrasing that Isabella rather liked for its raw American feel. I've spent more time than I care to admit in America, and though my agent says that you can tell it in my writing—especially when I get excited or tired—I simply can't abide this idiom. It is so like those hardy pioneers to mix animal fat with flour and consider it something wonderful enough to use as a metaphor for good things. Loving the prince was just gravy. (Or, if you're thinking in terms more appropriate to a proper Bisbanian woman, loving the prince was just a good fig relish.)

For as the wedding approached, Isabella came to realize on her own what someone really should have told her during all those years when she and the other suitable playmates were being lined up before the prince, pushed into his receiving lines, urged to dance, flirt, and spend time with him.

She came to realize there was no way she could decline an invitation to be queen. Perhaps you dispute that. Lots of people certainly do. Many insist that they would, in a second, turn it down. They echo Isabella's own words at that infamous ball, comparing a man with a crown to a man with a disease.

But for a woman of Isabella's age, in the era that Isabella lived, raised the way she was raised, saying "no thanks" was not possible. It was like winning the lottery. You know the jackpot can destroy a family, turn friends into wolves, and leave your life empty and directionless. You know that. But if your number comes up, you can't just throw the ticket away. You can't tell lightning to strike somewhere else.

So, at the moment when Isabella ventured down the path that leads through the gardens of Glassidy Castle, she might as well have already been walking down the aisle of St. Luke's Cathedral in that breathtaking dress. Her fate was sealed. She would be queen.

Except, of course, she never was.

Chapter 2

I know, I know. The youngest of you probably want me to drop all this ancient history and just explain the mysteries that surrounded the princess after she became wrinkly and stooped with age. Others of you, I know, would rather I cut straight to the single tragedy of her life, the events of that tempestuous day on the beach shortly after her fifth wedding anniversary.

And some of you want more about the wedding itself, want me to rehash all the details about how many thousands of people watched, to recapture some of the editorials that praised the union, to wax on about how Raphael and Isabella were each escorted to the altar by their parents without comment, finally killing the appalling custom of "giving away the bride."

But again, even if you are as much of a fan of Her Highness as I am, you can dwell on these things for only so long.

If you ask me, too much was written about the cloudy morning when she wed the prince, and the blustery afternoon when it became apparent that she had lost him. To understand Her Royal Highness, you must consider for a moment the early months of her marriage.

There was, of course, the honeymoon. I'm not talking about the deliriously romantic nights the couple spent in the quaint and picturesque village of Positano, Italy, where, with the help of sunglasses and the unflappable townspeople, the royal newlyweds roamed the streets freely without interruptions and ate at ordinary tables without reservations.

In those entire two weeks, Isabella was struck only once by her new status. Walking down a steep hill, she caught a glimpse of a girl in a second-story window. The girl stared quizzically at Isabella, who smiled and waved. A look of wonder and amazement passed over the girl's face, and Isabella saw her turn and shout to her family: "Principessa! Principessa!"

But the honeymoon I was talking about was the honeymoon with the press, with the people, with the advisers, with the world. Everyone wanted her to succeed. Her success would benefit the nation. And everyone was acutely aware of what a difficult transition she faced.

For though Isabella grew up around the royal family, right in the heart of the castle as often as not, even she did not know what it meant to be royal. As the prince's friend, and later as his date, she was often photographed going into various parties and dinners. As she got older, it was not uncommon, when standing in line at a bakery or theater, to hear a few whispers around her, as people sought confirmation that the woman ahead of them did look a bit like that woman Prince Raphael was said to be dating.

But it was only as the rumors of the engagement began mounting and were eventually confirmed that she started being followed by the photographers and openly gawked at by strangers. For several weeks, even that wasn't so bad, filled as it was with optimistic good wishes and refreshing enthusiasm.

It was only in the last few weeks before the wedding that she had any real hint of what would await her. That was when she began to notice how some of the articles about the wedding would include snide comparisons about how many meals for the homeless the cake budget would buy. And after a small misstatement regarding a historical fact at the dedication of a war memorial, and that rather splashy spill she took coming down the castle's grand staircase at the annual theater festival, a couple of newspapers even took to calling her "Dizzy Izzy."

"But I hate being called Izzy," Isabella complained to friends, rather missing the point.

Even so, things weren't all bad. At least not compared to how they could have been. For a while, Isabella was even able to continue meeting her sister and some old primary-school chums for a weekly brunch at a small sidewalk café, which was, fittingly for the new Princess of Gallagher, located in the Gallagher neighborhood, along the picturesque banks of the Kloster River. Soon, though, photographers—lured by the image of young women wearing straw hats and sundresses while sitting outside sipping imported ciders and eating spring rolls with the river traffic rolling behind them—began camping just across the street, snapping away at every bite.

The castle advisers, a group of stodgy and conservative men, wrung their hands and insisted that Isabella bring her friends to the castle for lunch. But Isabella ignored them, arguing that she would not live in fear, that the photographers would get bored eventually, and what would they gain anyway? Proof that she ate?

During one infamous row on the subject, Sir Hubert, the head of castle operations, angrily put his foot down, saying, "I'm afraid, Your Highness, I must put my foot down. The café luncheons will stop."

Isabella stared him down with cool disinterest before mustering a rather nonegalitarian response: "That's interesting. Because seeing as how I'm the future queen, and you're nothing but hired help, I'm afraid I must put my foot down and insist the subject not be raised in my presence again."

This caused, as you might imagine, quite a stir at the castle. And it speaks volumes that of all the goings-on during what came to be known as the "Isabella years," that particular confrontation was the only showdown not widely reported. Apparently, the people fond of leaking scuttlebutt weren't so fond of leaking their own comeuppance.

Even the queen, perhaps remembering the bullying she took in her own days as the Princess of Gallagher, was said to have enjoyed this little exchange, though she naturally feigned shock when Sir Hubert reported it to her.

But Hubert eventually got his way, and the luncheon custom was abandoned after the unfortunate incident in which the princess's sister, Lady Fiona, made a rather amusing crack about the prime minister—which, thankfully, the reporters did not overhear—and Isabella burst into laughter, blowing her water right out of her nose. I'm sorry to put it so bluntly, but there is no discreet way to get the point across.

Like so many royal crises, this one seems in retrospect a bit, shall I say, overblown. But it is hard for us to imagine what it was like for someone of Isabella's upbringing—she always curtsied when appropriate, knew her way around a twenty-seven-piece place setting, and generally had impeccable manners—to be plastered on the front pages of the tabloids with the headline: THAR SHE BLOWS, MATEY.

And while the advisers and the royal family and the commentators all publicly expressed the "Well, it could happen to anyone and why don't they leave her alone" sentiment, privately, everyone was rather aghast. For the picture was, and I don't think I'm exaggerating, absolutely revolting. Her face was contorted. The spray was oceanic. One of her chums was reeling back as if she'd been shot, a look of abject horror on her face.

The queen in particular was beside herself over the whole event, imagining the antics at upcoming state dinners as prankish foreigners tried their best gags in an effort to prod Old Faithful into a repeat performance. "And *do* remind me to give the princess handkerchiefs for Christmas," the queen sniffed to a lady-in-waiting.

All the tabloids reported that Isabella quipped afterward, "At least they got my good side." But she didn't really say that. That was the line Secrest and Raphael came up with to spread among the "friends" who would leak quotes to the tabloids. The advisers and Rafie hoped the comment showed a jaunty, self-mocking attitude that would please the people, rather than make them feel guilty for buying up the tabloids and snickering at the picture. The things Isabella really said were almost too pathetic to repeat. She cried and carried on and kept telling Raphael that she was a miserable wife and a miserable princess and why couldn't they leave her alone for one hour a week and it didn't matter, she might as well do what the advisers wanted and give up on the luncheons because her friends would give up on her soon enough if that sort of nonsense continued.

Raphael was sympathetic about the photo. (It could, after all, happen to anyone.) But he was mystified about why she wouldn't just have the luncheons at the castle. The prince had only briefly experienced, on his honeymoon and other foreign trips, the freedom of being able to walk in the street and to browse at shops and eat in restaurants without a fuss. It was, he supposed, fun in its way. But it didn't strike him, at least not in those days, as something you needed to do all the time.

Instead of moving the luncheons to the castle, Isabella gave up the ritual altogether, trying in vain to explain to Rafie that the feel of the luncheons—five independent women carving out precious time to meet, stand in line for fruit plates, and giggle at one another as they tried to adjust the table umbrella—would be utterly ruined if situated in the Glassidy Gardens with butlers tending to their needs.

"Explain it to him, Secrest," she'd say. "We're modern working girls, aren't we? You understand."

And Secrest—who was enough of a modern working girl to know that she would get nowhere by pointing out that Isabella wasn't, strictly speaking, working—would demur and flee the room.

In the days that followed the "thar she blows" photo, Raphael stayed up late each night, indulging his interest in the mechanics of communication by reading a speech therapy text called *Enunciation and Pronunciation. A Layman's Guide.* Between chapters, he would pause to think about his conversations with Isabella. He decided she needed to take up an interest herself and stop being so ridiculous.

And Isabella? On most of those nights, she went to bed thinking . . . well, to be honest, Isabella was thinking of Geoffrey.

Chapter 3

I guess I should explain before going further that I believe in princesses. Princes, too, of course, but especially princesses. A lot of people don't, you know. Not these days. Not for a long time, really. We look back on the biggest royal weddings of old, watch the video of the outpouring at King William's mum's funeral, and we say those were monarchy's glory days.

But that's revisionist history. We forget that there were protesters at those weddings and that people thought Will's father should step aside, giving up his place in the line of succession. If European monarchies ever had glorious days, they were not as recent as that. I'm not sure there was ever a time when the very concept of a monarchy was not ridiculed and mocked—at least behind the king's back.

Anyway, it's not that I believe monarchies are a good way to run a country. I don't. And it's not that the wealth of the ruling classes doesn't appall me. It does.

But my belief in princesses relates to my belief in good stories. It seems, for whatever reason, that every time you create a princess, you create a start to a good story. I guess it's because, not to put too fine a point on it, women's lives are more interesting than men's. Oh sure, if you review historic events, you'll find that men have, more often than not, played key roles. But day in and day out, women have been where it's happening. They've been giving birth and nursing the dying and debating the symbolism of name changes at weddings. Men, meanwhile, have been collecting paychecks and dabbling in office politics. Ho. Hum.

That is a gross stereotype, but I'm sure you see my point.

When a prince marries a less noble woman, which princes often do, the prince is always baffled that the crowds love the princess more, line up to see her, give her flowers, gush, and carry on. Meanwhile, the prince himself—the heir to the throne, no less!—is almost ignored. But it only makes sense. People look at the young princess and wonder, "How will she do? Will she bring out the good in her husband? Will she bear an heir and raise that child to be good and kind? Will she keep our fashion industry humming and give us a bit of spring on gray winter days? Will she inspire us?"

For the prince, they say, "Stick with dark suits, stay out of trouble till your dad dies, and please, try not to cheat on the pretty young thing."

I'm not saying it's right. But that's the way it is.

You may wonder, as you continue through this story, who I am. You may ask how I know the things I know: the secrets of the castle. You may question my motives for revealing all that I am about to reveal. But I think when the story is done, you will understand. You will see that everything I have documented here, I know either firsthand or from long, detailed, soul-searching conversations with others who know it firsthand. But more important, when this story is done, you will understand what exactly it is that I owe Isabella and what she owes me. You will see why I must write this story while I'm still alive to write it.

For in the end, the story is not completely Isabella's. Cruel as it is, princesses do belong, a little, to all of us. As a child, I was raised on fairy tales. Although, even as old as I am, I was raised on the less troubling modern versions, not the ones in which women are forever getting their feet lopped off and practically killing one another for a shot at the prince. Despite a fair diet of glass slippers and ornate coaches and magic spells, I didn't realize how much I loved princesses until adulthood, when my women friends and I, young and consumed by our careers, would gather for weekends at fancy hotels. We would splurge on expensive wine and sit in hot tubs and agonize about our futures and our pasts. We were surprised at how often the conversation would turn to the royal family.

Back then we talked mostly about Queen Regina, whom we had started following in her days as Princess Reggie. Our male friends assumed that we liked her clothes and her style, and she *was* rather something, and her clothes *did* interest us. Remember when she made red polka dots all the rage? My, my, I had this one dress that . . . Well, I'm getting off track again. Suffice it to say that the highest compliment a smart suit could draw was the simple "very Reggie."

But mostly, we were interested in her story. We wondered if she really loved the king. And did it break her heart when Rafie was a child and would dream of being an astronaut or a firefighter or a software designer or some other decent profession and she had to murmur softly, "Silly boy, you'll be king, of course." Did she mind terribly that even her father's funeral was not private? Or did she no longer notice the cameras?

And what of her much younger sister, the glamorous Lady Carissa, whose engagement to a Bisbanian count was called off on the very eve of the wedding, requiring embarrassing explanations to four kings and five queens, all of whom had traveled to the Selbar Isles for the occasion? What was the secret that Carissa revealed to her fiancé on the night before her wedding? And does it haunt the queen to this day? Does it explain why Raphael was never once publicly seen, nor even privately photographed, with his aunt, who was herself photographed quite a lot for the next several years, until she started putting on a bit of weight and took to wearing sweatpants in public?

And when, in happier days, Reggie's clothing budget was printed and criticized, we sympathized, having known firsthand a boyfriend's raised eyebrow, a father's terse words at expensive clothes—as well as we also knew their disappointment with women who did not dress prettily. (Consider the reaction to Lady Carissa in sweats.)

Things have improved since then. But it used to be, even in my lifetime, even after things had already improved, that a woman could not win. And Regina's struggle to win took place on a global stage.

We wondered about the rumors of her affair with her chauffeur, and we gossiped into the night about her battles with the Queen Mother, and we saw in her life a giant reflection of our own, the life we had lived and the one that still lay before us. Disappointments and joys and in-laws and friends. Her life was just like ours, only lived on a grander scale, one that gave the mundane things—clothes, shopping, and in-law problems—a dramatic edge. Let our boyfriends talk about hockey and soccer; we were talking about the game of life.

Then Isabella came along, and Isabella was so much better.

Those of us who believe in princesses are often laughed at. But I believe the world needs princesses and dukes and queens and kings. We need people who glitter and shine and make a room silent with their entrance. We need them the same way we need ice cream and soccer and music and stories. Oh, how we need stories.

And though the world didn't know it until now, Isabella's story—the sad one that you know so well and the grand one that is only now being revealed—began with Geoffrey.

Chapter 4

What? You've never heard of Geoffrey? You've spent your whole life, it seems, reading about everything that the princess ate or wore or did, but you're still unaware of the man who consumed Isabella's thoughts on those wistful, lonely nights when she lay awake wondering what on earth she had gotten herself into?

(I guess that proves my agent, Frederick, wrong when he said there was nothing new I could possibly reveal about the Princess of Gallagher!)

Geoffrey Whitehall-Wright, né Jeff Wright, was a friend, perhaps ever so slightly more than a friend, whom Isabella had met in America. The first time she mentioned him to

Raphael, the prince assumed Geoffrey was a former classmate from Yale. Isabella did not initially correct this assumption.

He was actually the man who fixed her car. Well, *checked* her car. You know, looking for bombs and wear and tear and bugs. The castle insisted on such inspections for all friends of the prince, and although Isabella sometimes vaguely wondered what would happen if she simply refused to show up for her weekly appointments, it never seemed worth the bother. Once she got to know Geoffrey, whom she had selected out of the phone book because his family shop was near her dorm, she actually came to look forward to visiting the garage.

Isabella's reluctance to reveal that Geoffrey was what Raphael's friends would call her "car man" had nothing to do with concerns about class snobbery or her upper-crust reputation. It was perhaps more sinister than that. She liked having a secret. She liked having a secret from Rafie, and she liked having a secret from the castle advisers. She liked having a secret from the whole world.

After the "thar she blows" photo and what she deemed as Rafie's unsympathetic reaction to it, she thought about Geoffrey more and more and finally decided to write to him. She did so—that time and the many times that followed—by going through an elaborate ruse. She would plead insomnia and wander the castle restlessly, chatting with the night guards and making quite a fuss about her inability to sleep. Finally, she would wander into the castle gift shop and slip the envelope—return address simply "Belle"—into the Royal Mail drop, which was established so that castle tourists could send postcards to friends for free.

(This was the reason that Isabella was the surprisingly passionate advocate of removing security cameras from the gift shop. "If I can't trust the people not to steal from me," she said dramatically, "then I'm quite sure I can't be their queen." This was the sort of thing that made Sir Hubert throw up his hands, roll his eyes, and curse the castle retirement system, which was so lucrative that it made it virtually impossible for any sane person to walk away from a senior job. "If it weren't for the royal pension, I'd be happily selling shoes!" he'd exclaim each night to his wife, who would smile weakly and say, "I know, dear," even though she herself rather liked Isabella.)

The first time Geoffrey received a note, he couldn't believe his eyes. He had walked down his long gravel driveway to get the mail. Thumbing through it in a disinterested way, noting the bills and the junk and so forth, he then saw a personal letter, which was rare even in those days. He noticed the elegant penmanship and thought, *Nah, can't be.* Then he saw "Belle," and he knew.

He rubbed his fingers over the ink and was almost scared to open the envelope. In any other circumstance, Geoffrey would have been thrilled, would have ripped the letter open, eager to hear what had become of his long-lost friend. But in this case, he *knew* what had become of her. How could anyone not know what had happened to Isabella Cordage?

Geoffrey, who liked eavesdropping on his wife when she gossiped with friends about celebrities, had heard a good deal about the engagement of the Prince of Gallagher before he realized whom the prince was marrying. He had heard the name Isabella, of course, but he had not thought to connect it with the former customer he had always called Belle. Then one day he saw his old friend smiling on the cover of *People* magazine, under a headline that said RAFIE PICKS A PRINCESS, and he realized. He was so incredulous that his mouth was still hanging open when his wife returned from work several hours later.

"This princess," he said, pointing to a magazine. "Or at least she's going to be a princess. This Isabella they're talking about. She's an ol' buddy of mine."

"Buddy?" his wife said, clearly expecting a punch line.

"I took care of her car," he said.

"*You* did?" his wife asked, speaking slowly, almost as if she were talking to the insane. She snorted. "I suppose you made her hot cider, too."

But the truth became apparent to Mae Whitehall, who had not yet convinced her husband of the wisdom of combining their names. (The change from Jeffrey to Geoffrey is a bit more complicated and, as you might imagine, involves various vanities and pretensions, none of which seems pertinent here.) Once Mae became convinced, she told all her friends. Word reached a local television station, where, in the final days before the wedding, reporters were desperate to find fresh human-interest angles on the woman they insisted on calling their "American princess."

But when a producer from the station called, Geoffrey denied it all. For at that moment, he realized it would be wrong to talk publicly about Isabella. On some level that he couldn't explain, he knew that Isabella's life was no longer hers and that it was unseemly for him to offer up to the public some little piece of it that she'd managed to keep to herself.

"We were buds," he explained to Mae. "She'd bring her car in each week, and I checked the tires and brakes. It seemed ridiculous, but all those Yale kids were nuts about security. She always brought her books in, but she never studied much. We just talked. 'Solved the world's problems,' we liked to say. She'd never heard of the Boss. Can you imagine that?"

Mae humored her husband with a surprised look, but really, she could imagine it. The Boss was an old nickname for Bruce Springsteen, a rock artist of much critical and commercial success. Mae had certainly heard of the Boss, but she was not surprised that Isabella had not. Mae was, after all, a born-and-bred Kentucky girl with rockin' dairy-farmer parents. She was not a noble lady from a distant and isolated land. "The boss of what?" would be the expected reaction from Bisbanian royalty, Mae supposed.

"I loaned her some CDs," Geoffrey continued. "And we'd talk about them some. She'd warm up peach cider in the break room. Put some sort of foreign spice in it." He paused. "That was good cider."

He ambled over to the refrigerator and started rummaging around in it while still talking. "Tell the news all that? It wouldn't be right. Maybe I'm kidding myself. She's a lady. I'm a mechanic. But I think we're friends. I don't talk about her on the news. It's like that Springsteen song where the lawman lets his brother escape. It's about loyalty."

Mae did not see how it was like that, exactly, but she had gotten used to her husband's strange habit of referencing the works of Springsteen as if they were Scripture, so she did not argue.

But even without the "big" story of a local mechanic's ties to the soon-to-be princess, the coverage of the royal wedding was exhaustive. Stories about the wedding preparations—the ice sculpture of the royal shield; the mild controversy over Isabella's decision to use hothouse tulips rather than native, in-season but somewhat odiferous Bisbanian mums; the security details—were on the front pages, even in America. Old professors were quoted saying flattering but vague things about her years at Yale ("I remember her as being, um, always there," said one professor. "And her work was generally well punctuated and perfectly adequate"). All the late-night comedians had some fun with the way that three American hairstylists each claimed to have held weekly appointments with Isabella, though her hair had in those days been long and straight and appeared to receive professional attention on more of a quarterly basis.

During all these stories, they ran video of Isabella—shopping with the bridesmaids, cutting ribbons at building projects for nonprofit agencies, planting mums in a community garden, and swearing, somewhat awkwardly, that if she ever got married again, she'd choose mums for her bouquet. "They're my second favorite," she said.

She was everywhere. (And so was Secrest, who was constantly being interviewed about the cake plans and the reception menu and was more than once quoted saying that she could not comment on the dress, other than to promise that Isabella would look amazing in it.)

Geoffrey watched the wedding broadcast and listened to his wife explain who all the various dignitaries were as the crowned prince of this, the heir to that throne, the Queen Mother, blah, blah, blah, filed into the church. Mae got positively misty-eyed at the gown, while Geoffrey only smiled approvingly at the embroidery around the wrists and neckline. "Detailing," he said, with a nod. "That works on cars, too, but I would have picked a color with less contrast."

When the happy royal couple emerged from the church and that ray of sunshine hit them and they looked up, Geoffrey's wife thought that Isabella looked blessed and radiant. But Geoffrey, he thought she looked kind of tired.

"Look at her eyes," he said. "It doesn't look like she slept."

He thought about writing to her, sending a gift, maybe. But he never did. He never could think of the right thing to say, and he couldn't imagine the right gift for a future queen. So he lapsed into an odd feeling of conspiracy. He watched the princess on television and read about her in newspapers and asked his wife endless questions about the machinations of royal life.

"Why is she the Princess of Gallagher if she's going to be the Queen of Bisbania?" he asked Mae over and over again. But no matter how clearly Mae tried to explain it, he never seemed to grasp why it would be customary in the tiny city-state of Bisbania to give the next in line to the throne (and, by extension, his wife) the title of the city's northernmost neighborhood, a chic conglomeration of over-priced boutiques, antique bookstores, and gift shops that specialized in herbal soaps and jewelry.

"It's the same in Great Britain," Mae would explain impatiently. "You know. The Prince of Wales becomes the King of England."

But Geoffrey would just shake his head and ask, "Then who's the King of Wales?"

Mae would sigh in an exasperated way and wander out of the room.

But whatever Isabella's title, and whatever the customs of Bisbanian royals, Geoffrey knew enough to see that she had become an important and sought-after celebrity, the sort of person who understands privacy only as a memory. One of his wife's food magazines published an argument that the princess was eating too much refined sugar, complete with photos of every plate she had been served at a public banquet in the last six months. And all the newspapers reported the arrest of a computer hacker who had traced the princess's keystrokes and found what was officially described as "personal correspondence" but which was widely rumored to involve Isabella's e-mailed exchange with the royal doctor about yeast infections.

So when Geoffrey saw what Isabella's life had become, he felt somehow like her secret champion, her valiant savior, the one guy in the whole world who wouldn't make a buck off her. He was faithfully keeping silent. Although when things got bad for her—with all the "dizzy" headlines and the nose-spray photo—he began to wonder if the news that she had often shared cider with a mechanic would make much of a worldwide impression.

And then he got her first letter. He stood in the driveway, running his finger over the ink, not quite believing that it could really be. Inside was elegant stationery; at the top was a curvy abstract rendering that he would later learn represented Bisbania's national bird. *So, he thought, I didn't dream this or make it up. I meant something to the princess.*

He did not know exactly what he feared. Did he fear she would cheapen his restraint by thanking him for his silence? Worse, by offering to pay him for it? Did he fear that she would appear to remember him only faintly or too well?

No, I think what he feared was that in some way, his life would be different after he opened that letter. Not obviously and not immediately. But slowly, over time, he might get swept up into a story that he wasn't ready for, had not requested.

The letter was simple enough.

> *Dear Jeff,*
>
> *Remember me? I'm terribly sorry for falling out of touch. My life has been rather a blur as of late, but that's no excuse. I often think fondly of our weekly chats and I hope things are going well for you.*
>
> *If you'd like to stay in touch, I've enclosed a card with my address. If you don't mind, use the return address "Lord Baron Dudley." I've instructed my staff that letters bearing that return address be forwarded to me unopened.*
>
> *Do tell me all about your life. I'm afraid mine is dreadfully dull, although I'm lucky in many ways and I know I should not complain.*
>
> *Belle*

And there it was. Nothing objectionable on any level. She had neither presumed that he knew about her life, nor condescended to tell him. Aside from the practical matter of instructing him on how to reach her, she had simply acted as if nothing had changed.

But things had. Even though you don't yet know what happened to the man who became known as Geoffrey

Whitehall-Wright, even you must realize that things had changed dramatically for him.

And they would change for Princess Isabella also. They would change the moment that Secrest appeared in the doorway of the royal bedchamber with a relieved smile on her face and a single envelope in her hand.

Secrest did not know then exactly what "this Lord Baron Dudley business"—as she came to think of it—was all about. The royal associate knew only that Isabella had been asking repeatedly if any mail had arrived from Lord Dudley, and that Her Royal Highness had seemed, alarmingly, a bit more crushed each time the answer was no.

Castle employees do not wish to see their royal charges depressed. It bodes badly in so many ways. Depressed royals might, for example, start eating too much or letting themselves go in some other way, getting the higher-ranking castle advisers all worked up and bringing down pressure on the likes of Secrest to urge the princess to start taking better care of her nails or to forgo fig pancakes for breakfast. Or perhaps depressed royals would turn their ill moods in another direction and sulk around, constantly complaining about the lack of light in their bedroom or proclaiming their lack of royal interest in the day's schedule of ribbon cuttings.

It made for such unpleasant company.

Already Secrest had overheard—she was very good at overhearing things—the senior advisers musing about some photos taken of Isabella at a garden tour, where she had carried herself in a glum, slump-shouldered way that Secrest would have described as "sullen and spoiled" but Hubert, with uncharacteristic charity, described as "looking pale and tired." Secrest's initial relief at Hubert's kind description dissolved when she realized it was motivated by his suspicion that Isabella was tired and pale in a joyous, expectant way— if you catch my meaning.

Secrest thought that sullen and spoiled was more likely.

And not just because she knew that Raphael was up late reading speech pathology texts alone while Isabella was roaming about the castle in her nightclothes pleading insomnia. Secrest had the unglamorous duty of serving the royal birth control pill on a china plate each morning and restocking the royal—how shall we put this?—feminine products each month. She thought Hubert was being wildly optimistic.

Hubert might be the head of castle operations, while Secrest was only a glorified chambermaid. But Hubert was a provincial, small-city, same-haircut-he-had-in-high-school kind of guy, while Secrest was, you see, a woman of the world.

Over the years, Secrest had lived in other countries and pursued other careers while waiting for her mother to give up the castle position. Most of the other castle help, by contrast, had never left the confines of their own tiny nation. The Huberts of the castle had spent their pre-castle years helping out in the legendary but struggling royal fig orchards, so vital to the national self-image but slowly choking on the Bisbanian smog. Or they had worked in Bisbania's troubled auto industry, which exported the flashy but unreliable (and, needless to say, smog-producing) Bisba convertibles. These experiences meant Secrest's colleagues had trouble imagining a worldview that extended beyond the petty neighborhood politics that so often dominated Bisbanian affairs. They also had trouble imagining working for a dynamic, profitable, up-to-date operation, but never mind that.

Or maybe you should mind that. For that was precisely where Hubert was making his mistake, Secrest thought. The nation's misguided approach to fig production and auto production was, in her mind, related to Hubert's old-fashioned notions of royal reproduction. He did not see any reason to move the fig orchards away from the city center. He did not see any reason to reengineer the Bisba, and he did not see any reason that Isabella would view her royal wifely duties any differently from the few hundred princesses who had come before her over the past few thousand years. He thought that Isabella would quickly set herself toward producing an heir because that was what previous Princesses of Gallagher had quickly set themselves toward doing.

Secrest, though, could imagine other worldviews and other sorts of affairs. She had begun to suspect that this Dudley fellow was not a "distant uncle," as Isabella had originally, if somewhat nonsensically, suggested. Secrest could imagine all too well the sort of cross-class, cross-culture friendship that a lonely member of the nobility might be tempted by while being schooled in a casual, classless country, the sort of undisciplined place that teaches young nobles to hand out silly titles like "royal associate."

But Secrest didn't allow herself to worry too much about all of that on the day when the slightly rumpled envelope with a Connecticut postmark arrived in Isabella's mail, mixed in with the usual tea invitations, fan letters, and credit card solicitations. ("H.R. Highness is already approved!") Secrest simply snatched up the envelope and dashed off to Isabella's room, confident that, whatever problems lay ahead, the immediate problem was solved—no more slightly sullen-looking princess.

Later, Secrest would wonder if she should have told Hubert about the letter. Later, she would promise herself to keep a wary eye on this Dudley correspondence. Later, she would vow to sneak peeks at anything Isabella left lying around the royal desk, vow to pick up crumpled drafts from the royal wastebasket, vow to keep her royal associate ears open—especially when Isabella was busy chatting on the phone and not paying much attention to who was emptying her wastebaskets or straightening her bed or laying out her clothes.

But on the day the letter arrived, Secrest was only happy and relieved as she burst into Isabella's room, announcing with uncharacteristic breathlessness:

"Your Highness, I think, perhaps, you are expecting this."

Chapter 5

*N*early a year separated the start of Lord Baron Dudley's long-distance advice and the time when Isabella's myth-makers first marked a turnaround in the princess's "performance." But to appreciate the turnaround, you must first appreciate how bad things had gotten.

Far too often, biographies of the princess have merely breezed through the first year or so of her marriage, chronicling the well-known "thar she blows" photo, a few fashion mistakes, and the "Dizzy" nickname. I can understand how this happens. I myself can hardly bear to repeat her many missteps. Remembering them is like remembering the most awkward thing you ever did in the seventh grade, or some really flawed attempt at flirtation. It just makes you shiver all over. Egad.

But I feel obligated to remind people, especially my younger readers, just how badly the princess struggled at first, after the honeymoon and before the miraculous remake. I will try to be as brief and discreet as possible. I've included the tabloid headlines as a handy reference.

☆ Isabella glibly visited an overseas factory widely rumored to be experimenting with biological warfare and, with a goofy grin on her face, praised their "exciting work." Headline: DIZZY IZZY SAYS: GO GERMS!

☆ On two occasions, she was photographed dancing at nightclubs on St. Teresa of Calcutta Day, then considered the most holy of the modern saint days. Headline: HOLY GO-GO? IZZY TANGOS ON SAINTLY TOES.

☆ She wore shoes made from cloned alligators, a practice long banned in Bisbania. Headline: HEELS FROM HELL: IZZY'S WRONG AGAIN.

☆ Surely, I need not rehash the infamous incident involving the Prime Minister of Algeria. Headline: SLURP AND BURP: IZZY'S DINING DISASTER.

And she was forever dressed wrong. Not that such things should matter, the commentators would always note. But there was just something off about her. She would be all frilly when sleek would have been better. And she would be all sleek when lacy would have been better. Ethelbald Candeloro, who wore an overgrown handlebar mustache on his pasty, somewhat flabby face in the photo that ran alongside his column, once remarked that he wouldn't have imagined there was a bad time to be sleek until Isabella came along.

Things reached their nadir, I suppose, a few months after the wedding, when Isabella was rushing out of the castle to catch a flight to Russia for the baby shower of a minor duchess in the recently restored but, needless to say, much humbled Russian royal family. (The Russian royals had, by this point, taken to calling the Russian Revolution and the century of communism that followed it "the experiment," and they were calling the slaughter of most of their ancestors "the accident.") Isabella was running late because of some sort of security scare that had been triggered by a wayward raccoon rustling about in the royal garbage. So she was not quite herself as she dashed off to the airport. That is how she came to be photographed climbing into a stretch Bisba, wearing a denim peasant skirt and carrying in her right hand a goblet of ice water. Her hair was somewhat askew.

The tabloids had a field day.

First off, they dubbed the skirt a "prairie" skirt, which was not correct in the fashion sense, but perhaps was close enough from a political standpoint. "How have we reached a point," Ethelbald Candeloro wrote in what became an infamous column, "where the wife of the Bisbanian heir scoots off to represent us among the nobility of other continents, wearing the fashion of rough-handed American cattle herders and carrying glassware into motor vehicles, as if the royal family could not afford a proper, lidded thermos cup?

"Moreover," he continued, "the goblet appeared to be German, an insult to the hardworking glassblowers of Bisbania's Eighth Street Glass Factory. While the water, I understand, was imported from Morocco. Morocco! As if Bisbanian springs did not produce water as fresh and tasty as that of a desert country most famous for playing it again, Sam.

"All of that would be reason enough to leave His and Her Majesty beside themselves, but it also appears," he concluded, "that the Princess of Gallagher could stand to be introduced to a comb, a tool the rest of us use, often daily, to arrange our hair into pleasing—or at least nonoffending—configurations."

Ethelbald was being awfully unfair. While I'll be the first to admit that carrying crystal into a car does seem a bit gauche, the goblet in question came straight from Queen Regina's kitchen, and thus if anyone owed an explanation to the Glassblowers of Local 808, it would be the queen. Meanwhile, Isabella had planned, as was the custom of royal travelers, to change her skirt and comb her hair on the plane en route to Moscow, which at last report was located in Europe, not another continent. (Besides, given the Russian royal family's then-recent stint as peasants, it would seem unlikely that they could make a case for being offended by the humble styling of Isabella's skirt.)

Finally, I have it on good authority that the water came straight from the royal lavatory sink, not from a well in Casablanca. Isabella had drawn the glass herself while packing up her toiletries, although Ethelbald would surely think both activities were beneath her station in life. (She had insisted she would handle those tasks so that Secrest could check the royal mail one last time. And it was the last time Secrest allowed herself to be dissuaded from doing her own job, I can assure you of that.)

But the truth did not matter. This is exactly the sort of nonevent that tabloids can drag out for several weeks, with new rounds of leaked criticism and rumored backlash. FORMER BUTLER SAYS IZZY ALWAYS INSISTED ON IMPORTED STEMWARE, one headline would say. QUEEN ORDERS MIDNIGHT RAID OF IZZY'S KITCHEN, DIRECTS ALL FOREIGN WATER DUMPED IN ROYAL TOILET, would read the next.

People not in that circumstance have trouble understanding how hard it is to turn your public image around once it has taken this sort of battering. Isabella was seen as someone levelheaded enough, but just too awkward, frumpy, and ill at ease to represent a country that wants potential tourists to believe it is good-looking and laid-back. People who were far more awkward and frumpy and ill at ease resented her, saying she made them all look bad. She'd tread off to some obscure nation and sit in bleachers with other dignitaries at some silly dedication, and fifty-five-year-old, balding, overweight, badly dressed factory workers would yell at the screen during news accounts of the event: "Look now what's she done, she's grinning during the prayer, she makes us all look like fools." Or "What's that? Wearing black to a coronation? They'll think we're all rubes." And it mattered not that, at Yale, young women wore black everywhere. "This ain't Yale," the commentators would say, snickering a little at what they considered their clever use of American slang.

The queen became so distressed that she brought in one of those disastrous British princesses. I can't remember her name now. It's become so hard to keep them all straight. But whatever her name or title, she was, at that point, just beginning to live down a series of dating disgraces, misguided forays into pop music, and unsuccessful dieting ads. She was no help at all.

"I can't imagine why they want you to take my advice," she said, in the marvelously blunt way of the British. "The best thing that ever happened to me was Will's mum dying. It somehow reminded people that, princesses or not, we're still mortal, still human beings, we still bloody bleed and die. Even then it took years to pull my image out of the loo."

You can imagine what that did for Isabella's spirits.

In fact, the visit of the British princess only succeeded in getting King Philippe, who had been moping about the castle in a fretful way, thinking along very unhelpful lines. His staff insisted that whenever he and the queen dined together, he would whisper, "Divorce worked out well enough for King Will's father."

The queen would invariably reply, "Widowhood worked out even better."

The problem is that once people are expecting you to

be awkward and ill at ease, there is almost no way to appear to be graceful and at ease. You can glide across a room like an angel, but any photographer worth his press license can still manage to get a picture of you blinking and in mid-swallow. No one in the room even saw such a moment, but it looked great next to a headline with the word "dizzy."

Once you've made a few clumsy mistakes, there's almost no point in coming out with a wonderful, insightful speech. People just assume someone else wrote it.

I could compile a book about exactly what went so gloriously wrong in the first year or so of Isabella's marriage. I could debate whether it was bad advice or bad karma. Was it that Isabella, for all her celebrated levelheadedness, wasn't up to the job? Or was it that no one, really, is up to that job?

That book has been written many times already. If you're looking for a good one, I'd recommend *Dizzy Izzy: Deconstruction of a Postmodern Princess* by Camille Paglia, although it does dwell a bit much on the silly psychobabble of the time period. (And the constant comparisons to King William's mother will just bore many of today's readers to tears. You have to remember the book was written relatively soon after Will's mum's death, and people of the time actually thought she would be of more lasting significance than Isabella.)

Still, I'm telling the story not of Isabella's missteps but of how she found her footing. Change rarely happens overnight, and this change most certainly did not. But there was a moment when it became marvelously apparent, and that was the moment when Ethelbald Candeloro published a column under the headline: I'M DIZZY FOR IZZY.

Ethelbald, with amazing candor, wrote of how he had been cruelly delighted when the engagement had been announced, because Isabella had shown all the signs of producing years of juicy copy. Yes, he had joined the throngs praising the prince's choice at the time. Who would, on news of an engagement, be tactless enough to predict a rip-roaring disaster? But that was, Ethelbald now admitted, what he had privately expected. From the way her name so easily lent itself to mockery (Dizzy Izzy, indeed) to her absolute daring (her wedding dress was lovely, but anything so bold portended years of fashion mistakes ahead), it all added up to a sure sign of a terrific fiasco.

When would princes learn, Ethelbald remembered asking himself at the wedding, that they must marry only crowned heiresses of other countries, creatures who were neither glamorous nor down-to-earth nor mature nor level-headed? A successful match, Ethelbald had thought, would come only when princes marry silly, selfish women who demand their butlers bring food right to their room and insist on wearing only the gowns of their great-grandmama the Queen of Someplace Distant and Tasteful. Ethelbald noted in passing that Rafie's sister, Princess Iphigenia, was a prime example of a proper princess and was sure to suit some foreign prince very well.

All this rubbing shoulders with commoners and dressing like a modern woman and living like a modern woman, it just wouldn't work at all, he had thought. Isabella's so-called down-to-earth quality—which he viewed as more of a stubborn, selfish insistence that she should have the same right to breeze about the public streets as the average commoner—was the surest sign of disaster to come. Ethelbald had thought Isabella's desire to eat in ordinary cafés and to have tea with commoners, however charming on the surface, would inevitably cause her to blunder into disaster. Isabella was so unassuming, he had argued, because she did not fully appreciate her new role; therefore, she never understood her own privilege, could not fathom the danger of dining in public spots, spending her own money extravagantly, or trusting those who seemed kind.

Ever since the marriage, Ethelbald had half expected to

find photos of her straddling a motorcycle and French-kissing some long-haired American auto mechanic with a criminal record. When, instead, the "thar she blows" photo appeared, the only surprise was that it wasn't much worse and much sooner. That's what he said at the time, and that's what he believed. He had considered it only a good warm-up for a rocking few decades.

But—and here is where the tone of the column made a dramatic turn—something had changed. And for the life of him, Ethelbald said, he didn't know what it was. Sometime in the last year or so, Isabella had become a real fairy-tale princess. The cynical old coot actually used the phrase "real fairy-tale princess."

He talked of how she worked tirelessly for charity, how she dressed in plain but pretty pastel suits set off to perfection by the tweaking of the tiniest detail—a thin bejeweled belt, a series of miniature bows down the back, some fine needlework on the bodice. "Her fashion staff reports that she calls this 'detailing,'" he said. "But photographers call it dazzling."

And speaking of photographers, he noted that she never frowned at them even when (he admitted!) they were quite beastly. On St. Teresa of Calcutta Day, Isabella gave blood.

He could not fault her for not being generous. She was generous with her time, her money, and her smiles. He could not fault her for not being glamorous. She was glamorous. And while it was undoubtedly true that she spent more on her clothes than the average woman in the kingdom, she routinely wore the same clothes several times over—just in stunning new combinations. Consider, he said, the sleeveless cloud-colored shift dress she wore to a children's ward on Valentine's Day. Posed with the nurses in modern blue scrubs that day, Isabella in her white dress looked like a sweet, old-fashioned angel of mercy. Florence Nightingale herself could not have been easier on the eyes.

Then, a couple of months later, when Rafie was speaking to war veterans on the National Day of Remembering, she wore the same dress, this time set off by a tailored jacket with subtle military styling and just enough crimson trim to bring to mind the nation's naval uniform.

No matter what Isabella's clothing allowance actually was, Ethelbald said, the princess had proved herself a fine example to frugal women everywhere who wanted to find sensible but stylish and fresh ways to liven up an old dress. Besides, he noted, the average woman would spend more, too, if she were photographed so often. And if she looked so beautiful in everything she wore.

In a final flourish, Ethelbald, with no apparent shame, praised Isabella's good humor and self-deferential quality, applauding her decision to give to an eBay charity auction the goblet she had carried to the Russian baby shower.

"I thought I'd spend the rest of my career writing about Dizzy Izzy," he famously concluded. "But the joke is on me, because now 'I'm Dizzy for Izzy.'"

Chapter 6

*N*o one else knows this. But Isabella told me once. She got a faraway look in her eyes, and her voice took on a distant, dreamy—some would even say goofy—quality.

She told me that, on the night before she was to leave Yale and return home, the buzzer in her room went off. When she heard his voice on the intercom, she realized that she had, in some way, been waiting for that buzz for three years. She didn't know why he had waited so long.

They talked for hours, under the stars. She invited him up, but he declined. So they stood there, leaning against his truck, listening to music that drifted down from a fourth-floor dorm room. It seemed to Isabella that the sky was higher that night than it had ever been. She looked up once and felt faint. It seemed, also, like all her thoughts and feelings and insights had never been so fresh and original and profound.

That is what she said. And since she is not generally inclined to speak about events in such a silly, gushing (dare I say?), romantic way, I can only suppose that is truly the way she felt.

She said she had always admired Geoffrey's muscles and laughed at his jokes and appreciated his kindness, but she had never, until that night, noticed—not consciously, at least—that he was this tiny thing. In the garage, he seemed to loom large as he moved about, the master of his environment. But here, she could see that there was, all around him, this huge world: big stone buildings, ancient tall trees. Geoffrey did not seem in control here. He was small and vulnerable. In that moment, he seemed not like someone who kept her car safe and thus her life secure, but like someone who was small and alone and who might need a hug.

So she hugged him. They hugged for a long time.

Then they kissed.

It was not, quite obviously, her first kiss, but it was so tender, sweet, and passionate that it evoked memories of teenage love and shared ice cream and broken curfews. At least that's what Isabella said it did for her. And I guess hearing her talk this way made me think of those things, too.

Then Isabella said to Geoffrey, "I'd better be going."

Then she said, "Good night."

She never knew why she did it. She never knew why she pulled away. Why she didn't go right on kissing him for hours, following those kisses wherever they led, which would have most certainly not been marriage, but might have been a painfully passionate few months. You know, the sort of relationship with such incredible highs and lows that the whole world seems to spin on the mood of your beloved, where it feels at times like you've caught hold of an angel's wing and it's burning you up but keeping you so splendidly warm, the kind of relationship that when, years later, happily married and content with your life, you see someone who resembles your old beau on a street in a big foreign city, your stomach churns, though you wouldn't take him back for a second. I think Isabella considered her failure to climb on for that ride a sign of her emotional immaturity, of excessive, even royal, rigidness.

But I also think she was too hard on herself. I suspect she realized that it was simply too late. Had Geoffrey knocked on her door and stood in that parking lot even a month sooner, she might have given it a go. If either of them had believed in each other enough to pucker up before they were about to be separated by an ocean, it would have indicated something—some real chance, some real daring.

But by the time he showed up, her clothes were already in boxes and her roommate was already gone. Isabella and Geoffrey had shared drinks and talks and life philosophies and had stared into each other's eyes and held that stare for just a bit longer than was comfortable and had flirted and complimented and bantered. But they had lacked the courage to do more.

As she kissed him there in the parking lot, she knew that their lack of courage was a fatal error, a deal breaker, a sure sign that they had no long-term chance. And given that, she knew that nothing they could do or say or share over a few passionate months could possibly make him mean more to her than he already did.

They could carry on long-distance and she could suddenly take an interest in getting a doctorate and Geoffrey could thrill her by calling and break her heart by not calling enough and they could soar together and crash together and when it was all said and done, he would still be what he already was, a fond and tender half-regret, a road not fully taken. So she might as well walk away now, without all the dramatics.

Some practical part of her heart knew that.

They would not end up together, not because of any differences in class or culture, not because of the distance or her degree. It was far simpler than that. He was a rebel who showed up at doors of women who were leaving. And she was, then, a very good girl who left on the day she was scheduled and did not fiddle with long-distance love. Neither of them could have imagined then that she would someday lead him into the worst trouble of his life.

So why did they kiss at all? It was so that years later, when Geoffrey said things like "Maybe I was kidding myself" and when she wrote letters that began "Remember me?" they would be only words, uttered in the form of humility. They did not mean anything. He knew he had not been fooling himself. She knew he remembered her. For there had been that kiss.

Chapter 7

You can imagine, of course, what a stir Ethelbald's "Dizzy for Izzy" column caused at the castle. The queen spun into a tremendous, envious funk, which she did not fully shake for many years. The king was rather relieved that the words were kind, at least, but he was sorely afraid that it would only encourage Her Highness into more high jinks. Prince Raphael was delighted. Sir Hubert was mortified.

Isabella was scared to death.

She read it that morning over tea. Her husband handed it to her and told her that though he normally discouraged her from reading the columns, he thought she should see this one. She smiled pleasantly at the end and said, "That's nice." But she was thinking that it wasn't nice at all. It was the most awful thing that had ever happened. *Ethelbald Candeloro knows about Geoffrey!* she thought.

Ethelbald, she was convinced, was like a cat batting around the mouse rather than biting its head off. She realized suddenly that she hated Ethelbald. She hated his ugly mustache and she hated his sick grin and she hated the way he was looking up from that column, smugly, as if to acknowledge that he was toying with her.

It was, she thought, quite apparent. For out of the whole column, one line stood out starkly: "I half expected before the first year was out to find photos of her straddling a motorcycle and French-kissing a long-haired American auto mechanic with a criminal record."

Strictly speaking, Isabella knew that this warning, which she was certain it must be, was a bluff. After all, her one kiss with Geoffrey had been leaning against a pickup, not straddling a motorcycle. Besides, it wasn't a *French* kiss but a good wholesome Bisbanian kiss, she could assure you of that. Geoffrey didn't have a criminal record. (That high school marijuana charge would not have been considered criminal in most of Europe.) And she would have noticed if cameras had been sported by any of the dozens of people who had passed them that evening in the dorm parking lot where she and Geoffrey had lingered and talked and hugged and finally kissed. Wouldn't she have noticed?

In fact, the only person she particularly remembered passing by that night was Jimmy Bennett, a classmate who was himself leaving—unenthusiastically, it must be said— that same weekend for his home in Green Bay, Wisconsin. He had been entertaining friends for months by loudly lamenting his return home, portraying it as a place so remote in location and so insular in attitude that some of the more cynical townspeople claimed Elvis Presley was living out his waning days there, unnoticed by his neighbors.

"Trust me," Jimmy would say, "it's possible. Elvis could jog up and down the streets of Green Bay every day for years, and no one would notice. They're an unobservant lot."

"Jog?" Isabella would ask. "Wouldn't Elvis be rather old by now?"

"They also can't count," Jimmy would say.

Isabella thought Jimmy was a harmless, funny guy, and so she'd never thought much about how he'd seemed to linger longer than strictly necessary that night when he came by to pick up something that Isabella's roommate had left for him. But now that Isabella was thinking about it, she was beginning to remember a few troubling details. For example, the "something" her roommate had left for him was a camera. Also, the camera was one the roommate and Jimmy had used on a class project—a journalism class project.

Jimmy had seen her in the parking lot with Geoffrey. Isabella remembered that he'd approached in a hesitant, curious way. She had told him to go on up to the dorm room. She'd probably gestured to the window of her room, three flights up and with a direct line of sight to where Geoffrey's truck was parked. She'd said that the door was unlocked, that the camera was on the desk. "Help yourself," she said, and added with a giggle, "Have fun in Green Bay."

Jimmy had rolled his eyes and grimaced a little and headed on up. A little later, she saw him leave. At least she thought she remembered that, though she could not say for sure now if "a little later" had been minutes or hours. Time had seemed to stand still that night. And so much had happened in the time since.

She'd never thought much about Jimmy's visit before. But after Ethelbald's column, it was the only thing she could think about. And she didn't at all like what she was thinking.

For while the details of the column—the motorcycle, the French kiss, the criminal record—were sufficiently wrong to give her hope, they were sufficiently right to give her pause.

It is hard for us to imagine now the terror this struck in poor Isabella's heart. To an objective observer, it would hardly seem that a photograph of a youthful passionate kiss, even if such a photo suggested more of a relationship than actually existed, would have caused anything more than the slightest, most fleeting embarrassment for the princess. After all, the time she had spent with Geoffrey was while she was single. She and Rafie had not even dated. In fact, during that same time, the prince was often photographed with a bevy of beautiful women on his arm.

But Isabella's fear was not the rational fear of a woman who was considering the possible existence of an embarrassing photograph. Isabella's fear was not that Ethelbald knew her secret actions, but something worse. She feared he knew the secrets of her heart.

It seems crazy. But from Isabella's perspective, it was the only possible explanation. A man who openly admitted to loathing her writes a column praising her and dangles in it a sentence that describes her one secret almost perfectly. Was it a warning? A public bid for a photo that he knew must exist? Could it be just coincidence?

Isabella excused herself, went into her largest closet, and pulled from her safe the only thing of Geoffrey's she had dared to keep—his first letter. She read it again, closed her eyes, and repeated it, convincing herself that she had memorized it. Then she shredded it. The letter, even if printed in full in Ethelbald's column, would not have created the faintest stir. No one could have imagined that it meant anything to anyone. It was all froth and bubble. The notion that it had somehow converted the unsuccessful Princess Isabella into the "I'm Dizzy for Izzy" phenomenon would seem preposterous. But Isabella had to do something, and it was the only thing she could think to do: destroy her one physical link to Geoffrey.

That is the reason the letter does not exist. But I read it

a time or two before it was destroyed. So I know what it said:

> *Dear Belle,*
>   *Glad to hear from you. Don't worry about losing touch. I've been pretty busy myself, so I know the score. We'll just do better from now on.*
>   *Dreadfully dull, eh? I know how that is. Same old, same old. Easy or hard, life gets dull if it's too predictable. That's when you should kick back, listen to some good tunes, and remember that life is what you make of it. Remember, the Boss will never let you down.*
>   *Will write more later,*
>
>   *Jeffrey*
>
> *P.S. I got married myself. My wife told me to tell you, "Keep your chin up."*

Chapter 8

The ramifications of Ethelbald's column did not end with the torn-up letter. Outside the castle, the column unleashed a frenzy that never really died. You can hear echoes of it still, all these years later, in the commentary about Isabella being one of the "faces of the century."

When a longtime royal watcher like Ethelbald writes a column like that, it gets picked up everywhere. The theme was beaten into the ground, and suddenly, there were little feature stories on the news, even in America. The Yale gift shop, I'm told, started selling T-shirts that said, FROM PRESIDENTS TO PRINCESSES, WE PREPARE YOU FOR LIFE. (I *think* it was some sort of American joke. But you know the way they are. You never can be sure.)

You'd think it would have become boring—and if there were any complaints, they were from people like my old hot-tub friends, casual, unprofessional royal watchers who rather liked a good scandal now and then. Too much flawless pizzazz gets boring so quickly. "Well, she's a bit much," such people would say with a sniff. But then, just in time to save the tabloids, Isabella would manage to stir something up to sell a few more papers. There was the way she proclaimed often enough and loudly enough that it was sure to be leaked that she wouldn't be producing grandchildren until King Philippe agreed that her firstborn, be it a boy *or* a girl, would be next in line to the throne. (The king finally agreed, officially changing the line of royal succession to treat male and female offspring equally.)

And there was the time when Isabella nearly caused that poor reporter to faint by volunteering during a gardening interview what she thought of the parliament's move to repeal a long-standing ban on the once traditional Bisbanian "sport" of urban bunny trapping. The sport had become distasteful to almost all the nation's citizens, and not only because the phrase "bunny trapping" looked so bad in tourism brochures. Let's just say the traditional traps were about as efficient as the nation's signature motor cars and thus were considered cruel. Not to mention the unpleasantness of encountering, during a stroll in the park, a not quite successful trapping.

Still, it was unprecedented for a member of the monarch's family to take a stand on even such a clear-cut issue. Yet Isabella did so, almost nonchalantly.

"I know my responsibilities as princess require me to remain removed from politics," she said, sounding a little sad. "But surely my responsibilities as a person, and a citizen and a Christian, are more important. They require me to speak out on matters that are as simple as right and wrong. And this is wrong for our country on so many different levels."

The majority leader, a member of a trap-building family, nearly wept, he was so livid at her statement. He demanded an apology and hinted vaguely that Isabella was not fit to be queen. But his words backfired, as more and more people demanded to know why, exactly, he believed that a person, a citizen, a Christian should *not* speak about what she believed.

Even the nation's by then quite large Islamic population was utterly delighted by Isabella's invocation of her religion, for they thought that she used it in a humble, charming way. "It's hardly a matter of introducing a royal religion," explained one religious leader. "She didn't say trapping should be banned because it's unchristian. She said being a Christian requires her to speak out, something that a member of any principled religion can agree with."

By week's end, the majority leader had done a complete reversal, holding a press conference to announce he'd vote no on his own bill. He wore a button that said I'M DIZZY FOR IZZY.

On the street, the rusty bumpers of the Bisbas driven by many young people sported stickers that said IZZY FOR PRIME MINISTER.

Back at the castle?

Sir Hubert retreated to his chambers and cursed for hours. "Sell shoes? Sell shoes?" he said to his wife. "Did I say *sell* shoes? Harrumph. I'd *make* shoes, I tell you, if it weren't for that pension fund."

Queen Regina seemed to be considering a cobbling career herself about then. She kept watching the clip over and over, fixating on the stunning line about Isabella's responsibilities as a citizen being more important than those of a princess.

Her Majesty was aghast, muttering repeatedly, "Well I never."

And King Philippe would reply, "Neither have I."

It was clear what the people thought, however. Isabella's

public career, right up until that awful day when it all fell apart, was unparalleled. Sometimes, even all these years later, I wish she could have kept it up. I still feel robbed that it was cut short. Part of me agrees with the conventional wisdom of the time, which was that something had to give. She couldn't keep going that way forever. It was just a matter of time before she got fat or, at least, pregnant. Soon enough, she would have gotten old and inflexible and would have started muttering about teenagers needing to have more respect or about good help being hard to find anymore. It was only a matter of time before some other new, young, mysterious princess in some other small, glamorous country pushed her aside on the global stage. Or, you know, some television starlet.

But part of me believes Isabella could have done it. And oh, wouldn't it have been something to see!

But alas, I'm getting ahead of myself again. The important thing to note about the royal family during those wonderful Isabella years was that gradually, a certain giddy, reckless atmosphere developed. Steeped in tradition, ruled by decorum, frightened by change, the rest of the royal family did not come close to emulating the princess, but they did slowly begin to exercise a bit of self-will and ambition.

Queen Regina boxed up her royal furs and sent them to a museum. "I think fur's ghastly," she told Hubert. "I don't care what the furriers think."

His Majesty took to wearing imported suits and watching American football, even though his advisers thought it would unsettle the country.

And Prince Raphael? Well, Rafie did several things. Most notably, he began to admit to himself that he was in love.

Chapter 9

This love he admitted surprised Rafie, because he had convinced himself that his marriage was one of convenience. And it was convenient. Because, despite Ethelbald Candeloro's initial private cynicism, Raphael and Isabella's marriage was one of the soundest royal matches of the last two centuries. They were, even at their worst, an extraordinary public team. Whenever they stood before the people, they played off each other and supported each other and bucked each other up in ways that only those who were close to them could appreciate.

Being a royal, after all, is very much a lifelong performance art piece. And Rafie and Isabella, for the most part, ad-libbed with ease and flair. Rafie would somehow call attention to himself just when Isabella was becoming a bit weary of all eyes being on her. She would dress most attractively on the days when he felt his small speeches were the weakest. She would snort water out of her nose, and he'd come up with the line "At least they got my good side."

The Prince and Princess of Gallagher were quite rare in that they genuinely liked each other. Modern royal couplings are usually either strictly practical or wildly romantic. The idea of a comfortable companionship was almost unheard of and usually came only by accident and after a good many years.

But it came immediately to Raphael and Isabella. So they did not engage in the competition and petty jealousies that unravel the marriages of many young heirs. It was unremarkable to them. That was part of being a team.

It is true that, like many newlyweds, they struggled during the first year of their marriage. Isabella's public stumbles created nights of icy arguments and heated silences in the couple's suite in the west wing of the castle. In their worst nights, they confronted demons and nursed regret and wondered about former loves. Despite all that bumbling and mumbling, despite their misgivings and wonderings, their public face never faltered, and of all the charges lobbed at Isabella during her dizziness days, it is a compliment that no one once suggested she was a bad wife.

Later, when she became the phenomenon that defined a century, she managed to do so without seeming to ever intentionally overshadow her husband. Perhaps it was a testament to their humility and companionship, but I think it was because the magic that Isabella spread worked the best on people she was close to. And Raphael was the closest. So he would look at a sea of well-wishers, notice that 80 percent of them were reaching for Isabella's hand rather than his, and his only reaction was to be sorry that he'd distracted the other 20 percent. At least that is the impression he always gave in public, and in my experience, it is the impression he gave in private, too. He was, simply, a team player and she was his team.

This is not to suggest that they were just friendly coworkers. Far from it. Neither the prince nor the princess was raised to engage in mushy banter and sweet nothings, but oh, how they laughed and giggled and shared conspiratorial looks and phrases. (In the entire time that the royal couple lived at the castle, neither Secrest nor Vreeland could figure out the meaning of certain code words that Their Highnesses would exchange with each other, prompting gales of laughter.)

In fact, if things had only turned out differently for Raphael, I am quite sure that his marriage to Isabella would have been remembered as one of the greatest love stories ever lived on a global stage. And that is saying quite a bit for what was, after all, the relatively sensible pairing of two well-positioned people. Usually, great love stories must have great suffering. There must be valiant struggles and cruel ironies and tremendous sacrifices. They can't just be cavorting about European resort towns in a souped-up Bisba, making a splash by going through drive-throughs while wearing tuxes and diamonds.

("Those stuffy royal banquets always leave me wanting," Isabella reportedly said to a Bisbanian White Castle employee one late night, as she pulled up to order twenty burgers to go. The employee—dubbed Burger Boy by the low-rent tabloid that bought his story and published it under the headline WHITE CASTLE PRINCESS—claimed this comment was awfully suggestive, given that it was uttered in a breathy voice, while Rafie, who was in the passenger seat, moved his hand along Isabella's thigh and stared at her in a slightly drunk, leering way. Her tiara, Burger Boy said, was slipping off the side of her head. Most commentators, including

Ethelbald Candeloro, did not believe Burger Boy. I was never brave enough to ask either Isabella or Rafie, so I don't know for sure. But I must say it sounds just like them to me.)

The true story of Isabella and Rafie's love actually does have cruel ironies and great sacrifices and valiant struggles. But no one knows that story. The story that the world believes it knows, with Raphael's sudden death and Isabella's long exile, is just too short. You'd think the decades during which the widowed princess wore her somber brown and roamed American streets would have permanently etched the Isabella-Raphael love story on the world's romantic psyche. But it somehow just made people forget Rafie altogether.

Nevertheless, I'm getting ahead of myself again. First I must finish explaining Isabella's glorious recovery.

The improvement noted by Ethelbald Candeloro had, as I already stated, started right after Isabella read Geoffrey's first letter. That first occasion was not at all like the last one. When Isabella read the letter the final time before destroying it, she wept. For the letter had come to mean a great deal to her. But when she read it the first time, she laughed bitterly.

She had not known exactly what she was hoping for. The letter was in fact much like what she should have expected. Geoffrey's simple, uncomplicated observations were, after all, what she had always liked about him. But she had somehow entertained the notion that her life and the strange turn it had taken would have merited more than a paragraph, especially a paragraph that suggested she listen to the Boss.

Isabella appreciated the works of Springsteen as much as any European princess could. She rather enjoyed the CDs Geoffrey had loaned her while she was at Yale, and she had even downloaded some more. She had listened to songs about the romance of the roads that lead out of dying small towns as she was flying back into tiny Bisbania, with its petty neighborhood politics and struggling industries. She had listened to songs about working-class couples being torn apart by economic hardship while she was being courted by the prince.

But she stopped listening to the music when she moved into the castle, where the music was always selected by Hubert or the queen and where the king required that 86 percent of any playlist be national.

Somewhat irrationally, Isabella thought Geoffrey should know about the castle playlist rules, so it irritated her that he suggested listening to a retro American songster, and it further irritated her that Geoffrey seemed to go out of his way to point out that he had married—though this seems unfair, coming from a woman who had been the star of the most celebrated wedding of the century. (Especially given that Geoffrey mentioned his wife only in passing, and not until the "P.S.") But fairness was beside the point. Isabella was experiencing the same sort of jealousy that makes all of us prefer to believe that none of our ex-boyfriends ever really got over us, even when the evidence would suggest that they were over us before the relationship was officially over.

Despite Isabella's rather pronounced initial disappointment, she saved the letter. Sometimes when she was lonely or sad, she would pull it out of her makeup drawer and reread it. These readings became daily and served to elevate and solemnize the simple words, and soon she found herself taking comfort in them. She came to like the notion that she could listen to a working-class American songwriter for advice, since it seemed to dignify her duties as real work. It also eventually came to please her that Geoffrey's wife had sent her advice. It suggested, somehow, that despite all the "Dizzy Izzy" headlines, Her Royal Highness the Princess of Gallagher had a following, an appeal, a "people," if you will. There were real human beings out there—an American car mechanic's wife among them—who were rooting for her.

So she ordered (she would say "asked") Secrest to bring

her headphones, and the princess began listening to Springsteen while writing letters or signing proclamations or dining alone. They gave her energy, put a bounce in her step, and helped her to laugh at herself. Many a day, she'd head off for a round of ribbon cuttings humming "Working on the Highway" and giggling a little. Often she would attempt in her speeches to toss out a poetic image that she thought might have suited the Boss—most notably in a commencement address at Bisbania Community College, in which she compared a degree to a beloved and well-tuned car.

More and more, she found herself relying on Springsteen for inspiration and comfort. Then one day, while lifting weights to one of the rocker's lesser-known tunes in the castle gymnasium, she came to believe that somehow the Boss was speaking directly to her.

She had the headphones turned up loud. She was attempting to keep pace with the music as she did her modest bench presses—less weight, more reps for toning. Suddenly, the lyrics jumped out at her. The song, entitled "Cynthia," was a silly little ditty about construction workers admiring a classy lady. She doesn't stop or greet the men, but they don't care. In a gloomy and glum world, the workers appreciate simply knowing that such loveliness exists.

Isabella was so enthralled with the song that she stopped in mid–bench press to listen to it. She had, like many princesses before her, struggled to know her job. She was not an actress who entertained, nor a stateswoman who governed. What should she do? And here was the answer. The construction workers saw the classy lady as an excuse to take a break from their daily labor. When she passed by, it was a reason to "stop, stand, and salute" her style.

In the days that followed, Princess Isabella couldn't get the lines out of her head. They seemed, she thought, to be written particularly for princesses of her generation. Suddenly, she was at ease. Her taste in clothes became

unfaltering. At the same time, her knack for picking appropriate causes became unwaveringly accurate. She learned
how to look directly into people's eyes, even when looking
at six hundred people at once. And, in an unexplained twist,
she even finally developed nice skin, which allowed her to
wear less makeup.

Her newfound knack for capturing the public fancy
became, perhaps, most apparent in what became known as
the "sock incident"—the near disaster that ensued when
Isabella was photographed hopping off a train in celebration
of Public Transport Day wearing one black sock and one blue.

We are not, I'm sorry to report, speaking of a mere flash
of color peeking out from a royal trouser leg. There was, in
this outfit, a lot of sock. Isabella was wearing knee-high stockings with a short plaid skirt, capturing the so-called schoolgirl
look that the queen thought was questionable enough for a
woman of Isabella's age, even if the colors were right.

But, in this case, the colors were quite clearly wrong.

Secrest had, needless to say, been on vacation.
Otherwise, she would have personally checked the tags for
dye-lot numbers and held them up to the window, as was
her routine, to detect any unfortunate fading issues, which
can sometimes occur even with the best laundries. Yes, the
clothes were as right as rain whenever Secrest checked them.

But Secrest was lying on a beach in southern Spain that
day. So the niece of one of the castle gardeners, a young
intern originally hired to walk the royal dogs, had taken
Secrest's place in handling the princess's clothes. Although it
appears that by "handle," we mean only that she "handed"
them over, because the subsequent investigation found
evidence of slipshod work from toe to top. In addition to the
color problem, the socks were from two different designers,
and one of the princess's bobby pins had a speck of rust.

Isabella herself, I suppose, could have saved the day by
glancing at her feet herself. But she was not accustomed to

paying much attention to such things and probably could not have been expected to notice the coloration differential in the dim light of her dressing room.

However, the difference screamed for attention in the early-morning train-station light and caused gasps of wonder and astonishment from the crowds bottlenecked at the station. (It is one of the ironies of Public Transport Day that the efforts to accommodate visiting dignitaries make everyone else late for work.)

Hubert was beside himself with rage and hurt. He fired two laundry maids and, of course, the inattentive intern and further launched a review of the castle vacation policy.

"Why on earth would Secrest be on vacation on Public Transport Day?" he kept asking the other senior advisers, who all agreed that they could not imagine a legitimate reason.

The queen herself launched the internal review of how the intern came to replace Secrest, and the review provided weeks of surprising revelations. I'll spare you the sordid details of how an unrequited crush on the dog groom had served to distract the young worker. But I will say that the entire staff was beside itself with shame and self-loathing after the investigation turned up an ominous memo, carefully filed away but never followed up on, from the head of kennel operations, who complained just days before the sock incident that the intern had twice walked Grover, the royal greyhound, using a leash that did not match his collar.

"The leash was red. The collar blue. Dear Grover is a rare milky white," the kennel chief wrote. "The poor dog looked like the flag of France! Scandalous!"

Hubert, who had found the memo in his own file cabinet but could not remember it ever crossing his desk, turned green with rage every time he thought about it. "This is the person put in charge of the princess's clothes?" Hubert said. Ever after, he became obsessive about reading every memo addressed to him, often twice, to the exclusion of all other duties.

The castle maintenance staff was soon charged with installing an elaborate lighting system in the dressing room of all the principal royals so that they could direct their dressers to adjust the lighting to mimic eighty-six distinct environments—from a cloudy day at the racetrack to a dusk trip down a red carpet to, needless to say, a clear morning in a train station on Public Transport Day.

(As a quick aside, I must report that among the ramifications was a personal one for Secrest, who met the chief of kennel operations over a hot morning cider to discuss the unfortunate chain of events. They found comfort in each other's words and eventually in each other's arms and were happily married soon after. Secrest was a blubbery, happy mess at the wedding, but was as ramrod strict as ever when she returned to work from her weekend honeymoon.)

But even as the sock crisis reverberated throughout the castle, ending a few careers and several carefree vacations, it played completely differently with the public, thanks to an anonymous freethinking public relations professional who was helping out at the anti-domestic violence organization known as Battered Women No More. The young public relations executive was a student of something called "guerrilla public relations," in which do-good organizations with little funding grab media attention by "hijacking" news stories and taking credit for celebrity fashion errors or marriage breakups.

So if a lovely young starlet and her leading man break up in the midst of a movie, causing massive budget overruns and stiffly acted love scenes, a dedicated animal rights group might quietly leak word that the relationship ended over a disagreement about whether, say, the starlet should wear fur slippers to bed—prompting all sorts of gossipy news stories that touch on animal rights and quote officials from the agency that leaked the completely fabricated story.

Battered Women No More had been looking for the right opportunity to highlight domestic violence. And when

Isabella stepped off that train in the lovely short skirt and those distinctive mismatched stockings, the freethinking PR professional knew he had found it. He printed up a press release and had it out to the media before the fired castle servants could even cash in by selling their own stories to the tabloids.

The release was simple and short:

"Battered Women No More wants to thank Her Royal Highness the Princess of Gallagher for helping launch the organization's new slogan: 'If he leaves you black and blue, then sock him with a summons.' We know the royal family does not normally take stands on public issues, but one as vital and as uncontroversial as this is surely worth an exception. Lives will no doubt be saved by the princess's adoption of this cause."

In retrospect, the PR agent only wished that he had worked on that slogan a bit, for it sounded awkward to him when repeated on the newscasts. Still, it was *on* the newscasts, and that was the most important thing. He held his breath and waited for the castle reaction. Privately, Hubert said, "Hmmm." Privately, the queen said, "Ummmm." Privately, the king said, "Sock him with a summons? Shouldn't a batterer be arrested outright, not just asked to appear in court at a later date?" Privately, Isabella said, "Huh?"

But publicly, they said . . . nothing. They just let it lie.

So that is how wearing colored socks replaced the earlier custom of wearing a loop of colored ribbon as the preferred way for celebrities to silently salute favorite causes. Actors accepted awards wearing designer tuxes and red socks to show their continuing concern about the AIDS crisis. "Sock it to AIDS," they'd say. Artists protesting the famed African coffee ban wore cappuccino-colored socks known as "No-doze hose." Things finally went too far, in my humble opinion, when Bisbanian men—Ethelbald Candeloro notably among them—started wearing nude nylons to show support for

some sort of legislation aimed at protecting cross-dressers and
the transgendered. It was a dreadful campaign idea made all
the worse by the complicated slogan "Cross-dressers have
nothing to hide." It seemed to presume that legislators would
understand that nude nylons reveal rather than hide—an out-
rageously generous assessment of the hosiery expertise of the
male-dominated Bisbanian legislative body.

(I feel compelled to explain that I love cross-dressers
and the transgendered as much as everyone else, and I'm
sure the legislation was good government and all that. My
quibble is not with the cause but with the medium. It seems
to me that the purpose of these sock statements was to
evoke the cause, not to *become* the cause. And why would
anyone, transgendered or otherwise, wear nude nylons anyway? It is so completely common. Your hose should match
your shoes. Please.)

Isabella's sock crisis, you might notice, was resolved
without any input from Isabella, who can be credited only
with the wisdom of not denying the lie when it was conve-
niently told for her. It goes to show you that when things are
going badly, things go badly. And when things are going
well, they go spectacularly.

It was, as it turned out, the sock incident that prompted
Ethelbald to start thinking about how well things had been
going for the princess, though it took him another several
months to acknowledge this change in that famous column—the one that put such fear into Isabella's heart. It
would have been a tragedy for all of Bisbania if Isabella had
let Ethelbald's column scare her off. If the apparent reference to Geoffrey had prompted her to take off the headphones and get a grip on herself, it would have been a
tragedy for her, the royal family, even the whole world.

But what happened instead, well, it was mostly a
tragedy for me.

Chapter 10

*O*h dear! I really shouldn't have said that. Now you're going to spend the next several chapters worrying about me, when obviously I'm fine. I'm old, no debate there. Time is quickly running out for me. But I'm alive and well and still enjoying a brisk walk every day. When it's all said and done, I've had a good life. I'm happy. And I have the princess to thank for much of it.

But lately, I've been in a fatalistic mood. When I'm in such a state, one of my great sources of entertainment is tracing back the events of a lifetime, determining at what specific point things went wrong or right. It is a pointless exercise. I know this. Look no further than the day when I, just a young wisp of a thing, turned down a perfectly good editing job at a small newspaper in middle America. When I look back on that now, I imagine promotions and leapfrogging career moves to larger and larger papers. I tell myself if I had taken that editing job, I would have been the editor of *The National Times*—Bisbania's only nontabloid daily newspaper—by the time I was fifty. Instead, all my dreams of news-management glory died that day. I sputtered and struggled along, doing mediocre but dependable reporting work. I churned out the sort of stories that pleased my bosses by being on time and easy to read but neither won awards nor changed lives. I never did the big work of journalism, setting the public agenda, shaping the national conversation. All because I didn't take that editing job. That's what I tell myself. And eventually, of course, I left news altogether.

But on the other hand, I never would have met my dearly departed husband if I had gone off to middle America to edit news. And what of the work I did do? Not that it compares to editing *The Times*. But I enjoyed it, and I think others did, too. So was the day I said no thanks to that editing job the best day or the worst day of my life? It was both. It was neither. It's not worth thinking about.

I can make the same kind of case for the events that unfolded shortly after Isabella tore up Geoffrey's letter and became obsessed with covering herself from Ethelbald's alleged photo hunt. She did three things that week.

First, she sobbed on the shoulder of Princess Iphigenia, who was alternately puzzled, disturbed, and strangely flattered by the sudden returned weakness in her sister-in-law, whose rocketing career and presumed fertility had made all but meaningless Genia's status as second in line to the throne. By the time anything happened to the fit, spry king, it was assumed, Isabella and Raphael would have a slew of children, all of whom would have stepped in front of Genia, who had so little respect among the tabloid writers that they had shortened her name yet again to the vulgar French-sounding Princess Gene. (Amazingly, they weren't even *trying* to be insulting; they just didn't care enough to make an extra letter seem worthwhile.)

Second, Isabella dispatched a mystified Secrest to America to hire a discreet private investigator—a saucy, sassy, heavy-smoking woman with a big tattoo and a licensed semiautomatic—to dig up Jimmy Bennett, the college chum with the worrisome camera.

Finally, Princess Isabella asked Geoffrey and his wife to leave America and move to Bisbania.

It was really inevitable. From the moment that Geoffrey responded to Isabella's first letter, there was little doubt that he would someday be safely ensconced in the castle, working at the royal garage and taking smoke breaks by the lapping waters of the Bisbanian Sea.

Things might have been different if Geoffrey had simply replied with the fawning, gushing sort of note that Isabella was accustomed to receiving. But two sentences sealed his fate. When Geoffrey suggested listening to the Boss and then passed along his wife's encouragement, he assumed—without even realizing it—the role of royal adviser. As of that moment, he was destined to live at the beck and call of the princess, on the very grounds of the castle. Ethelbald's frightening column did little more than hurry him along.

As you might imagine, Geoffrey and his wife were overwhelmed, flattered, and a little put off by Isabella's request, which was presented to the young couple by Secrest one drizzly night in a royal houseboat permanently stationed near Martha's Vineyard. The deal was, by any standard, fair. Geoffrey was to be paid 172,000 Bisbanian pounds, which even today is a lot of money, so you can imagine its appeal then. Moreover, Geoffrey was to receive two months of vacation each year, free lodging at the castle, a generous clothing allowance for both him and his wife—since they would be expected to attend some castle functions—and any assistance his wife wished or required in finding her own work. For a modest American couple, it was almost unimaginable. (In fact, it caused a bit of whispering at the castle among more senior staff members who had similar packages and had been led to believe they were more than mere mechanics.)

But there was something about the tone of the offer that annoyed the soon-to-be-hyphenated Whitehall-Wrights. Geoffrey and Mae, despite their intense admiration of the princess, and despite the greedy American notion that lots of money and prestige are the building blocks of happiness, couldn't help but feel that the presentation of this offer— which Secrest set forth with a sort of a patriotic call for loyalty and sacrifice—was a bit much. After all, Geoffrey and Mae had no real reason to feel patriotic about or loyal to the royal family, other than their friendly fondness for its apparent future queen. And they saw no real reason why their friendly fondness should lead them to sacrifice for the princess any more than the princess should sacrifice for them. That is, of course, an awfully American way to look at it. Secrest couldn't see their point at all. She found herself wishing she'd paid better attention to "American Perspectives and Philosophies" in school. She was sure this had something to do with the Boston Tea Party. ("You know it's called that," she would say whenever the subject came up, "but they didn't actually drink tea.")

But in the end, she had not needed to worry. Because 172,000 pounds won out. Was that the couple's wisest or worst decision? The best day or the worst day of their lives? Well, now, as I said, I don't editorialize until the end. You'll just have to draw your own conclusions along the way.

Mae experienced all the happiness and horror that a woman could bear. And Geoffrey had a delightful life. There is no way to know how different it would have been if they'd said no thanks and returned to their two-bedroom home with the scuffed-up hardwood floors and horrid robin's-egg-blue aluminum siding. We know only this: If they had said no, there would have been nights when they lay awake, looking at the ceiling, fretting that they had chosen the wrong path. They would have been tortured by regret and sadness.

But as it was, only Mae was tortured. Geoffrey died.

Chapter 11

Geoffrey, who finally acquiesced to his wife's hyphenation request and officially adopted the Whitehall-Wright surname upon his immigration to Bisbania, quickly took to life in the castle. He liked the simple pleasures of performing extraordinarily detailed maintenance on mostly unused cars. (Although given that the royal fleet was, by political necessity, made up entirely of the unreliable Bisbas, he worked a good deal more then you might expect.)

He marveled at the small office he was accorded in the garage, where he kept window-box herb gardens, spent slow afternoons shopping on tawdry American websites, and listened to the best imported stereo system on the market—a gift from Her Highness. On weekends, he took up hobbies that would have been only daydreams in his past life. He learned to weave baskets, pilot small planes, and tap-dance.

Mae, who was building a career writing steamy, overly complicated, and too heavily plotted novels (under an assumed name, so as not to embarrass the royal family), often visited him in his office. They would stretch out end-to-end on the handmade African rugs, bare feet touching bare feet, and stare at the ornate ceiling, planning their next vacation and giggling at the marvelous turn their life had taken.

Mae spent much of her time, all of her clothing allowance, and no small part of their income on magnificent garments that always stood out at the various castle functions. She was even once featured in *HELLO!* as one of "ten common women who dress like royals." That headline caused Hubert no end of grief from Princess Genia, who complained for months afterward, bristling every time anyone uttered Mae's name.

"Dress like royals?" she'd say each and every time. "I hear she has a reputation for dressing like royals. I suppose she must be dressing like the royals of some struggling third-world country where they don't mind garish jewelry and loud-colored gowns with"—here she would pause dramatically and lower her voice—"neutral shoes and nude hose." Her voice would return to normal, and her tone would brighten. "Because she certainly doesn't dress like any royals I know."

But Mae was, at that point at least, oblivious to Iphigenia's attitude. So the only source of tension in the Whitehall-Wrights' lives was also the source of all their happiness, and that was Isabella herself. The effortless elegance, the casual classiness, the spontaneous sensibleness that Isabella projected during the height of her popularity took a lot of work. It took planning. It took strategizing. It took endless late-night debates, and occasionally, as Mae and Prince Raphael each noticed with a bit of jealousy and concern, it took a bit of flirtatious persuasion on the part of Geoffrey.

It was Geoffrey who convinced Isabella just before the last holiday season she spent at the castle to go with a series of velvet gowns, even though all the fashion magazines predicted another year of satin. "You set the trends, Belle," he said. "You don't *follow* them."

It was Geoffrey who helped Isabella summon the courage to publicly align herself with the efforts to remove the stigma from what was, in those unenlightened times, called "streetwalkers' stress." "Whatcha 'fraid of, Belle?" he'd ask. "Being too kind to the downtrodden?"

And it was Geoffrey who found that perfect Springsteen line, the one about ascending into a beautiful dawn and meeting a loved one further down life's highway, that allowed Isabella to so memorably finish her elegy at the televised funeral of the Native American priest turned pop star who had so captured the fancy of the young before dying in a horrible Jacuzzi malfunction.

Geoffrey's form of flirtatious persuasion was a miracle to watch.

"I don't know," Isabella would say in that vaguely whiny voice she would use when she grew tired. "I don't think the people really care how I exercise as long as I don't get all flabby."

Geoffrey would agree, but then he would soar into a beautiful, rambling, seemingly pointless, and yet so pointed monologue. Yes, it was true, he'd say. The sort of exercise she took up didn't matter. After all, she couldn't be a fabulous, trendsetting fairy-tale princess in every possible way. If she was fabulous and trendsetting and fairy-tale in *many* ways, that ought to be enough. So if she was still using a snowboarding simulator when the hottest actresses, the

most gorgeous models, and even the dear Princess Gene—
who, he would note, had been dubbed Lean Gene recently
by the tabloids—had taken up the NASA-inspired body-
building program known as Astrofit, that was just fine.
"You've got it all over them, Belle," he'd say, not noticing the
way Rafie would bristle at the nickname. (The prince would,
often enough, visibly shudder, even if he did not actually
look up from what he was reading, usually a dry textbook
about the effect of mouth cancers on locution or some other
aspect of human speech.)

"You don't have to worry," Geoffrey would continue,
eyes locked with the princess. "You're all right."

Isabella would purr at the compliments and then set out
to ensure that he was correct, taking up the more advanced
Astrofit Pro before the week was up.

Aside from the shuddering, Raphael mostly appeared not
to notice the conversations, although he seemed somewhat
deliberate in his not noticing. But Mae would sometimes raise
her eyebrows or roll her eyes or let her mouth hang open a
little. She would stare at Geoffrey in a quizzical way, and she
was curious about whether he was consciously manipulating
the princess. After conversations like the Astrofit one, and
even on the more important matters, like whether the royal
family should comment on the prime minister's embarrassing
goat scandal, Mae would sometimes try to ferret out
Geoffrey's real thoughts. But she did not get far. He would
utter the same sort of vague observations to her.

Mae noticed this especially after Geoffrey advised
Isabella on how the royal family should handle the funeral
of Lady Carissa, the queen's sister who had been essentially
disowned by the family after the called-off engagement
many years earlier. Lady Carissa had, in fact, been so well
hidden by the royal family after her horrible sweatpants-in-
public phase that the newspaper obituaries felt obligated to
point out that she had still been alive before recently dying.

After Isabella consulted Geoffrey, Mae asked her husband point-blank what he thought the princess should do. Geoffrey did not answer her directly. Instead, he mused about one of Springsteen's less respected albums. "I was tuning in to *Lucky Town* yesterday," Geoffrey said. "Man, the critics did not do that CD justice."

He paused, looked out the window. "It was awesome. So real, you know, so wild. Like that dude knew how to talk about class. He spoke for us working stiffs and got rich speaking for us. That's insane, and he knew it. He's got that great line about how funny it is for a billionaire to wear a poor guy's shirt."

I suppose you have no idea what Geoffrey was talking about. Mae didn't either, though she probably had an advantage over many of you in that she had at least heard the album—about a thousand times on one long drive to Euro Disney alone.

But she later learned that based on this "observation" from Geoffrey, Isabella advised Rafie, and Rafie advised the king, and the king made his case to his wife, and the royal family decided to treat the funeral of the long-ignored Carissa as if it were that of a long-suffering and loyal royal servant. She would be a royal woman in a poor woman's ceremony—and perhaps in a poor woman's blouse, for all anyone knew. The funerals of servants are not considered public events.

This way of handling the funeral, Rafie noted while pitching it to his father, would give the occasion a quiet dignity and an understated majesty but would not raise too many uncomfortable questions about why there were more pictures of the royal family taken with Lady Carissa's casket than had ever been taken of the royal family and Lady Carissa.

The king, oblivious to the tortured history of this advice, took to it immediately and thought it was the soundest suggestion he had heard in a long time. He remarked to the queen, who had been tearfully meeting with her tailor to create a suitably mournful suit for the funeral, that their son had grown into a wise man and, using the cliché that Bisbanian royals always used about a worthy prospective heir, said, "Rafie will keep the throne warm."

So everyone who knew enough to have an opinion thought that Rafie's idea about how to handle the funeral was perfect. Except that it was really Isabella's idea. And except that she would have claimed to Rafie that it was Geoffrey's idea. But Mae, the only other person to actually discuss the plan with Geoffrey, and who knew him as well as anyone, was not at all convinced that Geoffrey had anything so concrete in mind when he rambled about rich pretenders and poor shirts.

Still, it wasn't as if he had talked about the lack of satisfying programming on commercial television or the plight of war veterans. He had, for whatever reason, chosen a Springsteen lyric that could, with some effort and creativity, be applied to the situation.

So Mae did not know what to think. Sometimes she thought that her sweet husband was really just a handy mechanic who made bland observations that seemed "wise" only to the extent that Isabella projected her own wisdom into them. But other times Mae thought her husband was crafty and conniving and that he was playing the princess as if she were his puppet. Mae was never sure which she would prefer him to be.

She was at even more of a loss about Isabella. Did the princess not see the way that Geoffrey was, intentionally or unintentionally, manipulating her? Did she not question his merit as an adviser? Did she not think his constant turning to Springsteen lyrics a bit, well, *odd*?

Apparently, she did not.

For when Geoffrey used the Springsteen song "Cover

Me" to suggest that Isabella start wearing summer gloves, Isabella promptly headed for the nation's fanciest accessory store and purchased every glove they had in stock, which was not many, because summer gloves had been out of fashion for most of the past century. Then she called all the nation's top designers—and truth be told, a few French ones that the royal family did not care to publicly do business with—and asked for custom-made gloves.

She wore these gloves to luncheons, on shopping excursions, and while making hospital rounds, delighting the photographers by peeling them off finger by finger before shaking hands with the patients. Of course, you know what happened. It brought gloves back from the grave, setting off an unparalleled fashion frenzy that—aided by the increasing worry about UV rays—has not died down yet, all these decades later. Gloves reemerged as a European classic, suddenly becoming a symbol of continental femininity and grace. At first the gloves stopped right at the wrist, but they gradually got longer and longer, reaching to the elbow and beyond even for daytime wear, though old-timers like, well, like the queen, would roll their eyes and sniff and snort and mutter something about strippers.

There is, after all, no way to stop a trend once it's started. Old glove companies, which had grown resigned to relying on scarves, belts, and lowbrow dickeys for their livelihood, were in demand again, pulling out old patterns and retraining seamstresses on the fine art of finger seams.

Geoffrey's role as the princess's somewhat questionable adviser fits into a long tradition. Royal women and presidential wives are always being accused of such nonsense. The czar's wife had Rasputin, and virtually all the powerful women who came after her were supposedly using tarot-card readers or psychics. But it never worked out for any of them.

So, no matter how vapid Geoffrey's advice appeared on

the surface, you must give him this: It worked for Isabella. Certainly no other famous advisee made so much out of so little as did the Princess of Gallagher, who became an international icon and fashion setter with nothing more than perfectly ordinary looks and the crown of a tiny, out-of-the-way country with a few big horse races, a long fig season, and a reputation for making unreliable but attractive automobiles. No wonder Isabella thought Springsteen lyrics, as filtered through Geoffrey, worked just fine.

If you ever wondered why Isabella and Raphael gave up the tropical vacations that were typical of the royal family, now you know. Springsteen, a New Jersey boy, did not sing much about palm trees. That is why the prince and princess, in the last months of their public life together, were so often seen walking down the aging boardwalks of Bisbania's touristy cold-water beach neighborhoods, where the royal couple delighted locals and the paparazzi by buying cotton candy, climbing into rusty carnival rides, and taking turns trying to win stuffed animals for each other. Geoffrey called these their *Greetings from Asbury Park* vacations, a reference to Springsteen's first album. The queen called them "pure insanity."

"Does the heir to the throne really need to be hanging upside down?" she would ask. "In public? On something called the Psychedelic Monster, no less?"

Whatever you called the vacations, they were brilliant public relations. The contrast between these low-budget and low-maintenance trips of the Gallaghers and the yachting vacations of the less popular members of the royal family could not have been more stark.

While Isabella had embraced this idea and insisted to Rafie that it was Geoffrey's stern advice, Mae could not help notice that when the princess had first consulted Geoffrey about vacations, he had actually mentioned another album entirely.

The subject had come up during a lighthearted, casual conversation that the mechanic and the princess shared while sitting on the garage patio, their feet irreverently propped up on a rather amateurish bust of Michelangelo while they sipped what they claimed was iced nonalcoholic raspberry cider but which Mae thought smelled of whiskey. (Her assessment, however, is suspect because she made it from several feet away and from the other side of a partially opened sliding glass door, while she was working on a steamy romance about, of all things, a missionary from Alaska.)

"If we don't come up with something, Geoff, it's another fortnight on the yacht for me," Isabella said. "It's simply excruciating. The queen arranges nightly domino tournaments." She sighed and leaned back to examine her carefully manicured pink-painted big toe, which she positioned just below the right eyebrow of Michelangelo. She squinted at it and called out, "Pinkeye!"

Geoffrey and she both laughed at that in a slaphappy, giddy, or perhaps slightly drunk way.

Geoffrey was normally rather protective of the bust, which the castle had accepted from an Italian count while under the mistaken belief that it was a sculpture *by* Michelangelo, rather than a sculpture *of* him.

The bust was actually the work of the count's daughter—if you can correctly describe a project undertaken in art therapy sessions as "work." When the queen realized the mistake, she ordered the sculpture hidden from her sight forever, an awkward order given that she had signed a legal agreement with the count promising to "prominently display" the bust "for now and as long as King Philippe and his heirs fill the throne."

The castle advisers solved the problem by placing the bust on Geoffrey's patio, a decision that was explained to the count in a flowery letter that continually referred to

Michelangelo as the "first great mechanic" and described the slab of concrete off Geoffrey's office as the Garden of Engineering.

Geoffrey loved that, loved talking about "the garden," and always got angry if visitors leaned on Michelangelo's likeness or otherwise showed disrespect. But now he put his own big, hairy, calloused toe over the other eye and said, "Corn eye!" He and Isabella both laughed some more, until she leaned her head over on his shoulder and looked up at him in a pleading way.

"Help me, Geoff," Isabella said with exaggerated drama. "I know you'd never want to vacation with the in-laws."

A cloud passed over her face then, and she glanced quickly at Mae, sat up straight, and pulled away from Geoffrey. "Nothing personal," the princess said, smiling weakly to her confidant's wife. "Any in-laws, I mean—even when they're honest farm folk like your family." She looked at Geoffrey, lowered her voice a little, and continued as if she had never uttered the aside to Mae. "It's inhumane."

That was when Geoffrey began musing about the Springsteen album *Nebraska*, which was named after a large and empty American state and which can only be described as a dark and grim collection of tales about unlucky characters who are forever poking dead dogs, chasing outlaw brothers, and using maps as napkins after eating greasy fried food.

Isabella's giddy mood grew more and more somber, and she stared at Geoffrey as he prattled on. She bit her lip and looked for all the world like she was developing a renewed appreciation for her mother-in-law's domino tournaments on the yacht. Then, finally, Geoffrey's monologue ambled up to a point, which was this:

"Of course, Bruce also talked about beach boardwalks."

"Well," Isabella said, springing back to life. "It wouldn't be my first choice, but you know what I always say: 'The

Boss will not let us down.' I hear Oceanside is delightful this time of year. I'll ask Secrest to make arrangements—once she gets her head out of the loo."

(Secrest and the kennel chief were expecting their first child, a blessed event so late in life, but it was proving to be a difficult pregnancy.)

Isabella jumped up and was gone before Geoffrey could finish saying he thought that sounded like a great plan. Mae replayed the conversation over and over in her mind and asked herself many things that I'm sure you can imagine and also asked herself who was really giving the advice.

Isabella directly questioned Geoffrey's advice only once that I know of. He had suggested she wear a snakeskin suit to a ceremony marking the opening of parliament. This advice would have been suspect enough, even if it had not been gleaned from the lyrics of one of Springsteen's seedier songs, an early work about street life in America called "The E Street Shuffle."

The song is populated with a greasy lot of characters— boy prophets, teenage tramps, a riot squad, a man-child, and someone called "Power Thirteen." Not saints, I'm guessing, and probably not the smartest dressers either.

Isabella apparently guessed the same. "Snakeskin?" she said, in a higher voice than usual. "An entire suit?" She wrinkled her nose, rubbed her hands along her arms as if imagining the feel of such a thing. She cringed. "I can see, perhaps, a nice pair of shoes."

She looked at Secrest and Mae. Secrest shrugged skeptically. Mae just looked away.

"Or maybe a handbag," Isabella offered.

Geoffrey smiled patiently but did not change his advice.

Mae knew Geoffrey had long nursed an inexplicable fondness for "The E Street Shuffle," a mysterious jumble of words and clichéd nicknames. Mae considered the song positively nonsensical and finally broke the awkward silence

by saying so. But Geoffrey relayed Springsteen's own published explanation that "The Shuffle" was a dance with no set
steps—the dance created by people shuffling through life.

Needless to say, this insight, while interesting, did not
really convert any of the three women to the merits of
snakeskin and did not, truth be told, even elevate the song in
their eyes. Isabella, Secrest, and even Mae were not the sort
to be sympathetic about that sort of thing. Each was a firm
believer in picking up your feet and walking properly. "I fail
to see," Isabella said, "how shuffling could help anyone!"

But even in the face of this dubious counsel, she ultimately
did not really argue. She simply looked at Geoffrey for a long
time, then sighed. "I'll talk to my designer," she said.

That is how Isabella came to parade before the assem-
bled legislators of Bisbania in a dignified cream business suit
with a striking rattlesnake skin collar that was tastefully set
off with a matching belt, shoes, and handbag. It was not her
most celebrated look. It was not featured in splashy photo
books about Isabella's style and it was not mass-produced
by the "designers" who specialize in rushing cheap knockoffs
into European department stores. But it was, at least, not a
complete embarrassment. Most of Bisbania never even knew
she wore the thing. After all, when was the last time *you*
watched a parliamentary ceremony?

Geoffrey never confronted Isabella about her rather
loose interpretation of his recommendation. At least, he
never did that I know of. But I have often suspected they
had conversations that did not get back to me.

Geoffrey's final advice to Isabella was interpreted with
similar flexibility. Isabella, weeping and wailing, called
Geoffrey home early from a family vacation to help her
decide what to wear to the investiture ball, the event during
which Princess Gene's coming-of-age would be celebrated
and she would be officially named Her Royal Highness the
Princess of South Main Street.

"I was going to wear that stunning red gown by the designer Burlle," Isabella said, sniffling a little in a message she left on Geoffrey's phone. "You know, the one with all the beading and the train. But now it turns out that Genia's wearing red. I can't look like I'm trying to show up my own sister-in-law. But the queen is wearing orchid, and Rafie hates me in yellow, and the king threatened to remodel our kitchen again if I show up at another event in black. I'm at a complete loss."

She dispatched Geoffrey to search the Boss's lyrics for advice. He spent the afternoon with his headphones on and ended the day by humming the song "Tougher Than the Rest," in which the love interest wears blue. Secrest, recently returned from a twelve-week maternity leave that had failed to soften her up one bit, was certain that Isabella would positively blanch at this advice. Isabella had long sniped about navy as being the boring default color choice of overly sensible royal women who usually desire the slimming effects of dark colors but invariably lack the courage to buck Bisbanian tradition and wear black.

Isabella did not blink at all. Instead, she summoned her bodyguard and had him drive her to Bisbania's trendiest designer that very afternoon. That is how Princess Iphigenia was outdone at her own investiture ball by her sister-in-law in a quickly designed but dazzling peacock-blue gown.

Isabella's choice of peacock blue is another bit of crucial evidence in understanding Mae's questions about Geoffrey's advice. Peacock blue is barely even blue. "Why'd you wear green?" Geoffrey was overheard asking Isabella.

She just laughed and dragged her hand over his cheek. "Don't be silly," she said. "It's peacock blue."

"Ah, yes," Geoffrey said, "when you step out into the light there, I can see what you're talking about."

But whatever its color, and whether it was selected because of Geoffrey's shrewd advice or Isabella's own fashion sense, it did look breathtaking in the famous photo of Isabella twirling on the dance floor with the president of the United States, her elegant wispy scarf floating behind her.

If you look carefully at the photo of Isabella and the president dancing, you can see Princess Genia, freshly returned from the Canadian school where she'd gotten a degree in Internet publishing. She is sitting forlornly and wondering why exactly she had requested that Isabella not wear red.

(Oh, all right, it's not obvious from the photo that she is thinking that, but come on, what else would she be thinking?)

That is the famous photo from that night. But another photo taken that night has been largely forgotten, because its significance is understood by few and its place in history is less obvious.

In that photo, which I love and loathe, which repels and attracts me, which I stare at and grow sickened by, Isabella is dancing with an unknown castle mechanic. His hand is resting on her slim back, just below the plunging back line of that stunning "blue" dress. Isabella looks like she is happy and safe and very comfortable, and the car mechanic looks proud and pained and like he senses danger.

In the background is Raphael, who, to the untrained eye, looks merely distracted, as if he is staring off into space. But that is how you read Raphael's expression when you know that he is a prince, the heir apparent to the throne, and when you think the man in the foreground is just a car mechanic. But knowing what you know now, I think you can understand why I read more into Raphael's expression, why I see a certain rigid irritation, a cold resentment, a tired worry. Am I imagining it? I don't know, and certainly no one else does.

For as you must remember, the story of Princess Isabella's life changed rather dramatically on the morning following Princess Iphigenia's investiture ball. That is the reason the photograph of Isabella, the apparent future queen, dancing with the young U.S. president in front of the relatively dowdy Princess Iphigenia, became so poignant. Everyone in the world knows the momentous event that happened to the royal family the next morning.

Just a few hours after those lovely ballroom photos were taken, hours after Isabella had seemed to make peacock blue the next hot color, a lowly royal mechanic, Geoffrey Whitehall-Wright, died when the single-engine plane he was piloting plunged into the stormy, icy waters of the predawn Bisbania Sea. Such a sudden, violent, unexpected death of a trusted, albeit low-ranking, castle aide is exactly the sort of thing that tabloids feed on, compose conspiracy theories about, and make up long backstories for.

But Geoffrey's death got little attention, because the world's eye was turned that stormy morning to a more important matter. For, as you must realize, His Royal Highness the Prince of Gallagher, the man known everywhere as Prince Raphael, the heir to the Bisbanian throne, was Geoffrey's passenger.

Chapter 12

I never did get back to Jimmy Bennett, did I? I'm getting old, you know. I sometimes lose threads of conversations. I go off on tangents. I ramble and wander. Then, several pages later, I realize I just left you wondering about the elusive Mr. Bennett, while a saucy, big-boned, husky-voiced detective roamed the streets of Green Bay, Wisconsin, looking for an unhappy Yale graduate. I can't do that, can I?

I told myself I would not fall into the traditional trappings of royal biographies in this account of Isabella's life. Those books—"those damn books," as Secrest always referred to them—are all predictable enough. They draw a picture of royal life in which the reigning monarch always desired the throne—longed for it with an aching, pathetic intensity and schemed for it to a degree both embarrassing and indecent. Or else he or she never really cared to be the monarch; it simply didn't make much difference one way or another.

The purpose of such books is always to buck conventional wisdom, by showing that the royal subject was either completely underappreciated or entirely overrated. The conventions of the genre demand that every prince and princess, every king and queen, be terribly put upon by the bullies who make up the castle help, a group of universally out-of-touch and stubbornly overformal advisers who insist on doing everything exactly wrong. To be able to enjoy a royal biography, you must be able to believe that crowned rulers, with their inherited titles and inherited wealth, with their lives of constant indulgence and ever present help, are always more in touch with the common people than the castle workers who clean the royal toilets, cook the regal meals, and study questions of protocol and politics for a living.

So, hemmed in by this stifling state of affairs, the royals (at least the ones who merit books about their lives) are forced to turn for advice to all sorts of unlikely sources, tarot-card readers or dream interpreters or, you know, Rasputin. And often, like the wives of presidents and prime ministers, they enjoy an occasional enema. You don't understand it. I don't understand it. No normal person understands it. But apparently, if you wore a crown and ate a lot of dreadful chicken dinners, you, too, would enjoy regular colonic irrigation. Such is the beauty regimen of the glamorous.

The narrators tell all this in, depending on their agenda, either a sympathetic, apologetic tone or a scolding, disapproving voice, and it turns out that the narrators themselves are always terribly crucial to every turn of events, which usually spin on seemingly mundane details. Did the princess's staff cook mistakenly use a cream sauce when the lactose-intolerant prime minister came to lunch? That, then, must surely explain why hemlines went down that year and why the economy collapsed soon after. Oh, if the cook had only listened to the narrator, the whole thing would have been avoided!

The exception to all of this, I suppose, are the biographies of the Russian royals, who were mostly slaughtered in the Russian Revolution, except for the ones who, according to the books about them, miraculously escaped but tragically could not prove their identities. I guess if you've got a story filled with people who may or may not be dead, you don't need to dwell as much on problems with luncheon menus. Although I'm pretty sure I once read a biography that claimed the czarina received frequent enemas from Rasputin and was terribly embarrassed by an overcooked leg of lamb at a state dinner. Also, supposedly, she was a man. Those books play by different rules.

And I will, too. Not by the Russian rules. But by different rules than those generally applied to contemporary royal biographies. Nevertheless, I suppose I ought to follow some of the basic conventions of good storytelling. So if I start to tell you about Jimmy Bennett, then I eventually ought to get back to him and put that part of the story to rest—not that an old narrator like me likes to use phrases such as "put to rest," bringing to mind, as it does, all sorts of ugly end-of-life musings.

Secrest was, as I said, in charge of the search for Jimmy Bennett, and she talked to the detective almost every week, though she milked these conversations into daily reports for Isabella. I happen to know that Secrest was very concerned about the whole situation. She wasn't sure exactly what Isabella hoped to accomplish. Secrest didn't know, at least not yet, about Isabella and Geoffrey's kiss, and so she wasn't sure what danger Jimmy Bennett presented to Isabella. The only theory she could come up with was the obvious one. She thought that Bennett himself was an old love interest of some degree or another. And given that it was Ethelbald Candeloro's column that had set Isabella off, Secrest feared he was a love interest of the leather-clad, motorcycle-riding variety. This, she reasoned, could not be good.

If the detective found him, Isabella had authorized only minimal action. The detective was supposed to watch him, complete a report, and keep her distance while Isabella considered the options. But from where Secrest sat, there were no good options. If Bennett was the long-haired boyfriend— Secrest constantly assured herself that there was no need to imagine words like "lover"—contacting the former classmate would only serve as the confirmation that Ethelbald Candeloro might be waiting on.

And if Bennett hadn't gone to the gossip columnist? Secrest worried that contacting him might just give him the idea that he could. The last thing Secrest wanted was for the person whom she sometimes referred to as "this Geoffrey fellow" to get involved in the decision. "I hate to think what the lyrics to 'Born in the U.S.A.' would do for this situation," Secrest would say, barely suppressing a smirk to Isabella, who usually ignored her.

In a sense, Secrest usually ignored Isabella. For while Isabella was dying for news, eager for any tidbit, Secrest passed on to the private investigator a nonchalant attitude, a spirit of what you might even describe as indifference. The investigator would call and wax apologetic for not making more progress and ask for more money or for permission to try a new lead, and Secrest would manage to be encouraging to the point of being discouraging. "Don't worry so much," she'd say. "Take your time. It's very important that we move slowly on this."

Secrest told me all of that a few hours after Geoffrey's funeral. She and I had slipped out to the Garden of

Engineering to get away from the stifling grief inside, though slipping outside didn't really help, because the whole country was awash in grief. Not for Geoffrey, of course. But for the future king.

Standing on the patio, we could see the castle courtyard, with the lowered flags and black-draped windows. If we looked to the west, down the hillside, we could see the darkened, eerily still city below. All the theaters, restaurants, and other entertainment facilities were closed for a period of national mourning. Litter left over from the processional that morning fluttered in the empty street. It was a respectful sort of litter. Wadded-up tissues, spent subway passes, a map here, a commemorative pamphlet there. No soft-drink cans. No hot-dog wrappers. A happy crowd might leave that sort of rubbish, but this crowd had merely shed some of its sadness. A torn tabloid cover with a black-and-white picture of Rafie was fluttering along the cobblestones of the courtyard. OUR LOST PRINCE, it said.

In the distance, a marquee sign said, WE MOURN RAFIE. In smaller letters, it said, AND HIS PILOT.

Those were the sort of obligatory references made to Geoffrey. People would add his name to convince themselves that they valued life equally, that they didn't place a prince above a pilot. Smug women stood up in churches all over the country to ask for prayers for Geoffrey's family. "We must remember he died, too," they would say. They were right, I suppose. Mae—who vacillated between numbness and violent weeping—certainly needed prayers. But I suspect the women who were standing up in churches to say so were a little too proud of themselves for pointing this out to their fellow worshippers. I suppose I shouldn't say that, because I wasn't spending a lot of time in churches in those days and don't have much firsthand knowledge. It's just that I've always observed that when someone stands up in church and asks that prayers be offered for world peace or homelessness or the disease of the week, they often seem a bit proud of themselves. "You people are just hoping that the service ends in time to get home for the football match," they seem to be saying. "But I have world events on my mind."

Or humble servants doubling as pilots. Either one.

Perhaps I'm too cynical, but that's the way I read things.

I was thinking about all of that on the patio as Secrest stood silently next to me, flicking her hands the way ex-smokers do sometimes in situations that call for a cigarette. She leaned for a moment on the Michelangelo bust and then, seeming to remember how such casual touching of the bust always bugged Geoffrey, moved away.

Secrest had never really liked Geoffrey. That had been obvious. But he was dead now, and she apparently felt the need to make up for that, to draw a connection between the two of them, to share in the mourning. Maybe motherhood had softened her up after all. She started with familiar territory.

"Those damn books," she said. "Read those royal tell-alls—and who doesn't these days?—and you get the impression that every dumb thing a prince or princess has ever done was because of the castle help."

I sighed.

She squinted into the distance. "Did the queen order a cheeseburger at a kosher restaurant? Did the earl start wearing pinstripes a season too early? Did their majesties go and have themselves an ugly, stupid child? Well, then it must be the maidservant's fault somehow." Her voice was bitter, but then softened a bit. "Or, you know, the mechanic's."

She swallowed hard, looked out over the square. "They're all about exaggerated crises and manufactured drama, those things," she said. "You read them and think that an ill-chosen ball gown or a photograph with an unfortunate nasal shadow was all that mattered in the world.

"No one ever writes our story. I'll tell you that much. They don't write about how we curtsy ourselves silly and whisper during transatlantic phone calls with trashy American detectives to keep the college flames secret. Or how we miss our son's primary school graduation because Her Highness has some sort of hat emergency."

If I hadn't been so sad and tired, I would have smiled at that. Her son was under four months old, and she was already worrying about missing his primary school graduation.

Secrest lowered her voice. "Or sock crisis." She looked down at her black skirt, flicked a bit of lint off it. "No one writes about how we have to just straighten our backs and steel our nerves when the tabs come out, because if the news isn't good, they're sure to blame us. If some grand duke gets caught urinating on the Princess Grace Memorial Rosebush, it can't be his own fault. That's for sure. He must have been given some 'bad advice.'

"And now," she said, "look at what happened to Geoffrey." She paused respectfully and looked at me, then the ground.

I nodded but didn't meet her eyes. I didn't want to go into all this. I just kept looking off in the distance.

"I didn't want him to move to the castle," she said, sounding old and bone-tired. "I thought it was a bad idea. I kept my eye on him, that's for sure. I let him know if he was spending too much time with the princess alone. If he was flaunting his influence too much. If he wasn't spending enough time with the cars. I wasn't shy, you know that."

She looked at me again. I said nothing, and that seemed enough.

"I was right, of course." She nodded as if to affirm this to herself. "But I suppose I could have been kinder to him. It wasn't ever personal, you know? It wasn't his fault. I was just trying to protect the princess. Do you think he understood that?" She turned to me. Tears streamed down her face.

I thought, *What difference does it make now?* I thought, *How could he possibly have understood that?* I thought, *When did it become my job to make you feel better?*

I said, "He probably understood."

And then I changed the subject. I asked her how she finally found Jimmy Bennett.

Chapter 13

*E*thelbald Candeloro is not what he seems. I planned to avoid telling you that. I'm not in the habit of hurting the innocent, and Ethelbald truly is an innocent in all this. He is absolutely critical to almost every turn of events in this story, but still ultimately a bystander. Everything he wrote, everything he said, everything he caused to happen or not to happen—it was all accidental. He was not trying to save lives or ruin souls. He did not know the havoc he created until years later, and he could hardly believe it then. He was just trying to do his job, trying to please the bosses and keep the raises coming.

He could not have imagined how his words would come

to haunt Isabella. Arguably as naive as Isabella herself, he did not dare flatter himself by thinking the princess would care one way or another what he thought of her clothes or her vacation choices or her college boyfriends. He could not fathom that anything he wrote really affected the royal family, and he would have been even more hard-pressed to imagine that his words had jerked a simple American couple out of their ordinary lives and taken them on a magnificent and fateful ride.

He was just trying to pay the bills. At least that is the way he would have put it. He had, after all, a leased Bisba convertible, the deluxe model, and a hefty mortgage on a penthouse spread in one of the most built-up and prestigious corners of Bisbania's Highlands neighborhood, which was nestled in the mountainous foothills and overlooked the sea. (Not all that far from Lady Carissa's home, actually—a constant source of worriment to the queen right up until the lady's death.) Rumor had it that he shared that penthouse with a steady stream of lovely young women who had expensive tastes.

But the rumor wasn't true. That is part of his secret. Though not the worst of it. Or perhaps I should not use "worst," an obviously value-laden word. Because the secret is not really shameful, at least not in my opinion. But I suppose any secret, if big enough and kept long enough, eventually becomes shameful. For example, there is absolutely nothing wrong with holding an office-administration degree from the seaside campus of Bisbania Community College, though it does have a party-hearty reputation compared to the more "serious" South Main Street campus. But to hold such a degree and to tell people that you have a master's in journalism from the College of Peter and Catherine the Greats, and to further describe that school as "the William and Mary of South America"? *That* is shameful. Especially when no such school even exists. And now you know another part of

Ethelbald's secret, though that is still not what I will describe as "the worst"—a judgmental phrasing I am using only for lack of a better word, you understand. (And please don't pretend to be surprised that the tabloid editors didn't check out his résumé.)

Regardless, his dedication to his work wasn't about the debt or the fine living. Let's be honest. Few people work hard for such things. There are exceptions, I'm sure, but most people who want fine living are not willing to work for it. Ask yourself this: What is fine about a life of hard work? So if you see a well-paid parliamentary lobbyist or an extravagantly successful stockbroker who tells people—his wife most of all—that he works eighty-hour weeks and he gives up the vacations and he stays indoors on nice days to pay for the home and the car and the catered parties and the imported, monogrammed sheets, be skeptical. This is not a person who would be a missionary if only it paid better. He likes the work. On some level, he loves what he does. He enjoys the job or he enjoys the prestige or he enjoys the excuse to be away from his wife and children. No one, at least no one who is observant and aware and awake, works through a spring day for penthouse money. That is something you do for groceries or something you do for love. No "extra" is worth it.

At least that is the case, I will argue, with Ethelbald. He didn't care about the Bisba and the penthouse. He enjoyed them. Who wouldn't? But he did not dish dirt on the royal family in order to live better. His motivation was good old-fashioned professional pride. It was his job to dish dirt, so he served it up as regularly as he could. I suppose he possessed a little of that Bisbanian work ethic that the Chamber of Commerce was always touting in efforts to attract new industry.

He rather enjoyed, simply enough, having the opportunity to comment on the ups and downs of the royal family.

That's all. In some basic, uncomplicated way, he found the task pleasant and even interesting. He meant no harm. Not even when he called the queen names. Not even when he questioned the parentage of the king's brother.

Somehow, Ethelbald did not see such comments as truly personal. He figured the royal family knew that, that they understood it was part of the bargain. You don't get to be queen without having someone pointing out that your ankles are thick and that your son is rather dim. You can't be the brother to the king and not expect people to comment on the way you resemble the bodyguard who was once assigned to your mother. In some vague and idiotic way, Ethelbald actually thought the royal family must enjoy such gossip, the way he enjoyed really nasty hate mail.

And he did enjoy hate mail. Nothing pleased him like getting notes from readers who questioned his intelligence, his qualifications, or his logic. Journalists, see, are not like normal people. We—and I use "we" because once a journalist, always a journalist—ask tough questions and second-guess everything and always ask for proof. No one gets a free ride with us. And true to the way we treat others, we develop a tough skin ourselves. So when you write a newspaper reporter a letter that says, "You are biased and wrong and pathetic and ugly," the reporter is not hurt. Instead, she passes the letter around to colleagues and laughs and posts it on the wall next to her desk and figures that if she hadn't angered someone, then she hadn't done her job. We're an odd lot.

So when Ethelbald, who had a lively style of writing that tended to agitate people and encourage them to fire off responses, would get a good hate letter, it would make his day. The more incoherently they babbled, the better.

He liked the one that said: "You sniveley little bastard commie. How dare you criticize the royal ankles of Her Majesty the Queen? I'd like to see your ankles. Thicker than a Clydesdale's I'm guessing. I can tell by looking at that jowl in your photograph that you'd need thick ankles to hold up that thick head of yours."

And he loved the one that said: "I am sick and tired of you and your paper trying to push your anti-monarchist agenda on the country. We know full well you were all educated at fancy schools with French teachers and that you all drive Eastern European cars. Get a real job."

And he absolutely cherished the letter from an American immigrant who displayed the extreme and inexplicable loyalty to the royal family that only immigrants can muster, and who was angry about a column in which Ethelbald called the king "overly simple and slightly ugly." The former American had, in addition to a convert's loyalty to the country, an American's misunderstanding of the name Ethelbald, which is a fine traditional name given to firstborn Bisbanian sons for hundreds of years, but which, to an American ear, sounds a little like Ethel, the name best associated with chunky, middle-aged sitcom women.

The letter attacked Ethelbald's journalistic credentials, his writing style, and his loyalty. It then concluded: "Also, have you heard of facial electrolysis? Read up on it. Judging by your photo, you could use it. You're the ugliest damn woman I ever saw."

Ethelbald laughed for days about that. For months, even. He called up his editor and read it aloud over the phone. He entertained colleagues at the office holiday party. He included it in his memoir. Each time he told the story, he would laugh in a jovial, extravagant, self-deprecating way, a way that a careful, removed observer might describe as being a little too hard. Because, you see, that was the last part of Ethelbald's secret.

He *was* the ugliest damn woman anyone ever saw.

And he (she?) really was named Ethel.

She was born Ethel Candeloro, the only daughter of a

Bisbanian serviceman and his American wife, a traditional woman who insisted on naming her baby girl after her great-grandmother, no matter how strange the name seemed to Bisbanians.

Ethel Candeloro changed her name to Ethel Bald upon marriage to George Bald, a mousy but intellectual engineer who thought his wife was beautiful despite her cheap hair-cuts and lack of makeup. All her friends tried to talk her out of changing her name. "Ethel Bald sounds like you're a first-born son," they would tell her over and over again. But she would say that it didn't matter, that she was, in some ways, as traditional as her mother had been and would not let occasional awkward confusions stop her from following tried-and-true paths. She had, she said, looked forward to changing her name with marriage ever since she was a school-girl, and she was not going to let a few snickers stop her now.

This made George Bald rather happy. In fact, everything about Ethel made him happy. Love is, after all, blind. So he did not notice that she had a jaw shaped like a crudely cut block, and he did not notice the tepid pool of sweat that sometimes collected on her upper lip on hot days. When George looked at Ethel, all he saw was beauty.

That is why he told her that she looked absolutely fine on the day when she headed out to interview for a job as royal writer for one of the lesser tabloids, even though she was wearing a rather mannish and somewhat ill-fitting black pantsuit.

Ethel's love for George, it must be said, was not so much blind as nearsighted. She had noticed a few of his faults, notably his lack of fashion sense. So she did not completely trust his opinion of her pantsuit. But she foolishly took his advice anyway. She had a bad cold that day and a crick in her neck to boot and didn't feel like changing. In her heart she had only wanted to be reassured. So when he said she looked fine, she was relieved.

The editor, who had spent some time on London's Fleet Street before being brought back home to Bisbania to turn the struggling tabloid around, was hard-pressed on deadline when Ethel Bald arrived, with her froggy throat, stiff neck, swollen eyes, and mannish pantsuit. The editor barely glanced at her and didn't look at her writing samples at all.

Instead, he surprised her by saying that she was the leading candidate and that it was "about bloody time a good heterosexual man finally applied for a royal column again."

That was the one moment he looked up at her. "You are heterosexual, aren't you?"

Ethel Bald was too stunned to think through the ethics of the situation and simply croaked, "Yes." And then, in a flourish that still surprised her years later when she replayed it all in her mind, she added, "Married, even."

"Good, good," the editor said. "Though you might not want the married part to get out. Better to have the reputation of a playboy. Name again?"

"Ethel Bald," she said.

"Ethelbald what?" the editor snapped. "I'm sick and tired of this one-name crap. Madonna is old news, and so is that fad."

"Ethel Bald . . ." She sniffled a little. Her head was full and slow, and her pantsuit was tight and uncomfortable. The thought of trying to explain, of using that raspy voice to go into detail, well, it was too much. Besides, the only reason she was getting the job was because he thought she was a firstborn son. So, by instinct, she reverted to her maiden name, the one she had used for most of her life. "Candeloro," she said.

So Ethelbald Candeloro was hired. He launched a satisfying career, working mostly from home and wearing a fake handlebar mustache whenever he posed for the column photo. I suppose by now it goes without saying that Ethel Bald was not a particularly striking woman. But when she

peeled off the mustache and gussied herself up in a black
strapless ball gown, she was obviously womanly enough
that she could mingle at balls with royal guests without anyone suspecting that she was the mustachioed man who so
often made the royal family's life miserable. (George Bald
had graduated first in his class from the Royal Academies of
Engineering and Other Practical Sciences, which meant he
was granted the lifelong title of "royal engineer" and was
invited to all the largest castle functions.)

This was the way that Ethel Bald picked up all sorts of
pertinent pieces of gossip and scuttlebutt. Her limited
appearances as Ethelbald only added to the mystery of the
noted royal watcher and made him seem even more fear-
some. How did he accurately describe details of events that
he did not appear to attend? How did he know royal secrets
whispered only in ladies' restrooms? He had, the royal family
believed, a frightening ability to get to the truth, or at least
an approximation of the truth exacting enough for tabloid
standards.

But no matter how dangerous Ethelbald seemed to
Iphigenia or Isabella or any other member of the royal family,
he was not, as I previously stated, what he seemed. He did
know the sorts of things that a middle-aged ballroom dancer
could pick up from eavesdropping and a trained eye. But
he—I always call him "he" when talking about his professional persona—could not know the secrets of the royal
hearts.

He did not know what Isabella thought of Geoffrey. He
did not know what Raphael thought of Isabella. He did not
know what Queen Regina thought of her sister, Lady
Carissa. He did not know what Iphigenia thought about
being queen.

He was just an ordinary woman, you know. Although a
bit more mannish than most and with the exceedingly bad
judgment to trust her husband's opinion of her business wear.

You, no doubt, wonder how I know Ethelbald's secret and why I have not told it until now. But that was, you see, the deal. I know his secret. He knows mine. We've been locked in this standoff for much of this past century. Mutual assured destruction. It's like the cold war. Neither of us can push the button without giving up our own secret as well. So I didn't tell his secret until I was ready to have my secret told.

Or at least I waited until now. When I am almost ready.

Chapter 14

I can't believe it. Looking back, I see I covered the entire marvelous few years that Geoffrey and Mae lived in the castle with just a chapter and a few anecdotes. When I started this book, I feared that, if anything, I would dwell too much on that time, detailing the antics of two American rubes as they discovered the majesty and mystery of life in Glassidy Castle.

But I guess time has softened me some. I am more sympathetic than I once was. I look upon those two dears and think they were, after all, just kids, well meaning and fun-loving.

Genia was, of course, still a princess then. She used to

cringe and carry on when she'd see Mae sitting by the castle pool, wearing cutoffs and drinking tea—made with tea bags, no less—out of a Kentucky Derby Festival coffee mug. Mae said it was a souvenir of the time her mother went to the Churchill Downs infield and watched War Emblem's wire-to-wire drive to win the Derby.

"Is the Lipton an inheritance, too?" Princess Genia would whisper in a nasty way, making the servants snicker.

But please don't be too hard on Genia, for she eventually recognized the shallow and snobbish traits that marred her personality. She has tried so hard to make up for it in her old age. Her life was, in its own way, quite difficult. The younger siblings of heirs to the throne always have a tough time. In Great Britain they call them "the spare," as in the "heir and the spare." No such vulgarity was uttered about the heirs of Glassidy Castle, partially because no such cute rhyme play worked in the nation's official language, which had too many consonants to foster the art of playful rhyming among the royal classes—the only ones still speaking the language.

Still, the heir-and-spare sentiment was obvious enough.

From the heir's perspective, the younger siblings have a nice life, getting all the perks that come with royal life but few of the responsibilities. But the spares see it quite differently. They are forced into the public eye for a waiting pattern that they hope never ends. If all goes well, they will live and die exactly as they were born, unused links in the chain of succession. In no other career do you peak at birth. But that is the way for most children of monarchs. They are born second or third or fourth in the line of succession. They might bump up a step when Granddad or Dad dies. But mostly, there are just more children born, so that by the time they're thirty-five or forty, they're so far out of the way of the throne that they're already has-beens. Their only hope is that when they show up at the coronation, the people who woke up early in the Americas to watch the pageantry will be saying things like

"Wow, she's held up well" rather than "Get a look at her, she used to be pretty."

The second (and third and fourth) children are left to amuse themselves by chasing love affairs or fine wines, or collecting art. They may take up a charity or two. But at best, their lives are shallow and sad. Perhaps that, as much as anything, was why Princess Genia looked so forlorn at her investiture ball as Isabella danced with the president. It wasn't just that Isabella, even when resigned to wearing blue, was gorgeous and radiant and glamorous. It was that Isabella, born a mere lady in the most minor house of the national nobility, seemed destined to be queen. Meanwhile, Princess Genia's greatest moment was to be that night, when she was officially proclaimed the Princess of South Main Street, the customary title for second-borns and thus the title unofficially used for her since birth.

(This custom, it goes without saying, had always been a sticking point with the Association of North Main Business Owners, and on certain holidays, the definition of South Main was stretched beyond all reason. But the thing about royals is that they don't run for reelection and don't need financial gifts, so the North Main shopkeepers could complain forever and it wouldn't make any difference.)

The morning after the ball, everything changed for Princess Genia. The princess had a nice apartment in the west wing of the castle. But she had slept that night in her childhood bedroom, where she was awakened at six A.M. by her mother, with the terrible word that the plane was missing and presumed crashed.

Genia trembled at the news. She tried to focus as she knelt in the castle chapel with her parents, praying for mercy on the frail and beautiful life of her dear brother, the very real human who had, as a child, played with her on the castle lawn, begged her to drill him for hours with flashcards on bird species, and who, as a teen, had teased her about boys, and who had, just the night before, as a dashing young man, danced with her and complimented her and told her that the world was hers now, that she could do anything and be anything.

"You know, they're doing amazing things with speech recognition technology," he said, showing again his mysterious preoccupation with the sciences of human oral communication. "You could get into that, if you wanted."

Genia loved her brother. But as she knelt in the chapel, she couldn't concentrate on his life or his soul or even his endearing little quirks. The only thought that pounded through her head as she contemplated the missing plane was this: *Please God, do not let me be queen.*

Later, after the funeral, she allowed herself to cry, and she told her mother that she knew it was a horrible, awful, selfish thing, but she was worried about it nonetheless. Her mother assured her that it was okay, she could tell her anything. Genia sobbed long and hard. "Someday," she said, blubbering into her handkerchief, "they'll call me Queen Gene. It sounds so *dorky.*"

Her mother, who had stood so stoically at the funeral and walked so tall down the long road to the church, laughed a halting uncertain laugh. Then she cried, and the two women, the queen and the future queen, hugged each other and held on tight.

As it was, there was no bigger victim in the tragedy than Princess Genia, and not only because she did become Queen Gene in the tabloids when her father died just a couple years later. (She insisted that only "Her Majesty Queen Iphigenia" be used in her presence.)

But in the days following the crash, the world's attention focused only on Isabella. The world mistakenly thought it was more tragic to have the apparent queendom stripped from you than to find it bestowed on you. They were wrong.

Not that it wasn't an adjustment for Isabella. The wife of

the king's first son is the future queen. The widow of the king's first son is, well, no one. Oh, she did retain her title. The king and queen made it quite clear that they would always consider Princess Isabella a member of the royal household, and she would always be welcome at family functions and castle events. Princess Genia, somewhat more reluctantly, said that would remain true once she became queen.

But no one expected Isabella to take them up on it. She was young, beautiful, glamorous. She would eventually want to date, remarry, have children. How could she do that in her dear late husband's boyhood home?

It is almost amusing to look back at the coverage in the days immediately following the crash, to see how much of it focused on Isabella and how it seemed the world and the media were mourning not just the death of the young prince, the heir apparent, but also his bride, though she was obviously very much alive.

The images were unforgettable, and not only because it was the first time she'd worn brown since the engagement. She carried such a sad regal composure as she stood there on the beach in the cropped khaki pants, a snug-fitting pair that had been carefully crafted by the nation's leading designer to look as if they'd been purchased right off the rack. She wore a similarly simple chocolate corduroy jacket as she greeted rescue workers on the beach, thanking them with quiet, shell-shocked dignity, refusing all sorts of offers of comfort. "Would you like a chair, Your Highness?" "Can I get you some coffee, Your Highness?" "Wouldn't you like to go back to the castle for some rest, Your Highness?"

She would shake her head, smile in a wan and hopeful way, and say, "You're too kind." The wind tousled her hair as the gray seas rose and fell in angry fits. The photographs were exquisite.

By contrast, everything Iphigenia did that day was wrong, starting with her clothes: a periwinkle polo shirt and a wrinkled pair of plaid Bermuda shorts. This was a terrible fashion misstep that the tabloids, for the sake of decency, did not mention right away, holding off in an unprecedented show of restraint until the initial shock had passed sometime later that evening. "Leaving aside the issue of polo and its rather lowbrow connections with a certain batch of English cousins," Ethelbald Candeloro wrote, "what sort of person would wear shorts while her brother's plane is missing? Especially shorts from Bermuda, where legend has it planes go missing all the time and never with happy endings."

Iphigenia also made the grave misstep of, upon being offered a chair, saying "Thank you" and taking it. This was regarded as insensitive by almost all commentators. "I hope Her Highness was comfy while the rescue workers were out in the cold," Ethelbald said later in the same column. All of Iphigenia's biographies, I must point out, say that she took the chair on the advice of Hubert, who had that morning taken a new interest in Iphigenia, believing for the first time that she might actually become the next in line to the throne.

"People do not want to see the future queen standing about as if she were waiting for a royal bus," he theorized, and so he practically ordered Iphigenia to take a seat when offered one.

By two P.M. it was obvious even to those with less of a self-interest than Hubert that the plane's occupants must be dead. But no one could bring themselves to point this out to either princess, both of whom had grown pale as the day wore on and who finally consented to moving to a nearby home when rain started pouring. That walk was the only time that Isabella cried during the entire ordeal. "I just started thinking," she said, "about Rafie out there treading water in the cold rain."

All the top news outlets devoted themselves to nonstop coverage. The main story on all the websites was a running update on the search-and-rescue efforts, and off to the side, there were macabre collections of the news stories produced throughout the prince's life. "Click here to see the news accounts of his birth." "Click here to see the archived coverage of his first day in kindergarten." "Click here to relive the minor scandal that occurred when, as a young teen, he sneaked out and colored his hair bright purple." PLUM PUTRID! screamed one headline.

And, of course, "Click here for the wedding."

I suppose none of us will know, until we die, if our lives really pass before our eyes at that moment. But we know this much: If a prince's plane goes down in an icy sea, his life passes before everyone's eyes.

The coverage was inescapable. Even the leading fashion website of its time, a little publication called WEAR!, put together a slide show of what the prince had worn on the opening day of every racing season since he was two years old and set off the trend for better boys' fashion with those little blue knickers and the matching bow tie.

But none of the images of the past could compete with the images of what was happening right then. Isabella on the beach. Her fine, flyaway hair whipping in a photogenic way with the gusty sprinkles. The search dogs in the background. The helicopters overhead.

And that afternoon, when they pulled the body out of the sea, the rain started pouring even harder. Ethelbald wrote that it seemed as if the heavens themselves were crying.

Throughout the stormy day, a somber Prince Louis, who, as the younger brother of the king, had supervised the search, periodically relayed messages to the house from the tent that served as the rescue operation headquarters. It was four P.M. when he made the last fateful walk up from the beach. His account of that conversation, as later reported in *The National Times,* is well known to those of us of a certain age. But I will recount it here briefly for my younger readers.

He said he remembered stepping inside the house,

which belonged to an acquaintance of Lady Carissa's and had been turned over to the family for their use during the duration of the emergency. As he walked through the foyer, he said he noticed how lovely the hardwood floors were, and he worried that his soaking clothes and wet shoes would damage the finish. "It was one of those odd things you think about," he said, "when it seems like you should be thinking of only one thing."

He made his way to the upstairs sitting room where the family had gathered. Before he opened the door, he noticed that he could hear nothing. The family was sitting together in silence. He cleared his voice and entered.

"I'm afraid I have some bad news," he remembered saying as he noticed Princess Genia, who had been slumped on an overstuffed love seat, sit up straight. Her body was rigid and tense. The queen put her head in her hands, and the king walked over to a window overlooking the gardens. Isabella's face was absolutely blank, but her body language seemed somehow relieved, as if she had long expected this and was just glad it was about to be over. At least that was Prince Louis's interpretation later.

"We found the prince's body," Louis said. "It washed up onshore twelve miles from Lancelot Beach."

"No!" Isabella cried. She buried her face in her hands, slumped to the floor, and began wailing.

Louis continued, somewhat unnecessarily, "I'm afraid he's dead."

The rest of the royal family did not react, but continued to stare at Louis, waiting for more. Secrest walked over and put her hands on Isabella's shoulders.

Louis went on. "I'm afraid, Your Majesty, that we've had to call off the search. There's simply no hope for the mechanic." His voice cracked, and he paused. "No one could survive this long in waters that cold, and the rescue workers are risking their lives out there. We can't ask them to continue."

"Of course," said the king. His gaze returned to the window. The queen walked over to Princess Genia and wrapped her arms around the young woman. Isabella was clutching Secrest and crying in an elaborate, showy way that the queen both detested and envied her for.

"Noooooo!" Isabella cried over and over and again. "Can't we go back? Can't we do it over? Can't we go back to yesterday and do it all over?"

(Many in the press thought these statements were odd when first reported, but when they interviewed psychiatrists, they learned that it was actually quite common for the survivors of those who die in accidental deaths to be overcome by the feeling that if they could just move time backward by a few minutes or a few hours, they could tell their loved ones to drive more carefully, not to take the plane, to stop at the railroad tracks, to refrain from blow-drying their hair in the tub. It is a manifestation of the horror that comes with seeing how random tragedy is and how quickly it comes and how easily, in retrospect, it could have been avoided.)

Isabella's showy grief lasted only a few moments and only in the privacy of her husband's family. In fact, some have questioned whether it was actually as Prince Louis reported, or if he invented it—either to show the humanity of the situation or to put Isabella's stability in doubt, depending on the theorizer.

In public, Isabella was as stoic and dignified as the king and queen. She was photographed leaving the home, looking red-eyed but pulled together. Twice in the following days, she stepped out of the castle to admire the flowers left by well-wishers. The next Saturday, she was everything you could ask a young royal widow to be: beautiful and weary and sad-eyed and straight-backed. Some people said she reminded them of the American Jackie Kennedy, who all those years earlier had walked behind the coffin of her husband, the slain U.S. president. But Isabella is remembered for walking in front of the coffin, leading the horse that pulled the carriage, occasionally whispering to it and patting its neck. Behind the carriage walked the king and queen, and behind them walked Isabella's parents.

Later that same afternoon, Isabella rode in the back of a limousine to a memorial service for Geoffrey. She was photographed holding Mae's face in her hands, peering into her eyes, and whispering something no one heard. One of the commentators noted that she cried at the mechanic's service, though she only looked exhausted at her husband's.

"It's no surprise," said Ethelbald, who wrote about the funeral for what seemed like months. "At that point, she'd been in funeral-related activities for the better part of seven hours. It had to be getting to her. Besides, it is just like Isabella to be broken down more by other people's woes than by her own."

You may suspect there is another reason that she cried so much at Geoffrey's service. You may think that she was in love with him. She certainly loved him. But was she "in love" with him? Well, that is the secret of Isabella's heart, and I, for one, could not claim to know it.

But having said that, I do know some of what was going through Isabella's mind as she broke into tears at Geoffrey's service. She was looking at the empty place on the altar where a coffin would have been, and she was thinking how sad it was that Geoffrey's family would not get to stand by a grave site and say their goodbyes as their loved one was given a proper burial.

They thought his body was lost at sea. But Isabella knew it wasn't. Geoffrey's body had been properly buried earlier that day.

In Prince Raphael's grave.

Chapter 15

*O*h dear! My agent, I can assure you, is having fits at this point. Calm down, Frederick. Take one of those pills of yours. You're going to ruin your health.

I know, I know, I can hear you before you've even said it. "If you're going to write a book that says the body buried in the Prince of Gallagher's grave isn't the actual Prince of Gallagher, then say it in the first paragraph of the first chapter, don't just slip it in at the end of the fourteenth!"

I know, Frederick. In theory, I agree. But like I said, I can't tell stories that way. All those years when I struggled with my mediocre journalism career, my editors were always nagging me about not burying the lead. "You buried the lead again, you buried the lead again." That's all they ever said. But me? I think sometimes leads should be buried. You've got to tell the story like a story. That's what I always say.

If you're going to rewrite it, then rewrite it. What do I care? I'm old, I'm moody, I'm too tired to keep up my usual refined decorum, and the only thing I've got going for me is that I know things no one else knows. I'm going to tell it my way.

So where was I? Oh yes, the Prince of Gallagher's grave.

The body in the coffin that Isabella so famously led into St. Luke's Cathedral, the body that is buried in the sandy soil of the royal cemetery, is not the Prince of Gallagher. It is Geoffrey.

Prince Louis's account of informing the royal family was reasonably accurate except on two counts. The first inaccuracy is simple. Throughout the entire account, the words "the prince" and "the mechanic" are switched. The news started with "We found the mechanic's body." And reached its climax with "There's simply no hope for the prince." In some ways, I guess, it was the opposite of what Prince Louis really told the family.

Isabella's reaction did not need to be altered. Prince Louis was able to reliably describe her reaction to the news of Geoffrey's death as being that of the death of her own husband. Some people may read something into it. But I don't know. Under the circumstances, with the fates of the two men so closely linked, perhaps that is what you would expect. Her husband was missing. His traveling companion was found dead. Under any circumstances, this was bad news. Who is going to quibble with her grief?

The second inaccuracy is Prince Louis's account of how the conversation ended. In fact, there was a long and spirited debate about how to handle the reality that Prince Raphael's body seemed unlikely to be found.

Isabella, who managed to collect herself somewhat, said

that a full accounting was owed to "the people" and that openness and accuracy, no matter how painful at first, would be the best in the long run for all involved.

But the king, who absentmindedly wandered over to the love seat and stood behind his daughter, lightly stroking her hair as if she were the royal dog, said they must be practical. How would it look to leave the heir to the throne merely "missing and presumed dead"? That wouldn't do at all. Poor Iphigenia would have enough problems as queen without a bunch of what he called "loonies" coming forth claiming to be the long-lost Prince Raphael.

"The people," the king said, too sad and tired to sustain his usual sense of politics, "are scam artists and idiots."

And Isabella? How would she like hearing all the wild stories they would come up with about how Raphael was really alive and well and living in some remote African camp with the lost Russian Grand Duchess Anastasia?

"Anastasia?" asked Secrest, the only person in the room calm enough to worry over details. "Wouldn't she be a little old for him?"

"The people also can't count," said the king, glaring at the royal associate and seeming to notice her presence in the room for the first time.

And then, as quick as that, his mind was made up. "We'll use the mechanic's body and say it's Rafie," said the king with a matter-of-fact air of regal confidence and authority. By this point in history, few leaders anywhere in the world would have been so audacious. But this king was the king of a small country. And small countries, like small towns, are the sorts of places where corners are cut and rules are often thought to be unnecessary. They do not lock their doors, and they do not do DNA testing on dead royals.

"There will be no autopsy," the king said without hesitation. "It will be simple enough."

Isabella stood up and looked directly at the king. The

young princess may have been famously headstrong and outspoken, but this was the only time she directly argued with either of Their Majesties.

"Your Majesty," she said, seeming to gather her courage. "I know you are the king and I am only the Princess of Gallagher. But I am his *wife*." She put her hand to her chest to emphasize this. "Or his widow, I guess." Her voice quivered with that but quickly grew steady again.

"You cannot ask me to mourn over another man's body. Besides," she continued with all the righteous indignation she could muster, which was quite a lot, "what about *Geoffrey*? What of his family? His wife? You can't just use his body as your . . . your . . . ."

She paused dramatically before spitting out the next word: "*prop*."

"This poor deceased royal servant is not just a tool for your convenience. Using him this way is just . . ." She seemed to search for the right word and finally came up with the perfect one. "It's just wrong!"

It was quite a speech. It was, in fact, the very sort of thing Isabella could always summon up, even in the most trying of circumstances.

But the king just waved his hand at her in a dismissive way, asked that Geoffrey's wife be brought to him, and told everyone to wait in the other room.

Mae—who had seemed serene as the rescuers searched for her husband's plane—was waiting in an adjacent room of the house with friends from among the castle staff. She would have preferred to be with Isabella, but Isabella had been invited to wait with Their Majesties, and you neither turn down such an invitation nor try to sneak in your common friends. Even when you are the Princess of Gallagher and the apparent future queen.

But Mae's calm seemed shaken when Secrest stepped into the room and told Mae that the king wished to speak to her. Mae gasped and turned white and walked on somewhat shaky legs.

Moments after Mae stepped into the room, people heard her cry "No," and there were loud wails. The king and Mae were alone together for over an hour.

The other staff members thought he was comforting her and noted that he was a fine and good king who, in his own time of grief, comforted a servant's wife more than his own family.

But he was, of course, trying to sell Mae on his plan.

When she emerged from the room, she ran directly to Isabella, who had taken to sobbing again after getting a phone call from her sister Lady Fiona's home. Isabella and Mae hugged for a long time. Isabella said, "I'm sorry. I'm sorry. I'm so sorry."

Finally, she took the American's face into her hands in exactly the way she does in that famous photo of the memorial service and said, "Listen to me. You don't have to do what the king wants. I'll stick with you. I'll expose everything. I'll call for a full and thorough investigation. I'll ask for an autopsy. They can't deny me. I'm the widow. I don't care what happens. Do you understand? I don't care how things turn out. I'll do it if that's what you want."

And Mae said . . .

But I can't tell you what Mae said, can I? It wouldn't make any sense. Knowing only what you know now, Mae's words would be just so much gibberish. To make sense of Mae's response, you have to know more than you now know.

See, the great irony of all this is that the king took this drastic step, spent a small fortune to bury an American commoner in his own dear son's grave, because the grief-stricken king feared that if people knew the rescuers had been unable to recover his son's body, the people would

entertain fanciful tales and hold out hope that the prince
was alive and trade conspiracy theories as entertainment.

The poor sad king thought he was doing a good thing.
But his actions were filled with irony for one simple reason.
Well, actually for two reasons.

1) There WAS a conspiracy.
2) The prince WAS alive.

Chapter 16

I suspect I'll have to get a new agent once Frederick gets to this point in the story. He'll surely have had a heart attack by now. I told him there was plenty of new material to explore, but he kept wanting me to write about King Will's granddaughter, the one who seems to be bringing hats back into style on the streets of London. Poor Frederick. He really has no sense of history. Hats? My word!

But I do suspect that even those of you more strongly constituted than Frederick must be getting a bit weary of the twists and turns. I can't help it. It's not as if I'm making this up! The facts are the facts. And I am confident you will find, if you bear with me for just a while longer, that the story of the Prince and Princess of Gallagher is the most beautiful and romantic and touching and tragic story ever told.

At least Isabella thought so. I guess Mae did, too.

It started out as a conspiracy of four. The plan had been hatched in those long sessions between the two couples. The dream had started with Rafie himself.

See, Rafie was a happy, happy man but an unhappy prince.

His unhappiness had dawned upon him slowly, after he had come to accept the fact that he loved Isabella. For most men the notion that they love their wives is not exactly news. They might be a little surprised to discover the feelings so fresh and alive if they, as Rafie did, were to find themselves overcome with adoration several years into their marriage. But they would take such a discovery as a small, unexpected, but much appreciated gift. For Rafie it was a crushing life crisis.

You see, Rafie had known since he was twelve that he would not, could not, should not even consider marrying for love. (Or have I said that already? Yes, I believe I have.) His mother and father had made that quite clear. They had also drilled into him what it was that he needed and wanted and felt. What did he feel? Loyalty, mostly. To the crown, to the monarchy, to the people. Duty, he felt lots of duty.

What did he want? To be a good king. To rule a prosperous nation. To help the poor. To ensure dignity. To pass on the crown as untarnished as it had been passed on to him.

What did he need? Solid advisers. A respectable wife. An heir and a spare, by whatever names you called them.

But in those wonderful, carefree Isabella years, Rafie began to realize that he didn't want or need or *feel* any of those things. What he wanted was to run off with Isabella and keep her all to himself, to steal away with her for long weekends and read aloud to her the most fascinating passages of *Accents and Affectations: Diagnosis and Detection.*

He wanted to cook meals with her in a small kitchen and to fill a tiny home with love and children and the smell of spaghetti, a popular Italian food normally shunned as "ethnic" by the Bisbanian royal family.

"Oh, you're silly," Isabella would say. "We can do all those things now."

"No," he would say, "we can't."

I'm not sure if Rafie ever explained it very well to Isabella. But one late night, he explained it to me. He was the heir to the throne. If he decreed that he would never work on weekends, that he would cook his own meals, that he and Isabella would live in one of the servants' quarters, there would be grumbling and wringing of hands and the advisers would sweat and swear and storm off, but it would be done. Even his father couldn't really stop him.

But it would all be a ruse. He and Isabella still wouldn't truly be an ordinary couple. There wouldn't be any richer or poorer or better or worse. "Oh, I suppose one of us could get sick," he said. "But we've got the best health care money can buy, and that's the best health care there is.

"It's not that I think Isabella married me just to be queen or anything," he went on. "But until recently, even I couldn't separate myself from the king I am to become, so how could she have made such a distinction? I don't want Isabella to be married to His Royal Highness the Prince of Gallagher. I want her to marry Ralph Gallagher, a workingman, a bird-watcher, a speech pathologist."

Rafie thought about abdicating, but there were already republican rumblings in the Senate, and he feared that the movement needed only a final push, such as the abdication of an heir—especially an abdication inspired by nothing more dramatic than a desire to go to speech pathology school. It is one thing to walk away from your own destiny to be king. But to ruin the royal gig for your whole family? That was too much.

He thought about getting involved in some sort of scandal that would force him out of the line of succession, but in researching the family history, he concluded that such an unprecedented scandal would surely have to involve a multiple homicide. That didn't seem quite right.

"The only way out of being king," he said with a sigh, "is to die."

And that was when the idea of faking his death came about. It was a grand, romantic plan. Rafie was especially proud of his decision to stage his death the morning after Princess Iphigenia's investiture ball, figuring the nation would be so gaga over the young, beautiful princess that they would love the notion of her being tragically propelled onto the throne, and the monarchy would be more beloved and stronger than ever. (He did not seem to worry what it would mean for Princess Iphigenia to be tragically propelled to the throne, or to ask himself what it would mean to her modest ambition to publish a children's version of WEAR!)

Isabella sometimes grew frustrated with Rafie's constant ruminating on the subject. "Is our life together so bad?" she would say. "Are you so miserable?" Coveting middle-class life is, she argued, unbecoming for a prince. "Just as unbecoming as it would be for a middle-class man to go about wishing he lived in a castle. If you have enough," she said, "you should be grateful for what you have. And you have a lot to be thankful for. You have a lovely home."

The prince rolled his eyes. "Dad makes all the decorating decisions," he said in what might legitimately be described as a whine. "I had to beg for permission to put up a football poster in my office. My office! And he only relented because it was a commissioned, one-of-a-kind, impressionistic watercolor on handmade paper. That's not even a poster! It's original art!"

"You have satisfying work," Isabella said, continuing with her list of blessings as if Raphael had not spoken. "You get to visit deserving projects, give attention to worthwhile charities, shed light on the important issues of the day."

"Yesterday," said the prince with a bored sigh, "I watched schoolchildren perform an ode to figs and attended a ribbon cutting for a cat museum."

"You meet interesting people," Isabella said. "You get to travel."

The prince shook his head sadly. "Next week I'm scheduled to tour a sewer project with the prime minister's wife, an awful woman who is always showing off her tawdry French manicures and insisting that the royal flight attendants bring powdered creamer for her tea." He exhaled slowly. "She likes to talk about her surgeries."

"You don't appreciate how nice it is to have a staff," said Isabella. (She had cleaned her own toilet in college, and she had not forgotten it.) "You don't even throw away your own toenail clippings. You just leave them on the bedside table for the maid. I'm sure I don't know what would happen if we didn't have a maid. We'd be drowning in royal toenail clippings."

"I said I didn't want to be king," Raphael said. "Who said anything about not having a maid?"

"And what about your family?" Isabella asked. "You'll never talk to them again? Never see them again? Your parents' funerals? Your sister's coronation? All the happiness and sadness of their lives . . . all the happiness and sadness of *your* life . . . how can you not share that?"

"I'll share it with *you,*" Raphael would say.

That was how the conversations went. The prince spent a year trying to convince Isabella of the plan. What a wonderful, romantic year it was for the two of them! He courted her then in a very unprincelike way, making dinner, giving her foot massages, winning stuffed animals for her at boardwalk carnivals, growing her favorite herbs in a small garden that he stole away from the professional gardeners. Leering at her, if Burger Boy is to be believed, at White Castle drive-through windows.

Isabella was charmed. (Maybe not by the leering part, but generally.) And so it was because of her love of Rafie—and, I think, because of another reason—that she agreed to the silly, extravagant plan. But to her everlasting relief and shame, she refused one part of the plan: She refused to fake her death as well.

"As if I could jump out of a plane!" she would say whenever Rafie and Geoffrey urged it as the most logical course of action. "Into cold water, of all things! All the columnists laughed their heads off at me when I climbed into that stupid old tank for the veterans' parade. Now I'm going to act like some sort of special unit military force? You can't be serious!"

And so in the late-night strategy sessions, the Gallaghers and the Whitehall-Wrights came to believe that only Rafie needed to fake his death, that Isabella would, as the widowed princess, soon lose her panache. The world's eye would turn to Princess Genia and would be content for Isabella to occasionally appear at royal family functions, such as the annual racing ball. Rafie even convinced himself that this was an ideal setup, because it would give her an opportunity to have intimate chats with the royal family and keep him supplied with the gossip and news he would otherwise surely miss.

It was, as you must realize, a horribly naive notion. Isabella lost none of her panache and, if anything, became even more famous and sought-after. Perhaps things would have gone differently if Geoffrey had not died. But it seems, in retrospect, inevitable that the widowed princess would continue to be the subject of much interest and scrutiny. It is hard to imagine that Geoffrey, Mae, Rafie, and Isabella really thought she could sneak off to America and live quietly with Rafie.

But that is exactly what they thought. The only subject

of debate had been over how to fake the death. Mae had urged a simple plan, and the plan was simply this. Geoffrey and Rafie would take off on an unscheduled predawn run to the royal lodge on the Selbar Isles for a "spontaneous" day of fishing. Geoffrey knew a spot where low-level flying was considered quite dangerous. Rafie would bail out. Geoffrey would put the plane on automatic pilot, on a course to fly into the gray cliffs, and then bail out himself.

Rafie would swim to Lady Fiona's seaside compound—which was closed for renovations but always open to the royal family—and would be drinking kiwi cider in the hot tub by the time it became clear that the plane had crashed and Geoffrey was found clinging to his seat cushion.

Geoffrey would send the rescuers off in the wrong direction, with a fanciful tale of the prince trying to swim for help. In the days that followed, as scuba divers, trained dolphins, swimming dogs, and more than a few reporters in wet suits would try in vain to at least recover the body, Rafie would be slipping out of the country, taking a small boat to Turkey. He would hide there for a few weeks and, with the aid of a fake passport that he had obtained during a long-forgotten presentation on passport forgery by the head of homeland security, Rafie would emigrate to a rural part of the United States. There he would wait for Isabella while preparing applications to online speech pathology programs and building a mansion with an interior courtyard in a remote and forested area near a small midwestern city.

Rafie's belief in this plan was unwavering. Mae would say, "Do you really think it could work?" And he would say, "I know it will."

Isabella's part was even simpler. She would stay in Bisbania for a few weeks to attend the funeral and pack her rather voluminous bags. Then she would ask for her privacy and retreat into hiding. Her first hiding place would be half a world away from Rafie, but she would join him once she was reasonably certain that the world had accepted Rafie's death and the market had dropped for pictures of the royal widow.

"It'll give you time to grow that beard, dear," she would say with a laugh. As it turned out, it gave him more than enough time for that.

Despite her doubts, Mae liked the plan's relative simplicity. (You may be thinking it sounds complicated, but consider the options. How would you fake a death? Would you care to attempt to orchestrate a train crash? Ask yourself this: How do you lose a body in a car accident? Would you try to fake a hospital death? With all those witnesses? Many of whom have medical training! Impossible!)

Still, Mae was gravely concerned that a plane crash would leave Geoffrey under a cloud of suspicion from which he would never emerge. After all, surviving a plane crash that kills the heir to the throne—especially when the heir's body is never found—is not the sort of event that seals your place in upstanding society. And Mae, in spite of her humble origins and neutral shoes, grew more and more concerned about upstanding society with each day she spent in the castle. She had taken classes aimed at expanding her vocabulary. She had carefully studied the habits and customs of the more senior servants and the more accessible royals. She had come to appreciate being able to throw around names (or even just her address) to get what she wanted in stores and restaurants. "Oh," she would say when calling the nation's finest restaurants, "you're not taking reservations for Friday night? Well, if you change your mind, please call me at Glassidy Castle."

Mae did not want to give all that up. She didn't want to move out of the castle, although she supposed she could hang on to a little minor celebrity if she could just be grandfathered in on the castle invitation lists. And she certainly didn't want Geoffrey to go to prison. Even given that Isabella would remain as a source of protection for

Geoffrey, the plane-crash plan seemed fraught with peril. "What if they ask him to take a lie-detector test?" Mae asked. "He'll fail! Then what?"

But Geoffrey was game. Rafie was game. Isabella was game. Mae, the sole holdout, couldn't withstand the pressure. It's unfathomable, looking back, that four worldly, sophisticated, decent people hatched and enacted such an evil, dangerous, and stupid plot. Rafie, I believe, thought he had no choice. The royal cage is a cage only of the mind. But a cage of the mind is the strongest cage there is. Rafie did not believe that he could escape his destiny to be king except through death. Royals can do anything, but they somehow don't realize they can do the one thing that almost all the rest of us started doing as toddlers: disappoint our parents. Rafie's decision was one of desperation.

Isabella? I'm not sure I understand her motivation even now. I think she wanted to make her husband happy. She wanted to prove that she did not need the glamour and the glitz of royal life.

And Mae? Mae was just weak-willed and too optimistic. She lined up all her reasons against the plan and then said, basically, "Ah well, it will probably work out okay."

But what about Geoffrey? He was the one with the most to lose, and he did lose the most. The risk he was taking was the most senseless, given that he had nothing to gain from the plan, not privacy nor happiness nor money nor love.

If the plan had gone as envisioned, he would have lost the life he so enjoyed. He surely would have lost his royal mechanic's job and the lucrative pay. And he would have lost the daily companionship of Isabella and Rafie. Geoffrey's act can only be explained as the generous act of friendship.

I guess.

But sometimes when I'm in a dark and foul mood, when I have lost my optimistic spirit, when I entertain demons that make me think ill of people and suspect that no one is generous and good, sometimes in those moments, I remember the last time I saw Geoffrey and Isabella together. It was moments after they danced at Princess Iphigenia's investiture ball. They slipped out onto a balcony and believed themselves alone.

Geoffrey said, "If you go through with this, you know, there's no going back. You can't decide a year from now or a decade from now that it was a big mistake."

Isabella just smiled, rolled her eyes toward the tiara she was wearing, and shrugged.

Geoffrey put his hand on her cheek. "It's not just that, babe," he said. "Not just the queen thing. If you do this, you can't ever leave Rafie. He'll be dependent on you. He'll have given up everything for you. You'll be more married than ever. You can't back out of that, either."

"I'm not going to back out of that," she said.

They just stared at each other for a moment or two. He nodded. "Okay, then."

She touched his face and leaned forward and whispered something I could not hear. He rubbed his hand along the heading on the waist of her peacock blue dress, and I felt something pass between them that I did not understand.

Many times since then, I've wondered if the words I heard Geoffrey speak that night were true. If he really thought that Isabella would be more married than ever, or if he secretly dreamed of what Rafie must have feared. I wondered if he thought that Isabella, for all her apparent ambivalence about royal life, had not merely married a crown. Did Geoffrey think he was helping Rafie and Isabella be together? Or did he hope that he was pulling them apart?

We do not know. Geoffrey took his motivations and the secrets of his heart with him into the icy, stormy sea. Rafie was never able to explain what had gone wrong to Isabella or Mae, and he also never adequately explained the long delay between the crash and the moment when Isabella finally received a call from Lady Fiona's phone.

"The plan was going just spick-spack when I bailed," Rafie said. "Dear Geoffrey, I can't imagine what happened."

Rafie would later tell the women that it took him a little over two hours to reach Fiona's home—an hour longer than they had planned—in part because he had to stay hidden on the rocky beach for a good half hour while some of Fiona's neighbors came out to watch the search planes. He was supposed to call Isabella immediately upon reaching the home, but he was so exhausted that he just collapsed on the sofa and napped. Or so he said.

Isabella clucked sympathetically and stroked his hair, but Mae noticed a faraway look in the princess's eyes and wondered if she had thought the same thing that Mae had. When Rafie had first broached the sea-crash plan, Geoffrey had opined that the people would never be satisfied if they did not find Rafie's body. Rafie had dismissed Geoffrey's concern.

Mae wondered, had Rafie been confident all along that there *would* be a body?

She could not know. She knew only that when Isabella held the American widow's face between her royal hands there in the home of Lady Carissa's acquaintance and said that she could demand a full investigation and that everything would come to light and that whatever that would mean is whatever that would mean, Mae made a split-second judgment that she sometimes regretted.

She said, "No, for then Geoffrey would have died in vain."

Chapter  17

*I*t's done now. Isn't it? I look down at my hands, and I see that I am shaking. It has been four days since I wrote the last chapter. I haven't slept well since. Secrets are hard to keep, but I am learning now that they are sometimes harder to tell. I don't even know you, but I have spilled to you my worst knowledge, the memories I have held in my heart even while shielding them from my mind for all these many long years. I have hinted to you the darkest suspicions of my soul. I wonder now if that is right. Or if I am just a tired old woman who has had too much time to think.

Rafie was a good man. I know not one bad thing about him, other than perhaps he used poor judgment in finding a way to get out of the family business. He was exceedingly kind to Mae in the years following the accident. "There, there," he would say whenever she got weepy. He would pat her arm, hand her a tissue. He would repeat himself as long as he needed to, because he understood that there was no way to elaborate. "There, there," he would say. "There, there."

He offered, in other words, only the good and simple kindness that you would expect of any decent human being. He did not seem motivated by guilt or shame.

In fact, he was kind enough to her even beforehand.

Perhaps I shouldn't have said as much as I did. But in the past four days, I have gone over and over the last chapter, and I cannot decide what I would cut. The story that I am telling is important and needs to be understood in all its appropriate context. I cannot presume to know what detail or suspicion or fear was insignificant. So I guess I must include it all.

Besides, I fear that writing it down is, in and of itself, going beyond where I can turn back. I have, if only while moving my lips silently as I lean over my keyboard, voiced the unspeakable truth, the unbearable suspicions. Deleting them now would make no difference. They have escaped my heart. They are loose in the world. I cannot get them back.

That is, at least, how I feel.

The castle's official mourning lasted one year. During that time, the queen and Princess Iphigenia always wore somber colors. The annual racing ball was suspended, and official banquets did not serve dessert—though after the first few months, the kitchen staff was able to slip in a final fruit course, which was often seasoned a bit with sugar and butter and sometimes cooked with a bit of flour. You know, sort of like cake.

The nation's mourning was much shorter. In the first few hours, the florists sold out of Bisbanian mums, then lilacs, which were the official flower of the Prince of Gallagher. Tulips, a nod to Isabella's Dutch heritage, were the next to go. During those first few days, nearly all work stopped, and bus drivers, cops, and other public servants were often seen blinking back tears. The smell of the flowers—first sweet, then sour and rotting—hung over the city-state for weeks.

Investigations were called for. "How did we get to the point," the prime minister asked, "where the heir to the throne is being flown about by a mechanic? Does the castle security staff do anything anymore?"

That sort of talk lasted for months.

And for years—even now, in fact—there were all sorts of rumors: that perhaps a missile shot down the plane, that maybe the engine had been tampered with, that surely the pilot had not wanted to fly through that storm but the prince, cocky and overconfident and used to getting his way, had insisted.

(Raphael could not help but be irritated by those rumors. "Cocky?" he'd say in the e-mails he exchanged with Isabella while they were in hiding half a world away from each other. "Since when have I been cocky? I'm positively unassuming. That's always been written about me!")

Mae did not sue the royal family, and that decision was seen as highly suspicious by the sorts of people who were suspicious about the whole thing anyway.

There were questions about why it took so long to get search boats out, and there was concern about the condition of the castle's aging plane fleet. In out-of-the-way Internet chat rooms, people with a loose hold on reality theorized that either the royal family had, at some point, been placed under a curse, or they had their own son killed to keep Isabella from eventually becoming queen.

("That's just ridiculous," Raphael would write to Isabella each time a tabloid featured that line of reasoning. "Wouldn't they just kill you, then?" he'd ask, leaving Isabella a bit too flabbergasted to reply. "Why involve me in it?")

Meanwhile, the more serious papers were attempting to

document how the tragedy had become a turning point for the nation. When Vreeland, Rafie's longtime valet, left the castle service and became a missionary, magazines held him up as evidence that the nation would become more giving now that it had lost its innocence.

But you know how these sorts of things go. It wasn't long before people were making jokes about the conspiracy theorists, and even the prince's worthiness was questioned. "He's just a prince," you'd start to overhear people say. "He wasn't the pope." And luckily for everyone involved, the nation's innocence was somehow restored so that it could be lost again a couple of years later, when the king died.

I shouldn't be so flip. It's predictable and trite, but it's real too. Those feelings—both the feeling that it is all too unimaginably awful and we will never be the same again, and then later, the equal feeling that we need to move on, we need to be the same again—are real.

People can't feel such sadness forever. So three weeks after the funerals, when the king and queen announced that Isabella had left the castle, seeking a private place to grieve, it seemed to mark the unofficial end of the public's mourning.

Their Majesties asked that the press and others respect this action on her part and not try to find her. "It is our sincere hope," said the queen, making a great effort to sound sincere, "that the Princess of Gallagher will be afforded time in a quiet place to adjust to her tremendous personal loss and to decide what role she would like to have in the royal family and the nation's public life. We eagerly await her decisions and bid her all the best."

Some people greeted such statements from the queen and king with much skepticism, but I think it was their honest attempt to rise to the occasion. They were, after all, mourning their own loss, grappling with the need to prepare their daughter for queendom, and, for the first time, facing their own mortality.

Naturally, the castle plea did not stop anyone from seeking the whereabouts of the princess. The foreign press was especially ruthless—tapping the Cordage family's phones, staking out all the princess's favorite vacation spots, and even following Mae for a few nerve-racking weeks, under the assumption that the two widows would stay in touch. But the national press was far more restrained, not out of respect so much. They were just looking for an excuse to let the story die. No one could take another day of it.

At any rate, they never found her. In what is considered one of the most stunning self-exiles since the dawn of the modern media, Isabella's whereabouts were completely unknown for two solid years. It seems hard to believe now. But her exile was so successful that, after a year or so, she was almost forgotten except as a dated icon. The thought of her would give middle-aged women faraway looks in their eyes and make them recall their own lost promise and youth.

Unimaginable as this seems now, the public was convinced during her exile that they had heard the last of the Princess of Gallagher and that her star had fallen with her husband's fateful plane.

But you know that they were wrong. On the second anniversary of her husband's death, when Isabella emerged from a hiding place that, until the writing of this book, has never been revealed, she became what no one could have guessed: an even bigger star. And it happened for all the wrong reasons.

Several months before the second anniversary of Rafie's death, the king and queen begged Isabella to return to Bisbania. The king was quite ill and did not have long to live. Both His and Her Majesties wanted Isabella to return for a commemoration of Rafie's crash and, more important, to be photographed spending time with Iphigenia, whom they were attempting to prepare for her rapidly approaching role as queen, but who was again having a bit of a rough time of it in the press.

At any rate, the king and queen explained to Isabella—through an elaborate system of forwarded e-mails handled by Secrest—that they suspected the public held a lingering perception that the young widowed princess had been drummed out of the castle. They feared this unfounded rumor was affecting the way the people saw Princess Iphigenia, viewing her as a petty, heartless, weak replacement for her dear, glamorous brother. Isabella wrote short pithy replies in which she assured Their Majesties that it couldn't be as bad as all that, and that she was quite certain the uproar of her return would only do the family more harm than good.

But when the king, obviously weakened, sent a video clip of himself pleading with her, she relented. Though they were never particularly chummy, Isabella had always rather liked the king, because he was the only member of the royal family who enjoyed a good slapstick comedy and who shared her distaste for fig pie. ("Why ruin perfectly good figs with all that syrup and buttery crust?" the king would always ask. And Isabella would always reply that she couldn't imagine a good reason.)

Plans were immediately set into motion. Word quickly leaked out from the senior staff members of the castle, and soon everyone was completely abuzz with excitement. Isabella was coming home!

I have always wished the queen would have talked about the day Isabella returned, for I'm sure her account would have been the most acid, biting, and astute. But she was much too discreet to ever say anything, although it was obvious enough that she was not pleased. The look on Iphigenia's face, likewise, was just too precious: filled at once with shock, sadness, anger, and confusion.

Knowing everything we know now, it's hard to appreciate how shocking it all was at the time. When the princess had left the castle two years earlier, she had been a sad but composed woman of pearls and pastels. (Allowing for the more somber colors she wore during the sorrowful days after the plane crash.)

In the weeks preceding her much anticipated return, the commentators had practically outdone themselves speculating on how she would look. Ethelbald said he thought she would look a bit sadder and wiser for the things she'd gone through. "But don't forget," he said, "this is a woman who defied all odds and hid herself for two years. If she's coming out now, it can mean only one thing: She's ready. I expect to see her step off that plane in a pink suit and polka-dot shoes."

This prediction caused the queen to work herself into a bit of a tizzy, saying to Iphigenia over and over again that surely the princess would have the good sense to wear something a bit more serious. "Not too serious, of course," she said. "But you can't wear pink polka dots to a memorial service for your husband. Surely she'll wear navy. Won't she? Wouldn't any sane royal woman wear navy?"

And Iphigenia said any sane royal woman would.

So both Her Majesty the Queen and Princess Iphigenia were positively aghast on the sunny day at His Majesty's National Airport when the door of the chartered plane opened and Princess Isabella stepped into the sunlight.

You've seen the photo a million times, so you are not shocked. But imagine what that photo would look like if you were expecting pink polka dots and pearls!

Isabella was wearing—on an unseasonably warm day— wool. Dark brown wool. It was sewn together roughly with darker brown thread and gathered at the waist with a bit of rope. The dress, if you could call it that, had no body or shape or styling. It hung in a clumsy, unplanned way and looked like a horrible home-economics project gone awry.

She wore sandals that appeared to be made out of reeds, though everyone assumed it was some new synthetic fiber.

But it wasn't just the clothes. Isabella, who had left a slim, attractive woman, was gaunt and bony. Her face, which bore not a trace of makeup, was pinched and thin. And her hair? It looked like it had been cut by holding two rocks together and rubbing them back and forth until the hairs in between broke away. It was cut awfully short at that, short and spiky, like something from that awful punk fad. No glamorous buns could be made with this hair. Not only that, but it was dirty, almost matted in places.

"She looks like a homeless woman," Iphigenia whispered to her mother, who just stared ahead, aware of the camera on her and concentrating on not making an expression. Isabella, frowning and sad-eyed, took a step toward the queen and curtsied. Then she took a step toward her sister-in-law, smiled awkwardly, and reached out to hug her.

Everyone at the airport that bright early morning was absolutely appalled. Isabella's sister, Lady Fiona, wept as she hugged Isabella and tried to pass it off as joy, but the rest of the crowd knew it was stunned fear. Ethelbald Candeloro was, perhaps for the first time, speechless. He was so distracted by the shock of it all that he tugged at his mustache in what would have been a telltale way, except no one was looking at him. He also crossed his legs in a ladylike manner and absentmindedly walked into a women's room. Luckily, though, he was not the only one doing things like that. Everyone there was rattled and thrown off-kilter.

The small crowd of subjects who had been allowed to gather on the runway seemed a little embarrassed and sad. "I thought, *Well, that's it,*" one of them later told me. "All that beauty, all that glory, all that glamour, it's gone. Now she's just a sad, crazy ol' hag with nothing to look forward to but years of ridicule."

But that just shows you that no one who is at an event

really knows what has happened until they see the news accounts the next day. Because the sole photographer at the scene, the one allowed in with Ethelbald, saw something that no one else did. He saw a split-second moment, in the endless time while Isabella had stood just outside the plane, dazed and tired and waiting for her eyes to adjust, when she had glanced up at the sun and given a small little smile.

And that was enough. The slight smile transformed her entire being. She looked, if not happy, at least normal. At least pretty. No one else saw the smile. I wonder sometimes if it was ever really there. Or if it was, somehow, a trick of light and shadow—a moment of gas or exasperation. But it hardly matters now, for what matters is perception. Isabella got off the plane looking and acting like a desert hermit, but the photo—the only one released of Isabella's arrival— was printed in the paper the next day and made her look striking and happy. So for the purposes of the story, as it was played on the world stage, that is what she was. Overnight, sackcloth clothing became the hot trend in clothes. Synthetic reed sandals replaced toeless slingbacks as the shoe of the season. Starlets started paying extraordinary prices for shampoo that, when used daily, would give their hair the not-washed-in-weeks look. Women the world over started starving themselves as Isabella's bony figure became the new standard of so-called fitness.

Isabella had been scheduled to do four weeks of appearances, and each day the crowds were larger and more enthusiastic than the day before. The energy was contagious. Soon Isabella seemed to be truly enjoying herself again. She gathered up flowers by the armful, appeared in several parades and two hot-air-balloon races, and inadvertently launched a multimillion-pound mail-order business for a modest cookie bakery by wandering into the small shop and proclaiming the macaroons "sinfully scrumptious."

Iphigenia—suddenly wearing simply cut brown suits,

sporting a new, spiky haircut, and forsaking dinner—basked in the reflective glow. Her approval ratings skyrocketed for no apparent reason other than her ability to root for Isabella during a balloon race and to comfort her when, as was inevitable, the homecoming became emotional.

During a ceremonial wreath-laying on Lancelot Beach, Isabella stepped away from the crowd of dignitaries and set float an origami seagull. She stood there for what seemed, on television at least, an excruciatingly long time, watching the waves carry away the bird and, occasionally, wiping tears from her cheek. Everyone else, the queen included, stood by awkwardly, not wanting to seem to rush the princess, but also not feeling like it was the sort of scene that should go on in public for too terribly long.

Finally, Iphigenia walked up, patted Isabella's arm, stared with her out into the sea for a respectful moment, then took her arm and gently led her back.

Later, at a ribbon cutting for the new His Royal Highness the Prince of Gallagher Elementary School, Isabella looked out upon the crowd of children and broke down in tears. Iphigenia hugged her sister-in-law and whispered in her ear. The two women smiled through their tears and even chuckled a little as the cameras snapped away.

Those are the lasting images of the relationship between the two princesses.

But if you think the two women were close, you are wrong. How could they be, when Isabella was keeping so many frightfully large secrets from her sister-in-law? Secrets that Isabella knew were the very source of all Iphigenia's sorrows and fears.

And how could Iphigenia love Isabella when she knew that she was the one thing that Iphigenia could not be? The tragic martyr, the princess who would never again be criticized because the poor dear had gone through enough, and who, by her very perfection, would make every day of Iphigenia's life harder.

To whatever extent that Isabella and Iphigenia shared a real bond, it was only of the foxhole variety. They both knew what it was like to live under fire, and clung a bit to anyone who was not firing directly at them, even if they somehow resented that the other person's presence drew some much unneeded attention their way. What else could they do but remain friendly allies?

In the last of the four weeks that Isabella was to be visiting, the king died. Isabella was forced to extend her stay in Bisbania to attend the funeral and, a few weeks later, her sister-in-law's coronation. To that event, she wore a long bronze gown and a gemless tiara that thrilled the royal commentators to no end and completely upstaged Iphigenia's rather dowdy crowning robes and overly bejeweled head-piece.

"Isabella is a gem herself," Ethelbald gushed. "She needs no jewels in her tiara."

The morning after the coronation, Isabella stood before the nation in a recorded address and announced that she was now renouncing her title, meaning she would henceforth be known again as simply Isabella Cordage.

Wearing the same rough wool that had become her trademark, and with the spiky hair that now looked trendy rather than grotesque, she explained her reasoning.

"I really should have taken this step two years ago," she said. "But I could not bring myself to give up the title that was my sole link to my dear husband. Now, however, I have come to realize my tie to Rafie is stronger than any mere words or name. My role in the royal family no longer has any constitutional purpose. I will continue to be a part of my in-laws' private lives, but I think it will be beneficial to everyone involved if I give up my public role and my title, which Queen Iphigenia may one day want to bestow upon one of her own children."

(Iphigenia had specifically asked for that line in an attempt to silence the mounting worry that her lack of anything resembling a boyfriend meant an end to the direct line of succession, a troubling prospect, as it would mean that one of Prince Louis's dreadful granddaughters, specifically the oldest one with the tattoos and French boyfriend, could be the next monarch.)

"To make the transition easier for all involved," Isabella continued, back on her own agenda, "I will be making a new home in a remote place, and I ask that I be allowed to live my life there in privacy and peace."

Iphigenia thought the speech went exceedingly well and was thrilled with Isabella's delivery of the line about the children. "She can put on quite a show," Iphigenia told the ladies-in-waiting. "I will grant her that." But once again, Iphigenia and Isabella learned how helpless they were at crafting public perception. The next morning, the headlines read:

MEAN QUEEN GENE BANISHES IZZY
TO NOWHERESVILLE
GREEN BAY, U.S.A., READIES FOR NEW ROYAL RESIDENT

Chapter 18

I guess I need to tell you how I learned Ethelbald Candeloro's secret. I don't mean to be cruel about this, to harp on his one awkward truth. But the moment when Ethelbald and I learned each other's secrets was a fateful one. And so I think any true accounting of what happened to all of us needs a detailed description of that encounter.

I had followed Isabella during her mysterious exile, and then I followed her home. After I returned, I attended one of the events that commemorated the king's death. They were all sad and solemn, of course. But the later ones had an underlying, shall I say, life to them, which made for politically tricky posturing. You had to appear to enjoy the party without seeming like you were glad there was an occasion for one.

I saw Isabella enter the building from afar. She was announced, and all eyes turned toward her and her beige suit (dubbed a "coffee-and-cream-colored confection of refined class" in Ethelbald's column the next day).

But she did not see me—just another face in navy—until we bumped into each other in the women's room. She surprised me by squealing with delight and hugging my neck and complimenting my dress, as if she sincerely liked the color. "You clean up great," she said.

I suppose I thought now that we were back in our old world, she would treat me in the old way. But the stress of returning, of once again being surrounded by so many things and so many eyes and so much excess, had unnerved her. She honestly seemed happy to see me.

She asked me if I'd had my first good cup of cider yet, and if I had been brushing my teeth all day long, as she had. "I had forgotten," she said, "how marvelous clean teeth feel."

I laughed and said, "Well, at least then you'll have a hobby in Green Bay. You can brush your teeth all day and night."

We were slaphappy and silly and feeling unreasonably clean and young. Right then we heard something hit the floor in the stall closest to us, and then someone cleared her throat. Isabella and I stared at each other, silently and frantically trying to remember exactly what we had said.

Had I actually said "Green Bay," or did I say something safe like "your new home"? In that panicky moment, neither of us was sure.

And then a heavyset, somewhat mannish woman stepped out of the stall and adjusted her strapless black ball gown.

"Well, hello," Isabella said in her brightest and most engaging voice. "I didn't realize we had company. I hope we haven't been boring you with our nonsensical patter."

Ethel Bald shook her head shyly, clearly wishing she had not dropped her purse and called attention to herself. "Oh, dear no, Your Highness," she said with the sort of awkward curtsy that commoners always offer up. "Were you talking? I was rather absorbed with a . . . " Ethel Bald's voice trailed off at this point as she apparently realized there wasn't much that she could claim to be absorbed with in a bathroom stall, especially to a princess. "Um. With a family, eh, issue." That had probably seemed like a good line when she started it, but she furrowed her brow in what appeared to be a regretful way when she got to the word "issue." Really, the word "issue" has an entirely different connotation when connected with bathroom stalls, doesn't it? Or perhaps she was worried that it sounded like some of her family members were still in the stall, because she continued by saying, "Thinking about it, I mean. The, um, issue, I was thinking of."

Another furrowed brow. "You know how family is," she continued, then gamely attempted a smile.

But that was all wrong, and each of the three of us winced, though Isabella tried to hide it. Isabella was, at least supposedly, still a relatively recent widow and attending a memorial service for her late father-in-law. This is not the sort of circumstance in which you joke about the trials of putting up with relatives.

"I suppose," Ethel Bald continued in a misguided attempt to cover up that mistake, "I should just be glad they're alive." She winced again. "Not that I wouldn't still love them if they were dead."

For a writer, she could be awfully awkward with words.

"Of course," said Isabella, trying to put on a chatty persona that would suggest it was perfectly ordinary for her to drag out conversations with babbling commoners who spontaneously and loudly emerge from bathroom stalls to say inappropriate things. Isabella needed to gauge who this person was and whether she had overheard anything that threatened Isabella and her not-really-dead husband. "Where is your family from?" Isabella asked, uncharacteristically ending her sentence with a preposition.

In all her years of sneaking about at royal balls and castle events, Ethel Bald had never faced a grilling like this. She looked positively panicked. "Um. Well. Here and there," she said. When Isabella did not leap in to fill the awkward silence, Ethel Bald made a rookie mistake. The first thing you are taught in journalism school is that you should *never* be the one to fill an awkward silence. You should always let the *other* person rush into the silence. That is how you get your best information.

But Ethel Bald was down on her game. She was nervous, and it showed. She panicked and kept talking, sharing the first thing that came into her head, which was, unfortunately for her, the truth. (It almost always is—that is precisely the reason journalists are taught to let the other person fill the silence.) "Mostly, I guess," Ethel Bald accurately reported, "from America."

"Oh," Isabella exclaimed, a bit too enthusiastically, I thought. "I went to school in America! It's a lovely country, you know."

There was another silence, and this time Isabella rushed to fill it. Neither of these women would have made it on *60 Minutes,* I could see that.

"It's so . . ." Isabella struggled to find the right words. "So casual and, well . . . big! Silly me, I haven't even introduced myself. I'm Isabella," she said, knowing full well that the strange woman was already aware of that. "They call me the Princess of Gallagher."

Ethel Bald nodded. "Pleased to meet you."

"And you are?" Isabella said in the royal way that seems absolutely nonjudgmental but nevertheless embarrasses people for not having already introduced themselves. "Oh," Ethel Bald said. "I'm Ethel." Pause. "It's an old-fashioned

American name, you know. But I consider myself Bisbanian through and through. Born here. Put myself through school by working in the fig orchards. Husband is in the royal engineer corps. Last name is Bald."

Something flashed across her face. Did she wish she hadn't said that?

Isabella said it was a delight to meet her, and she later told me that we were all clear. "We may need to be paranoid," she said. "But we do not need to be so paranoid that we're worried about the chunky and slightly mannish wives of royal engineers. Besides, we didn't say anything that interesting. It's not like you actually mentioned Green Bay by name."

But I wondered. For I have a lot in common with Ethel Bald. I know a little about ugly old-fashioned American names, and I know a little about awkwardly blurting out the truth, and I know the way a journalist holds her eyes when she does not want to reveal too much of herself to the subjects of her stories. And I thought I had used the words "Green Bay."

Besides, I caught something that Isabella didn't. The woman's name was Ethel Bald.

Then Ethelbald Candeloro broke the Green Bay story. So I knew. I called "him" and told him that I knew his secret. "He" said that was okay. He had been expecting my call. He'd been rattled by our encounter in the bathroom, so he'd been doing some research. He was pleased to tell me that he knew my secret as well.

Then he slipped into a dreamy, philosophical voice and told me he was almost glad that someone had found out. He had, for a long time, wanted to be able to tell someone, and he guessed that someone was me. He wanted to be able to say out loud that he never meant to do it, but the editor had thought he was a man, and he was afraid if he told the truth, he wouldn't get the job.

I said that was well and good. But I told him I wasn't the least bit glad that someone had learned my secret, and for the record, I could claim no such innocence. My secret came of a deliberate and conscious act, and I'd do it again if I had to. I had worked too hard for too long to let something like this humiliate me.

I said I wouldn't tell his secret, if he would not tell mine. And we agreed not to push each other's buttons. Until now.

Chapter 19

While Ethelbald and I were sharing secrets on the phone, pundits the world over were scrambling to outdo one another with moral outrage about "Mean Queen Gene" and her decision to banish Isabella to "Nowheresville."

The American press was a bit kinder. To Green Bay, I mean. Not to Iphigenia, who was immediately seized upon as the villain by all commentators. But even while waxing on about Mean Gene, the American editorialists saved a bit of venom to take umbrage at overly harsh criticisms of the princess's new home, which was not, strictly speaking, *in* Green Bay but was instead in a wooded region just north of there.

Although, make no mistake about it, even the Americans did not approve.

"While Green Bay hardly deserves the 'Nowheresville' label applied by European press snobs," wrote one Detroit columnist, "it is a bit remote and lacks some of the urban charms that the princess enjoys."

"She's not a princess anymore!" Queen Iphigenia whined to her ladies-in-waiting. "That was the whole point."

The ladies-in-waiting knew that it wasn't exactly the point. But they were too kind to say so to the new queen. Instead, they diplomatically tsked and tutted and said it would surely all blow over soon.

For her part, Isabella was terribly disappointed that the news of her location had leaked out already. She was, I suppose, still heady from her stunning and successful disappearance after the crash. And while she had no intention of going to the lengths necessary to do that again, she had hoped to keep things under wraps at least until she had quietly moved into the Green Bay home that Raphael had designed for the two of them.

It was, by royal standards, a small cabin—a mere forty rooms and fifteen thousand square feet. (Raphael had been siphoning money into a Swiss bank account for several months before the crash, although apparently not enough to build the eighty-room home he dreamed of.) But the locals undoubtedly still considered it a castle, with its showy architecture, its indoor pool, and most notably its Biosphere-esque covered interior courtyard, complete with riding court, hiking trail, and the usual mum garden.

Construction on the project, which Raphael had supervised while wearing flannel shirts and passing himself off as an eccentric and secretive Vermont billionaire, was not quite finished when Ethelbald Candeloro broke the Green Bay story—a scoop that seemed inexplicable and mysterious to Isabella at the time and which had not, until this book, been publicly explained.

Isabella's fear was understandable. She had sacrificed a great deal for this moment. Her title, the life of her beloved adviser, twenty-four months of adequate dental hygiene. More than that, really. I haven't even gotten to the big one.

Isabella had, in pursuit of Raphael's silly dream, spent the past two years living in positively miserable conditions. Most people, incorrectly assuming Isabella's gaunt look and sackcloth attire had more to do with fashion than anything else, thought she must have been living in some lush, well-staffed tropical resort. But it is no exaggeration to say that some prisoners of war lived better than Isabella did in those years. Her appearance might have shocked and offended the queen, but she had come dressed exactly as she should have, according to all royal handbooks. She had come to see the queen wearing the best that she had.

If the queen, if the world, had any idea how modestly Isabella had lived and dressed while she was away—I don't know that they ever could have understood it. I'm not sure *I* understood it, and I was living right there with her almost the whole time, sleeping on the same dirt floors and forgoing manicures just like she was.

So it was understandable that, after all the princess had gone through, she was upset when the location of her new home was reported before the construction was complete and before Raphael was settled into his basement bunker. He had planned to hole up there for several months, long enough so that his flannel-shirt-wearing persona would have softened a bit in the contractors' minds and would not seem suggestive of the famously dead Bisbanian prince—not even after they learned that the famously widowed Bisbanian princess was "buying" the place and moving in.

Instead, Ethelbald Candeloro's scoop spread around the world before Isabella could relay a warning to her husband. A news bulletin about her move came over Green Bay radio at perhaps the worst possible moment. Raphael was standing in the cabin's dining hall, a bit too regally, he thought later, complaining to the electrician about a glare from the secondary chandeliers. The radio announcer launched into the news bulletin, and the electrician turned toward the radio, seeming to listen carefully. The prince gulped but rallied gamely. He said "dang" and "golly" and then allowed that perhaps if the princess was looking for a new home in the area, she would "take this mess of a place off my hands."

"Assuming," the prince added with a snort, "she doesn't mind bad lighting." He then retreated quickly.

It was a close call, and Isabella was not happy at all when she later heard about it. Actually, she wasn't happy about a lot of things when she arrived in Green Bay. I don't mean to imply that she was not appropriately ecstatic to be back with her husband. They were, by all accounts, silly lovebirds in their first few weeks back together. (And when I say "all" accounts, I mean his account and her account, because for the first time in their lives, there was no one else present to watch them.) Rafie fussed over her constantly, urging her to gain back some of the weight she had lost and defying every royal sensibility there is by lovingly brushing her hair. Meanwhile, Isabella doted on her husband in unimaginably common ways, ironing his shirts, no less, and attempting to perfect a spaghetti-sauce recipe he found in a magazine.

Despite her happiness at being with Rafie, she thought he had made some questionable decisions in planning their new home. For example, there were no electrical outlets in Isabella's makeup and grooming room, forcing her to run an extension cord into the nearby closet. "Just when I was looking forward to an electric toothbrush and a regular blow-dry," she said.

Worse still, he had chosen, at the suggestion of the construction workers, a Packers color scheme, a look that required various green and gold combinations, none of them particularly pleasing. (In some parts of the world, the city of Green Bay is celebrated—mostly by the color-blind, I fear—for its support of the Packers, a legendary team in American football.) The unfortunate palette was carried into even the mum garden, which was inconveniently placed near the screened-in breakfast area. Have I mentioned that Bisbania mums are somewhat odiferous?

"Really, darling, what were you thinking," Isabella would say in a regular teasing refrain that grew somewhat less good-natured over the years. "We can't even have cider and toast out here, much less a full fig-pancake breakfast. I'm sure we'd become quite ill."

The whole castle made Isabella ill, truth be told. (I mean, obviously. Green and gold?) During the two years of what the press was by then calling her "mysterious first exile," the princess had developed some rather Spartan sensibilities. Don't get me wrong. Isabella was definitely ready to return to normal nail maintenance, pressed clothing, and brushed silk. Still, the huge Green Bay home and its garish color scheme made her uncomfortable in a way she could not have predicted before the crash.

Isabella was, however, smart enough to see the reality of her situation. She wanted to be with Rafie. To live with him again required a home so large and well equipped and self-contained that he could hide there for weeks or months or years at a time without leaving. Furthermore, it needed to be well off the beaten path of the worldly and wise and smack dab in the middle of the incurious and dull. Green Bay, she came to see, was perfect.

Oh dear. The Green Bay Chamber of Commerce will no doubt swamp me with complaint letters. But I assure you I mean no offense. I suppose it would be disingenuous to say that I mean the "incurious and dull," remark as a compliment. But when I say "incurious and dull," I mean a very specific quality, an outlook born out of honest self-satisfaction. Green Bay is a place that is happily content with itself.

A city with a less content populace would have been deeply suspicious of the princess's decision to live within it and would have picked and pried and nagged at her. But it made perfect sense to average Green Bay residents that a beloved princess would choose their city as her home. After all, hadn't their own great-great-grandfathers made the same choice? They had. And had any of their ancestors in the subsequent generations seen any reason to leave? They had not.

Those big cities with all their urban charms had less free parking, more crime, and fewer professional athletes per capita. If the most famous and photographed woman in the world wanted to move to their city, Green Bay's reaction was: "What took her so long?"

Ethelbald Candeloro's scoop may have caught Rafie and Isabella unprepared, but it ended up making no difference. The workers who built Rafie and Isabella's new home never questioned the identity of the flannel-shirted man who planned the building that the princess moved into. What were they supposed to question, really? Were they supposed to think he was the prince? The prince was dead. Everyone knew that. Besides, that guy was clearly from Vermont.

Incurious, dull, bad with accents.

I stand by my assessment.

Green Bay had one last thing going for it as far as Isabella was concerned: the city's year-round devotion to the Packers. It wasn't that the princess cared much about sports. She rarely took in even a real football game and certainly had no interest in the bastardized version that Americans play. Still, she appreciated that Green Bay's success in football not only served to distract the local populace but also significantly distorted the world's perception of the place. Oh sure, royal commentators the world over wrote stories about Green Bay's lack of urban charms, but truthfully, no one—not even Ethelbald Candeloro—thought it was as atrocious as the pundits let on. They thought it was dread-

ful compared to New York or London or Paris. Well, maybe
not dreadful compared to Paris, which Bisbanians detested
along with the rest of France. But dreadful compared to any-
place you would actually imagine the princess living. Green
Bay seemed, simply, too downscale.

But downscale is not, in the scheme of things, so bad.
It's not as if she was going somewhere without good cider.
So they poked fun with a sort of voyeuristic pity, but they
deluded themselves into thinking that Isabella remained
vaguely on the radar. Because of the football team and the
attention it had brought to Green Bay, even the Ethelbalds
of the world thought the city was a place quickly accessible
by plane travel and adequately represented by the social
arts. They did not realize, even when they looked at maps,
that it rested on the southern tip of a vast and unpopulated
region—a land of woods and vales where a celebrity
princess and her not-really-dead husband could cavort for
months, even visiting remote Native American gaming casinos
in off hours without being spotted.

(The prince tried hard to love casinos as much as he
loved horse racing, but he never quite succeeded. "It's utterly
random," he would say incredulously to Isabella each time
they ventured out for a night of slots. "There's absolutely no
handicapping involved at all.")

If Isabella had announced that she was moving to an isolated Montana cabin, the tabloids of the world would have
bought up the land around her and set up bureaus to keep
an eye on her. But in Green Bay, they falsely assumed she
was already under the eye of a vigorous and interested
press, a gossipy batch of neighbors. The tabloid editors did
not understand that the Green Bay press was trying to get
the details of the football coach's contract buyout, of the
quarterback's elbow surgery, and of the star linebacker's
felony charges. The tabloid editors did not realize the neighbors were busy shoveling their driveways and browsing

through snowblower catalogs. Isabella wasn't their primary concern.

So Isabella, having already pulled off one successful exile, pulled off another. She lived in hiding by appearing to live in the open. But I suppose I have gotten ahead of the story now. I should have stopped before this to tell you where Isabella had been in those two years she was gone. It explains so much, and it will become quite critical to the end of my story. I have a few secrets remaining, and the last one is the biggest, and it is my reason for writing this book.

Chapter 20

There was, in that time, a man named Jeb.

Not to sound all biblical about it, but those who know Jeb tend to speak of him in solemn, epic tones.

Jeb lived on a desert mountain that he often described as being near Nairobi, a desperate description that, for it was really near nothing. The bustling congestion of Nairobi was over three hundred miles away. Jeb liked it that way. He lived simply, without lightbulbs, running water, or any sort of worldly wealth.

Jeb had once been something of a radio celebrity in Mexico, hosting a fabulously successful polka hour under the name Juan El Baez. Despite published reports, he did not launch the surreal Mexican polka craze that was raging across the Americas at that time. In fact, he came rather late to the happy dance fad, which had gotten its start, strangely enough, in the Little Arabia neighborhood of Mexico City. (Mexico was apparently more cosmopolitan in those days than anyone on this side of the ocean imagined.)

But Jeb did a brilliant job of capitalizing on the trend, starting with his decision to include "El" as part of his radio name, a much appreciated nod to the Middle Eastern musicians who had essentially "invented" Mexican polka. He thought "El" sounded vaguely Arabic, but in a good old-fashioned Hispanic sort of way. Apparently, he was right. Because in many parts of the world, or at least in many parts of Mexico, polka fans to this day say that no one could introduce the "Fish Taco Polka" as well as the Chico Polka himself, Juan El.

Señor Baez was enough of a Mexican personality that his radical move to a life of chosen poverty should have made a splash in all the tabloids, women's magazines, and news shows, the editors and producers of which excel at lumping unrelated tidbits into celebrity-trend stories that can then be blown all out of proportion. You know: This young actress cut her hair short; this hot pop star bought a smaller than expected mansion; and this radio personality sold all his belongings, moved to the Kenyan desert, and symbolically pared his name down to his three initials. "Simplicity," the headlines would say, "is the next big thing."

But Jeb's career change was discussed in the media only obliquely and indirectly, for one unflattering reason: Everyone assumed he had lost his mind. His apparent break with reality came shortly after being dumped in a rather spectacular way by his girlfriend, the popular and quite attractive host of a Mexican cooking show. They had been a very public couple right up until the moment she announced, in a live television interview no less, that she was moving to L.A. to marry a man who became rich by investing in self-storage facilities.

Even the interviewer seemed taken aback and asked what had happened to her relationship with Juan El Baez.

"Oh, him," said the girlfriend with a dismissive wave of the hand. "Really, there's no future in radio."

Jeb mourned this rejection with a violent sort of grief. On one memorable occasion, he cursed during his show and said, shockingly, that he was sick of "perky polka poop." He then broke into sobs as a sound engineer quickly faded to a commercial.

Producers of the show apologized immediately and announced that they were offering Baez some professional assistance in grief and anger counseling. Baez declined that generous offer, marching out of the station manager's office in a dramatic way and driving straight to the airport, where he bought a ticket on the next plane out of town.

The plane happened to be going to Nairobi, and there you have it. The next thing you know, he was living in the desert, calling himself by a hillbilly name and mumbling about the evils of physical and emotional clutter. Junk mail stood as his enemy. Custom closet companies, with their false promises of organization, loomed as evil incarnate. (Perhaps you see where this is going.) Self-storage facilities were the work of the devil.

"There is no future," he would say, "in finding more places to put your stuff. Happiness lies in getting rid of plunder."

It was, I suppose, the right message for the right time, because citizens of the Western world truly were being plagued by an overabundance of paper products and unnecessary household items. Magazines wrote about fighting clutter in tones that suggested they were actually battling a deadly disease, and entire corporate empires were built on the notion that it's okay to fill your closets with clothes you don't wear, as long as you keep them in neatly labeled white plastic boxes.

In those brand-conscious, image-conscious days—when Isabella was still a young woman with a staff of people to manage her wardrobe—we were, as a culture, all about ever expanding square footage, bulging calendars, and excessively

busy kitchen decor. (There existed a ghastly tendency to display in the kitchens of middle-class homes uninspired and
unwieldy "collections" of chicken, cow, or pig figurines, often
alongside a "coordinating" wallpaper border. Chickens? Cows?
Pigs? As if anyone wants to be reminded of the barnyard while
preparing food!)

That was the way of the world in those days. So Jeb's
thoughts, when posted on an anti-clutter website, hit a
nerve. He spoke to people. He changed them.

A movement began, and that movement thrived. So we
are now living in spare and enlightened times and have been
for a few decades. Simplicity did become the next big thing.
But whenever anyone writes about this change, it is Isabella,
not Jeb, whom they use as their example. They point to her
self-imposed exiles from Glassidy Castle and her eventual
decision to dress mostly in desert hues. (Expensively
designed and carefully tailored desert hues, for the most part,
but still.) That's why Isabella's face graces the covers of all
those "faces of the century" books that are coming out these
days. She represents the "changing values of our times," at
least according to the editors, who invariably slap Isabella's
youthful face (they always use a photo from her youth) on
the cover of an otherwise dreary collection of ponderous
essays about important but ugly and badly dressed men.

I suspect they do this for cynical reasons (Isabella sells
books). But they are partially right. People have, on the
whole, come to emulate Isabella's solid colors, clean lines,
uncluttered shelves, empty drawers. You could argue that it's
just fashion, subject to change as soon as the next magazines
are out. But I think, I hope, that it is also a bit more than
that. Maybe people truly have discovered, as Jeb did there
in the desert, the peace that comes with living simply. They
have cleaned out their collections, purged unused files,
whittled down their wardrobes to a few simple, classic, well-
made, and easily interchanged pieces. In the process,

maybe, they have found a similar simplifying of their out-look. They have become less greedy and more gracious, less harried and more humble, less proud and more patient. The change is permanent. As it was for Isabella and Jeb and me.

Or maybe not. In a few years, we may be collecting cows again.

I don't know. And I can assure you that Isabella does not, either. I love her like a sister, like an icon, like a friend. But she is not, I am telling you, a great thinker. This is a woman who needed the advice of Bruce Springsteen lyrics to pick out a ball gown. Thank goodness she was not in charge of national security.

Perhaps that is the nature of icons. They sum up their times so well not because they deliberately set out to do so, but because if there is any truth to the idea that epochs have moods, then some famous people living in that time are bound to match the mood. And the ones who do so the best are the ones who do so obliviously.

But Jeb, dear Jeb, *was* a great thinker, a careful and deliberate man. His philosophy of life may have been influenced by his broken heart and wounded pride, but it was not casual or oblivious. Soon after his thoughts were posted on the Web, he was being joined in the desert by a steady stream of lively converts, all of whom sold off their barnyard cookie jars, pared their names down to one syllable, lived on a simple diet of corn mash, and wore sackcloth. Usually, they would return home after a half-dozen years or so and become examples of peace to their neighbors and friends.

I suppose you've figured out by now that one of them stayed for just two years and returned to become an example of peace for the entire world. She came in with the longest name but was known by the least personal name of any of Jeb's guests. Her Royal Highness the Princess of Gallagher, Isabella Cordage, was—during her time in the desert—known simply as Her.

Chapter 21

*I*sabella told me she couldn't sleep her first night back from Africa. She felt so ill at ease being in the castle again. The bed was nice, that was true enough. When her head sank into the down pillow, she wondered for a moment if she had slept at all during the previous two years. She vowed then that she would never, ever go back to the desert.

But all the stuff? All the piles of decorative pillows and the canopy and the forty-eight original oil paintings that seemed to cover every inch of the room and the vase of twenty-four "whispery pink" tulips and an assortment of handy items on the bedside table, from the magnifying glass and the tissues, to the crystal pitcher of water and matching goblet, to the alarm clock and the manicure kit and Queen Regina's recent autobiography, *For the Sake of Country: One Woman's Story*.

Isabella reported, with uncharacteristic hyperbole, that she had looked around the room and "freaked out."

That was, I suppose, my first sign that her years with Jeb had truly affected Isabella, had awakened in her a sincere desire to live simply, at least relatively.

Most of Jeb's followers were skeptical of her. Perhaps the skepticism goes without saying. "She's got a palace full of knickknacks waiting for her at home," the others would whisper while collecting water from the well. "What did she give up?"

I, too, initially assumed Isabella's interest in Jeb's camp was purely practical. We were sophisticated women of the world, the princess and I. We weren't fooled by Jeb. We knew his crusade to put self-storage companies out of business had nothing to do with the Zen-like peace of a minimalist lifestyle. And I suppose he knew that the princess and I wanted to live at his camp for reasons that had nothing to do with him.

Isabella needed a place to stay until the dust settled. A place without cameras or phones or people interested in selling stories to the tabloids and making lots of money. Jeb's camp and Jeb's followers, with their vows of poverty and lack of phone service, suited her purpose perfectly.

She did little during her first weeks at the camp to suggest that she was a true convert. Her usual royal reserve—the prized ability to hide any public displeasure and to feign interest and enthusiasm for any task—faltered in the desert. Perhaps if Geoffrey had not died during the attempt to fake Rafie's death, Isabella would have pulled it off better. Perhaps she was distracted by grief. Whatever the reasons, she stumbled early on in the camp. Once she embarrassed herself at dinner by absentmindedly asking for salt (which Jeb considered an unnecessarily fancy spice). Twice, when making sandals, she caused a camp scandal by rejecting the gathered reeds for being the wrong shade to accompany the camp's wool garments.

Not long after we arrived, the members of the camp sat around the fire and shared accounts of their newfound love of minimalism. Predictable stuff, really. One woman talked about how, in her old life, she had been chronically irritated and unhappy with her small kitchen, which provided inadequate storage for her souvenir mugs. "I wasted time longing for a bigger house, lusting after expensive kitchens in designer catalogs," she said. "Why didn't I just throw out some of those ugly mugs?"

Meanwhile, a man sobbed as he talked about how the pursuit of worldly wealth had taken him away from his kids. "I kept buying them toys," he said. "I wish I'd just played with them."

I was eyeing the crowd nervously. "I came here because the princess told me to," didn't seem to be the right answer.

Isabella's turn came first. She stared silently into the fire for a moment. It had been only a few weeks since the crash. She was not yet herself again. "I had a lot back home," she finally whispered. "Most of it was rather lovely. I enjoyed it."

The others were shifting nervously. This was not the sort of thing you were supposed to say. Even I knew that, and I wasn't myself yet, either.

"But I don't deserve nice things," she said. She shivered, nodded. "This is my penance."

Her words did not go over well at all. Jeb's followers didn't believe in giving up things as self-punishment. They believed in giving up things because things were not worth having. The crowd mumbled, grumbled, harrumphed, and splintered into shocked and angry clusters after Isabella's answer. People talked about it for weeks afterward.

"What's she doing here?" they'd ask. Occasionally, some of the more hotheaded members of the camp would suggest that Jeb had been paid in some way to hide Isabella, and despite all his talk of giving up worldly belongings, he had a cell phone buried in his hut and a castle waiting for him somewhere. But I don't think any of them believed that, not as the decades passed and Jeb stayed in the desert. As time wore on, they had to ask themselves this: If Jeb has a castle waiting for him, why doesn't he go to it?

I confess I came to respect and admire Jeb, despite his tenuous hold on reality. I came to think of him as a good, even holy, man. I suppose it's inevitable that if you spend years following a set of principles, even if you do so for cynical and self-serving reasons, something of the truth of those principles—assuming there is at least a modicum of truth—will rub off on you. Maybe Jeb found that the truth in his message—"less is more," basically—somehow sanctified him as time wore on. Apparently, Isabella did, too.

Isabella eventually stopped talking about simplicity as punishment. I think she, like the woman at the campfire with the formerly crowded cupboard, actually came to enjoy a less cluttered life, one that could be supported without a castle staff. In Bisbania, for example, she had two full-time shoe clerks who maintained, repaired, and rotated her shoe collection. By the time she got to Green Bay, she was happy with one small closet full of shoes, which she supervised herself. "You wouldn't believe how nice it is," she told me once, "to just walk in, grab some brown pumps, and be out the door."

(A fine argument for neutral shoes, perhaps, but this is not as frightfully common as it sounds. Remember, please, that in Isabella's case, brown always matched her outfit. It's not as if she was throwing on some tan sandals with a burgundy print skirt and calling it "good enough.")

In fact, after we left Kenya, Isabella refused to talk about the camp in anything other than fiercely nostalgic ways. She would not critically analyze Jeb's message or his lifestyle. She never let on that she knew he was crazy as a loon. She

utterly ignored my feeble attempts to make light of the difficult time we had there.

I would joke about the inability to engage in proper
dental care. "A few more months, and our teeth would have
looked like the royal dogs'," I'd say.

I would joke about the lack of hot water and antiper-
spirant. "It was like living in the Dark Ages," I'd say. "Or
maybe France."

I would expect an appreciative giggle but got nothing.
Maybe a bored sigh. Then she would launch into a glowing
monologue about the peace of the African desert or a sour
complaint about the overabundance of collectibles that filled
her own country and all of Europe and especially America.
"There is," she told me during one of our frequent phone conversations, "this utterly outrageous pony-print fad going on
here." (I was back in Bisbania, and Isabella seemed to enjoy
regaling me with this sort of bemusing American atrocity.)

"I went shopping yesterday," she said, "and there was a
display in which an *entire room* was styled with pony print:
sofa, rug, lamp shades."

I chuckled at the horror of it.

"Curtains," she continued, "pillows, tissue holders! It
looked like some sort of pony slaughterhouse!"

She sighed then and chuckled a little herself. Then she
asked the question that she asked too often for my taste. She
asked the question that always killed the laughter.

"Oh, Mae," she said. "What do you suppose Geoffrey
would have thought about that?"

Chapter 22

I think I need Frederick's help. I look back now and realize I've given up my identity. I had planned to keep it secret until closer to the end. But I confess that my plans for this story are all unraveling. I'm having trouble keeping the threads of this tale straight.

Frederick had cautioned me. He reminded me that my last novel had taken a bit of work. "You're not a spring chicken anymore," he said, laughing as if he had invented the cliché. He predicted that this story would be long, and "if you've really got those bombshells you're promising, it's bound to be complicated as well.

"Frankly," he said, "I'm not sure you're up to it."

I scoffed. I protested. I called my dearest friends and ranted about the injustice of it all. But now here I am, messing things up, slipping my name in when I had planned not to. I suppose I should go back and rewrite that last passage. But instead, I think I will just go ahead and admit that I am Mae Whitehall-Wright, Geoffrey's widow and perhaps the only woman Isabella ever befriended who did, in a period of foolish youthfulness, sometimes wear neutral shoes.

Perhaps you had already suspected as much. Secrest could, no doubt, tell a good story herself, and Ethel Bald knows things that she never wrote. I suppose Iphigenia could have written, if so motivated, a rollicking account of the last century of royal life. But none of those stories is this story. You had probably come to realize that only Isabella and Mae could know the things I know, and once you narrowed it down to those choices, then it has to be Mae, doesn't it? I guess there is no point in trying to hide it anymore. For though this is the story of Isabella, it is clearly not Isabella's story.

There are too many parts of herself that she kept closed off, even to me, though I think she was as open with me as she was with anyone. Except, of course, with her husband. And probably with Geoffrey. And possibly, for all I know, with Jeb as well. So I guess I should say she was as open with me as any other living person, since you know what happened to Geoffrey. And Rafie and Jeb are dead now, too. They passed away on the same day a few years back, on opposite sides of the world. They were old men, and long sick to boot. The timing of their deaths was one of those extraordinary coincidences that life sometimes offers up. Even I can't invent a conspiracy theory for it, but perhaps that just indicates that I'm sick unto death of conspiracy theories.

You know the photo I mentioned, the one taken at Geoffrey's funeral when Isabella held my face in her hands? She was whispering to me then, telling me—she would say asking me—to come with her to Africa. My husband was dead, and I was lonely and tired and scared. So I said yes.

As it turned out, it was a good thing I did.

Remarkably, she became my best friend while we were in Africa. Our time in the castle together had been inevitably strained. The princess's poise and her looks and her glamour were such that no common woman—least of all one whose husband was in the intimate position that Geoffrey was—could feel completely at ease with her. Besides, her relationship with everyone she actually knew was a little strained. She had that particular kind of magic—common to all icons, it seems—to be absolutely available only to those people she would never see again.

But she was transformed in Kenya. I suppose I was, too. We arrived with expensive manicures and overly pampered skin, and we each felt the eyes of the others on us, so we naturally fell into a conspiracy. We would make trips to the well together: only we would know how slow we were at hauling up the water, and how upset we got about breaking a nail, or how clumsily we handled the buckets.

On those walks, we talked a lot. Mostly, at first, Isabella just apologized. "I'm so sorry, Mae," she'd say. "I'm just incapacitated with the horror of it. We let Geoffrey down, Rafie and I. I guess we let you down, too."

But one day I told her I didn't want to talk about Geoffrey's death anymore, I wanted to talk about his life. That was when she began to tell me stories, giving me much of the information I have revealed to you in this book, including the story of the time she kissed Geoffrey, which was a strange first story to tell his widow, I guess. But I enjoyed it despite myself, for it all sounded just exactly like Geoffrey, and it did ultimately explain why Isabella had brought us to the castle, and it set what turned out to be the whole rest of my life in motion. So while I wished that Geoffrey had never kissed her, I thought about all that I would have lost if Isabella had not pulled us onto this ride. Geoffrey's life was too short, but he did so love working on the cars at the castle. I was able to give up journalism and become a novelist. And when we were not counseling Her Highness through some crisis or another, Geoffrey and I delighted ourselves by tramping around the stone streets of the capital and taking weekend trips throughout Europe and talking about art.

I loved Geoffrey. Hiding my identity may have hidden that fact, forcing me, as it did, to leave out so many critical chapters of our life together.

I never even told you, did I, how the young reporter who hung out in hot tubs with female coworkers and gossiped about the royal family eventually did a story about the perils of family-owned businesses and interviewed a young mechanic named Jeff Wright at his family's garage. I didn't explain how my heart leaped the very first time our eyes met and how that interview lasted about two hours longer than it should have, and how I liked the hot blackberry cider he made me, and how I was married in a simple white suit with a bouquet of red roses, and how dashing he looked, and the odd, endearing way that he saluted me as I walked down the aisle.

And I did not tell you how I helped proofread his letter to the princess and how I thought, frankly, that it was all wrong. He mentioned Springsteen in the body of the letter and put me in the postscript. The princess would think Geoffrey a rube. But then I thought she would never even read it, so I pointed out only that he had spelled "tunes" as "toons." "That's a comic strip, not a song," I said. He fixed it and mailed it the next day.

I also did not tell you, not directly at least, how I felt that I blossomed in Bisbania. How I finally had enough time to exercise properly and enough money to buy well-made clothes and to have my nails and my hair and my pores handled by professionals. I did not explain that in my newfound freedom, I at last gave up my struggling journalism career and indulged my overactive imagination, writing outlandish, fast-paced novels in which smart career girls with good taste in clothes were always falling in love with blue-collar guys who called them "babe."

While in Bisbania, I enjoyed my husband, too, loved him in whole new ways. Isabella may have distracted him occasionally, and she undoubtedly deserves much of the blame for the events that shortened his life. But at the same time, she somehow gave me more time with him. We could have worked for forty years in that house with robin's-egg-blue siding, and I might never have witnessed Geoffrey reading poetry or watched him as he studied the *Mona Lisa*. That was the luxury money bought us, although Jeb would be disappointed to hear me say it. You find time, he would say, or you make time, but you do not buy time. (Needless to say, he was completely opposed to the idea of "saving" time, as if it could be stored away in a rented garage in L.A. for later use.)

Maybe I'm a little like the editors of those face-of-the-century books—the ones who cynically place Isabella on the cover to boost sales. Not that I need help selling books; my novels have done well enough, thank you very much. But I suppose I have received more from Isabella than I ever gave her.

This is not to say that I gave her nothing.

In America, we once had a strange custom of appointing the widows of politicians to the position their husbands had held. As if marrying the man prepared them for the job. For a long while, Isabella—apparently likening Geoffrey's role to that of an American county sheriff—wanted me to keep her supplied with meaningful Springsteen lyrics. But I just didn't have the emotional energy or the desire to help her in this way. When she would not let it rest, I would make lyrics up. When she wanted to know what Springsteen would say about whether to leave Jeb's camp, for example, I demurred and pleaded tiredness and ignorance and even unwillingness. But she begged and whined and nagged, and I finally spun something out of air. I said, "I keep thinking of the song where he says, 'Ain't nothing holding me here, except for those smokes and a case of beer.'" It wasn't even a good attempt at faking a Springsteen lyric. I was not trying very hard.

Isabella seemed a little surprised and, I must say, suspicious. "Oh," she said. "I guess I'm not familiar . . ." Her voice trailed off, but then she looked around the dingy camp. By that time, she had grown used to living without things, but she did not at all like living with dirt. Her face brightened a bit. "It would seem to argue for me to move on." She looked at me as if for assurance.

"Yes," I said in what I believed to be a solemn voice, though I was laughing inside, suddenly wondering if Geoffrey had ever used this technique with her. I felt close to him again just by thinking it. "It would seem to argue for that," I said.

That is the awful way I sometimes treated my dear friend Isabella.

Now that you know who I am, perhaps you think you understand why I'm telling this story. You think I'm merely trying to give Geoffrey his due, to cast suspicion upon the spoiled prince who set in motion the events that led to my husband's death, to shed a bad light on the woman who took up a good part of my husband's time and no small part of his affections. I guess all those things are factors, though I'm rather appalled to admit the more vengeful aspects of my motive, and Geoffrey would have been uninterested in getting his due. (He comes to me in dreams sometimes, and no matter what I ask him, he merely wags his finger in mock scolding. "*You* always gave me too much credit," he says, then winks. "I never knew what the hell was going on.")

But I assure you, there is more behind this than a desire to honor my husband and seek revenge against Isabella. I'm motivated by a secret that sometimes keeps me up worrying at night. It is the secret that I long to tell and fear telling.

I am about to take something from Isabella, but it will not be a regular trade. That which I will take—a bit of privacy, a small amount of the public's good wishes—will not then be mine. Isabella and I will both be the poorer when this story is told.

So why am I telling it?

I want Milo, my sweet daughter, to be happy.

Chapter 23

I suppose I should tell you at last what happened to Jimmy Bennett. I should explain how Secrest's detective eventually found him. I should reveal his hiding place and resolve once and for all whether he actually had the photo that Isabella lay awake nights imagining and fearing. It's a critical question, really. For if he did not have that photo, then much of my life was lived in vain. Without the photo, there would have been no reason for Isabella to have plucked Geoffrey and me from our simple life. I could have whiled away years, writing my mediocre little magazine pieces and never noticing that my husband perked up a bit every time Isabella was on television.

The possibility of the photo is what prompted Isabella to lure Geoffrey to Europe. Geoffrey's arrival at the castle is what caused Rafie's jealousy. Rafie's jealousy is, I believe, at least part of what fueled his desire to sneak off to the Wisconsin woods and take Isabella with him. And Rafie and Isabella's sneaky plan is what killed my husband.

That tawdry chain of events all directly affected the circumstances of my child's birth and life. And the chain all starts with Isabella's fear about the photo.

So was the plan set in motion by something real? Did Jimmy Bennett have a photo of Isabella and Geoffrey?

It had taken Secrest's detective a year to find Bennett, a shockingly long time in the age of satellite photos and searchable Web-based public records. The detective had followed professional ties that led from city to city in an ordinary, traceable way, but she came to a point where Bennett had just fallen off the map and she could not unearth another clue. So she found his mother, then living in a nursing home in Milwaukee, and the detective spent many days with Mrs. Bennett, sharing cigarettes and coughing together, until the phone rang—on Mother's Day, predictably enough. The trace attached to the back of Mrs. Bennett's phone worked its magic, and the detective at last had Bennett's phone number. She called Secrest, and Secrest told Isabella, and it wasn't long before Isabella was chatting on royal phones with Jimmy Bennett as often as she talked to Geoffrey.

Which I don't think Rafie liked and I know Geoffrey didn't care for.

Those early conversations were awkward and stilted, filled as they were with unanswered fears and unspoken questions.

"Oh, Jimmy," Isabella would say. "It's wonderful to talk to you again. I can't tell you how often I've thought of you over the years. What fun we always had!

"Someday," she would continue with calculated casualness, "we'll have to get together, reminisce some, look at old photos."

Jimmy would be chatty enough when the conversations were all small talk and idle gossip about old classmates, but he would grow silent at that sort of suggestion.

"Perhaps," he would say after a pause. "But I didn't keep much from my college days. Most of my photos are gone."

"Gone?" Isabella would say. "Did you"—she would try to hide her excitement—"*burn* them?"

"Burn them?" Jimmy would sigh. "Throw them away? Sell them? What's the difference? All that matters is that they're gone."

The vaguer Jimmy was, the more often Isabella called. One thing led to another, and soon enough I was talking to Jimmy Bennett fairly often myself, though most of my conversations were in person. Sometimes, usually when I was too tired to be guarded, I would ask him if he had that photo. But even after we knew each other quite well, he would demur; he would hem, haw, roll his eyes, change the subject. Or he would ask me questions back: "Does it matter?" Or "Would it change anything either way?" Or "Why do you want to know?"

Until one night, when I was so tired, so weary, so lonely that I lost my temper. I cursed him—I regret that the most. I cracked a branch over my leg and let out a low animal howl. I glared at him and told him exactly why I wanted to know. I told him almost everything that I've told you and a few things I haven't told you yet, and I screamed at him, tears running down my face. "HELL YES, IT MATTERS!" I said. "My whole life is a chain of mysteries. I want to know one thing for sure."

He nodded, looked off into the darkness for a while. Then he said, "No, Mae." He flicked a pebble into the fire, got up, brushed the dirt off his jeans. He looked down at me. I was still seated. He patted me on the head, a gesture that should seem patronizing but somehow seemed only loving.

"No hay una fotografia."

And Jimmy Elvin Bennett, whom the detective had been initially unable to trace past an Evansville, Indiana, radio job, but who had moved to Mexico and changed his name to Juan El Baez and then, of course, moved to Kenya and changed his name to Jeb, turned and walked away.

Chapter 24

$\mathscr{S}$ecrest had been appalled. Somewhat relieved, of course. But totally appalled. Of all the places where she had imagined the detective might find Jimmy Bennett, she had not expected anything like this.

"A commune?" she sputtered into the phone when the detective called with the news. "A commune in the desert?"

It seemed awfully tawdry, and it made Secrest worry about what other sorts of people Isabella had associated with in America. The two she knew about so far—Geoffrey and Jimmy Bennett/Jeb—she did not like at all.

Former associates of the princess should be living conventional, upstanding, boring lives, not forgoing baths and living on dirt floors with a cell phone buried in their smelly hut, and not, needless to say, applying rock lyrics to world events or even royal fashion dilemmas. (Jimmy/Jeb was able to use his phone, by the way, because of a nearby celebrity safari ranch, which had built a series of cell towers so that Hollywood starlets could e-mail their wildlife photos home before they had even headed back to the lodge.)

"What exactly did you *do* with this man, or priest, or whatever he is?" Secrest kept asking the princess, who never gave a satisfying answer.

"Oh, you know," Isabella would say, affecting a breezy persona. "This and that, college things, nothing much.

"We studied, I suppose," the princess would add if pressed. "And, you know, made popcorn in the dorm lobby."

Secrest puzzled quite a bit over those comments, spending hours thumbing through an encyclopedia of American euphemisms in case "studied" or "made popcorn" had some scandalous meaning she was not aware of. In moments like that, Secrest wondered if she was in over her head and perhaps should write a memo about the whole series of events to Hubert, who would surely intervene and let her off the hook.

In her desperate worry, Secrest had seized upon the one whispered comment— something about a photo—that she had overheard Isabella make to Geoffrey. She could not imagine what sort of relationship Isabella had had with this Jimmy Bennett or what sort of photos might exist of it. He was American, after all. And something of a Packers fan, the detective had reported. "Please," Secrest prayed, imagining the worst possible photo of a wholesome Bisbanian princess, "if Isabella is wearing anything in these photos, don't let it be the jersey of an American football team."

"What if the headlines said something like 'Packer Backer'?" Secrest kept asking. (For all her street savvy, Secrest did not have the most creative imagination.)

Still, it had to be good news to find that the mysterious man with a camera was leading a movement that advocated giving up treasured personal belongings. "Such as photo albums?" Secrest wondered hopefully. And that he further rejected money and power. Such a person surely would have no interest in the princess or her secret. That is what Secrest argued, and we all more or less agreed.

But Secrest could not relax. I think on some level, she suspected that something was up. She had picked up on the reckless romance that charged the air around Raphael and Isabella—or was it the air around Isabella and Geoffrey? The air definitely seemed charged with danger when the princess was with either man. I did not fully appreciate this at the time, and I see it clearly only in retrospect. I thought then that I was suffering from a mood disorder, which I attempted to treat with organic herbs, various stretching exercises, and, on the advice of Princess Iphigenia, an enema or two (I found this unpleasant).

In those days, Secrest often took me with her on official shopping trips. She said that it made for less lonely travel and that she appreciated what she not very delicately called my "common perspective" on the venture. "I must know," she said, "how the princess will be perceived by the lower classes."

What I could actually perceive was the inside knowl-edge of Geoffrey's latest advice—prints or solids, studs or dangling earrings, bracelets or rings. There was an ever-changing and exhaustive list, often but not always loosely associated with some Springsteen song.

And I do mean loosely. You should have seen the incred-ulous look on the prince's face when Geoffrey used the song "Ricky Wants a Man of Her Own" to suggest to Isabella a summer of sundresses with rickrack trim. "How positively precious," the prince said. (That was not a compliment.)

Even at her best, Secrest had trouble keeping all of

Geoffrey's rules straight, and by the time she reached the latter months of her pregnancy, she was in no mood to even try. I would step in then, helping her sell Isabella on items the princess was unsure about.

(I don't know why I did this. I had *never* been particularly fond of Secrest and was, in those days, even less so. Her pregnancy had filled me with petty envy, since I had not been so blessed myself after many years of marriage.)

"I know you're trying to avoid shawls," I would say to Isabella after Secrest bought several different styles, not knowing that Geoffrey had banned that look without even a pretense of a lyrical connection. (Geoffrey had experienced a childhood trauma when wearing an older sister's hand-me-down, which his mother had told him was a cape but which his playground friends immediately recognized as a girl's shawl.)

"But this," I would say, borrowing on my mother-in-law's strategy and showing the princess one of Secrest's purchases in a confident way, "is really more of a drape."

"A drape?" Isabella would purse her lips, looking reluctant but intrigued. She had been disappointed when Geoffrey vetoed shawls, which she thought were pleasingly theatrical.

"Well, if you're *sure* it's not a shawl . . ." Isabella would pause and appear to think for a moment. "I mean, obviously, it's not. There's no fringe involved. A shawl always has fringe, doesn't it? That's practically the definition of a shawl—the fringe lining."

"I suppose you're right," I'd say, although I thought she was wrong. "And this goes so well with the dangly earrings you're wearing this season."

Suddenly, she'd be sold. Secrest would roll her eyes and knit her brows in an exasperated way.

On the last shopping trip I made with Secrest before her maternity leave, she grilled me over and over about just what level of celebrity radio personalities enjoy in America, and whether or not Isabella's association with Jimmy Bennett could be passed off as the innocent glad-handing required of any member of the royal family.

"She wasn't a member of the royal family then," I reminded Secrest. "And Jimmy Bennett wasn't yet a radio personality."

I said this as if I were trying to make Secrest feel better, but of course I knew it would make her feel worse, and I delighted in the way she tsked and tutted and fretted about it. After I realized that Secrest had in her mind some sort of sordid photo of an intimate nature, I stepped it up a notch. "But ultimately," I said with a bored sigh, "I suppose it depends on just how glad her hands seem."

This always caused Secrest to gasp, pat her pregnant belly, stare out the window of the stretch Bisba, and murmur to herself.

Needless to say, Secrest was fixated on what the proper course of action would be. Should the princess let sleeping dogs lie in their remote African camp, or should she reach out, clarify the status of things, see if a small gift of camels and donkeys could keep Jeb happy and remove any temptation he might feel to leave Africa someday.

"On the other hand," Secrest said, rooting through the size-six racks for tight jeans, another (more literal) suggestion from the "Ricky" song, "maybe we don't want to give this Jimmy any ideas."

Ultimately, she decided the princess should leave Jimmy/Jeb alone, a piece of advice she passed along from her hospital bed a few hours after giving birth. (Isabella had called to congratulate her, but Secrest launched into the Jeb question as if the previous twenty hours of labor had never happened.) Isabella listened, agreed, and thanked Secrest for her sound reasoning. She vowed to put the whole matter out of her mind. "By the time you're back from your leave," the princess said, "I'll have forgotten about the whole thing."

But that wasn't true.

For Isabella and Raphael were well into planning their fanciful escape and figuring out where they would each live during their separation. While Secrest was off singing lullabies, Jimmy Bennett's camp in Africa kept crossing Isabella's mind.

"Jimmy was a kind chap," she said to Rafie. "He was always picking up stray pets and giving rides to homeless people. I'm sure he'd take you in for a few months."

I saw Geoffrey suppress a smile at that. Did Isabella realize she'd just compared her husband, a prince, to stray pets and homeless persons? Did Raphael? I don't know. But I could tell Geoffrey realized it. And appreciated it.

Regardless of whether the prince noticed the insult, he certainly noticed the suggestion that he slip off to hide in a miserable desert camp. He did what royal people always do when they're trying to avoid saying what they really think. They ask questions.

That's why if you ever see members of the royal family in the midst of a parliamentary protest they don't want to involve themselves in, you'll hear them say, "What sort of poster board did you construct your signs with?" Or "Have you read that new book on the history of demonstrations? *The National Times* gave it a stellar review."

So in full royal mode, Rafie asked every possible question you can imagine about Jimmy Bennett and eventually retrieved every trace of information Isabella knew about her former classmate, from the model of the car he drove at Yale to the history of his habit of whistling a lot. (It was a nervous tic left over from a childhood in which he spent long road trips attempting to drown out his sister's singing.) Finally, Rafie asked some pedestrian question, the precise wording of which I've long forgotten, that prompted the princess to say, "Oh no, dear, Jimmy wasn't from Connecticut, he was from Green Bay. You know that little town with the big American football team. He hated it there. Said if you ever wanted a good place to hide, that was it. Claimed Elvis Presley was still alive and jogging about the streets there, unnoticed."

Raphael smiled broadly like a man who had stumbled upon an excuse to send his wife off to the store just before a play-off match was being broadcast. "Well, then," he said, "that sounds like the place I ought to hide."

And before Isabella knew it, her husband was holed up in Green Bay, and she was headed for Kenya.

Chapter 25

$\mathcal{S}$ix months after arriving at Jeb's camp, I was singing lullabies myself. Jeb's camp was destined to become Milo's birthplace, and she was immediately the most adorable person there. Babies always have beautiful crinkly faces, adorable toes, and the most wonderful yawns. But Milo was particularly distinctive, being born with especially wise eyes, exceptionally soft skin, and an extraordinarily full head of dark curly hair.

Once I saw her, I knew that perfect baby girl could handle the name Geoffrey had dreamed of for a son. Isabella agreed, which surprised me, given the Bisbanian bias toward feminine names that end with an "a." "Oh yes," she said to me moments after the birth. "She will make a lovely Milo."

During the christening, Jeb pronounced the name Mi-lo, stretching it out and thus emphasizing the two syllables. Not that they needed emphasis. To the ears of Jeb's followers, all of whom had followed Jeb's example and shortened their names, Milo was a lengthy, jaunty, extravagant waste of syllables. So I think it puzzled them when Jeb seemed to absolutely delight in the name, rolling it around on his tongue, laughing at it like an indulgent, patient parent.

Many of the camp's later arrivals assumed that Jeb *was* Milo's father. I was insulted by the suggestion, and a snobbish, ugly spirit would overtake me, causing me to curse the place that had offered me nothing but hospitality. "Milo was, thank you very much, conceived in a castle by parents with clean fingernails," I wanted to say, "not in some dumpy desert camp out of a sordid affair between dirty wretches like us."

I never actually said that. Instead, I would merely report matter-of-factly that Milo's father died in a plane crash a few weeks before I came here, six months before her birth. But my temptation to point to Milo's grander roots, even though I did not yield to it, shamed me at the time and troubles me even now. It goes against everything I say I believe about the basic equality of all people, the inherent rights of all children, no matter the circumstances of their birth.

But I held fiercely to those private thoughts, the spirit of which is arguably the motivation even now for writing this book. It seems to make no sense. Such hostility for a place that had offered me nothing but sanctuary. Such sneering at a place that I had chosen as home.

I guess becoming a mother does these things to you. You spend all your young adulthood cursing capitalism and proclaiming your lack of interest in material wealth, but you still want your baby to believe in Santa and to have presents spilling out from around the tree in a lavish display of luxury. You say looks don't matter, and yet you beam when someone compliments your baby's smile. Parenthood prompts not only unconditional love but petty pride.

I thought Milo was special, and I thought perhaps that pointing to a special start in life proved it. Although I never said that to the people in Jeb's camp. I never even said it to Milo, who did not, I'm embarrassed to say, get many explanations out of me. A child should know something about her family heritage, I suppose, but Milo does not. I never wanted to talk about it. Not in any specific way.

Except for one time when Milo was not yet two. It was the day Isabella left Jeb's camp. Rafie's parents, the queen and king, had been begging her to come, and I had sealed the deal with my fake Springsteen quote.

By that time, Isabella had won over all but the most skeptical of Jeb's followers. She quit talking about penance and talked about peace. She volunteered for more than her share of the kitchen duties. And she became quite a handy seamstress, making clothes for herself and many of the rest of us. (The haphazard look of the wool dress she wore to Bisbania should be blamed on poor sewing tools, not on Isabella's skills.) She sometimes even watched Milo for me, cooing and carrying on with such gusto that the other camp members would gather to watch and laugh with her.

(When all else failed to calm Milo's colicky phases, Isabella would twirl about the hut, shouting "coochie-coo" and flapping her hands above her head like some sort of mad pigeon. Her hips somehow seemed to swivel in the opposite direction of the twirling. It was an entirely ridiculous workout and, if ever videotaped, would have either ruined Isabella's reputation forever or launched a new line-dance craze. "You could call it the 'E Street Shuffle,'" I said once, more glibly than I intended. Isabella looked at me sadly, and I realized that for the first time in her life, she might understand what Geoffrey and Springsteen had been saying about the less-than-graceful steps people take in life.)

So despite her rough start at the camp, Isabella was quite popular by the time she left, and her send-off from Kenya was marked with as much fanfare, in the camp's own way, as her return to the castle generated back at home. There were hugs and tears, and Jeb sang a little song. Isabella worked the crowd with all her old regal flare, conveying to each camp member that he or she was surely the one who would be missed the most.

I remember Isabella gave Milo at least seven goodbye kisses. As she bent to kiss the child, I remember thinking not only that Isabella still had her regal posture, but if any of us had a camera, we could prove again why photographers love her. She never looked so beautiful as when she was miserable. And she did seem miserable as she kissed Milo and wished us all farewell.

Milo was oblivious to the sadness, concentrating on giving an adorable baby wave and asking an adorable baby sentence: "Where go? Where go?"

I answered with the absolute truth, using familial words that my little baby had not heard before and wouldn't hear again and could not possibly remember.

"She's going to see your grandparents in a castle," I said. "And then she's going to live with your daddy."

Chapter 26

So that, I guess, is the one thing you did not see coming. My child is the heir to the throne. My child's father is His Royal Highness the Prince of Gallagher. By all rights, I should hold the title last held by ol' Reggie herself. May she rest in peace. I should be the Queen Mother.

But I suppose such a title would never be given the likes of me, a tawdry American scribbler who was once married to castle help. That is fine. I do not desire the title nor the respect and certainly not the fame. I have always felt uncomfortable being the center of attention—at a graduation dinner, a surprise birthday party, a farewell gathering in the office on the last day of a job. At showers, I always felt sorry for the bride or the expectant mother, never envying the moment in the spotlight even as I envied the stage of life that had brought them to the moment. Though I didn't need to worry about the latter, as there were no baby showers for me, of course.

I did receive a few gifts, however. Isabella herself sewed a surprisingly soft camel-hair baby blanket while we were at the camp. "You can't wrap a baby in the scratchy stuff we wear," she said. And when I eventually returned to Bisbania, she set me up with a high-end Italian stroller, the same model that Isabella's sister, Lady Fiona, had famously used for her son and was always bragging about in interviews for parenting magazines. "She's very particular, my sister," Isabella said. "So this stroller must really be the bee's knees."

But it was Lady Fiona's nanny, not the lady herself, who took Isabella's nephew on walks, and I'm sure the nanny struggled as much as I did to maneuver the luxurious, yacht-sized stroller on the narrow, crowded sidewalks of Gallagher. I needed a lighter, more nimble baby mover, if I needed anything at all. After all, Milo was old enough to get around by herself most of the time. The stroller gift, in other words, made me feel awkward and uncomfortable on many different levels.

You're not surprised about my discomfort, I'm sure. And knowing all that you do, you will also not be surprised that the most difficult episode in my relationship with Isabella involved a rivalry over a man. You *may* be surprised to learn that the man in question was neither her husband nor mine.

The episode took place about three years after those eventful months in which Geoffrey died and Raphael's daughter was born. It occurred during a summer trip that little Milo and I made to visit Isabella and Rafie in Green Bay.

As you know, most of Princess Isabella's iconic reputation was made during the so-called Green Bay years. People older than I used to compare this phenomenon to Jackie

Bouvier Kennedy Onassis, who made the jump from run-of-the-mill celebrity to international icon only when she had lost her obvious claim to fame and attempted, or at least gave the appearance of attempting, to live an ordinary life.

In the same way, Isabella's life as a princess seems now to a lot of people like so much backstory. Now, when most people think of Isabella, they picture a wiry, dignified-looking woman wearing somber brown clothes—or, in the words of the fashion writers, "molasses and oatmeal-colored" clothes—and living out a (relatively) modest life in the Wisconsin woods.

But she lived that modest life with so much gusto! She was an active, dynamic, perpetual-motion machine. All those photos of Isabella plowing in the community garden or taking library classes on the latest in wiring your home for wireless home management made an impression on people. She took up golf and learned to yodel in the fine tradition of American cowboys. ("I suppose the alpine yodeling style is good for the Europeans," she famously said to *Yodeling Monthly,* building up to what I believe was a calculated compliment to her new continent. "But no one belts it out like a buckaroo.")

At first Raphael was a bit puzzled by Isabella's lengthy list of pursuits. Hadn't they planned to while away their time cuddling on the sofa and putzing around the house? But by the time Isabella's interest had turned to blacksmithing and she had built her own forge, Raphael had grown rather proud of her mushrooming interests and skills. He marveled that his wife could, even while living miles away from a major media market and even after officially giving up her royal title, still influence people the globe over. Women around the world, you see, were admiring how the princess looked in her blacksmithing goggles and saying, "Oh, all right, maybe I should at least take a needlework class."

In that sense, Isabella became a new sort of icon, the

sort that women would look to for inspiration when going through a midlife crisis. And not just the sort of crisis solved by heading off to the gym. That least of all. Women with grown children would suddenly take up painting. Or ballet. Or start learning to cook Thai dishes. Or—why not?—speak Thai.

The press was happy to give Isabella all the credit for this self-improvement fad. In one column, Ethelbald Candeloro called her "the princess who launched a thousand hobbies."

I was, in my own way, as surprised as Rafie was. All in all, Isabella had been a mopey and depressing presence during our time in Africa. But reuniting with Rafie seemed to do wonders for her mood. (Wearing more comfortable clothes probably didn't hurt, either.) She really did hit her stride there in America. And she did it all without any advice from the Boss. (At least as far as I know, although I suppose she could have searched the lyrics herself in a pinch.)

Maybe she was energized by the crowds that had greeted her while she was attending the king's funeral and Iphigenia's coronation events. Or perhaps her newfound energy came, simply, from eating again. I wondered sometimes if she was trying to fill up her new life, to make sure she didn't waste a moment of the time that Geoffrey had died to give her. Or did her remarkable pursuit of broadened horizons reflect something darker than that? Was she trying hard to stay busy, too busy to think about what she had lost? Was she trying to fill an aching void?

I don't know. But I do know that her hobbies would have been her own little secret if not for the work of Joplin Hughes, a photographer of little experience and less reputation who arrived in Green Bay soon after Isabella did.

Joplin possessed no historical perspective on the royal family and displayed no particular fondness for the princess. His interest was only in making a little money, just enough, perhaps, to pay off his student loans and invest in better photographic equipment.

He ended up doing a good bit better than that, happily earning an upper-middle-class living in a lower-middle-class kind of town by documenting Isabella's manic series of hobbies and her more ordinary exploits: trips to the grocery, that teary episode involving her futile efforts to chip away ice from her mailbox, the rather infamous outing in a shorter-in-back-than-she-realized "sandy-colored" miniskirt. The European tabloids snapped up those sorts of photos regularly and at a fair price, though thankfully not so fair as to attract more aggressive competitors.

I say "thankfully" because Joplin's lack of aggressive ambition is the only reason that his presence did not spell disaster for the princess and the not really dead prince who shared her home. Joplin was a singularly nonconfrontational, unquestioning type. He played by gentlemanly rules. If Isabella stepped out the front door, if she jogged on public pathways, if she dared enter a retail establishment, she would be photographed. But he never tried to get a glimpse of her interior courtyard. He was too lazy to note that she seemed to be buying at least twice as many groceries as a woman her size would eat. He did not waste time wondering about the shadowy figure whom he sometimes saw peering from an attic window. ("Probably a guard," Joplin said to me once. "Or maybe a ghost. That pilot who killed her husband probably comes back to bug her now.")

In short, Joplin did not really care about Isabella. He didn't care about the themes of her life, and he didn't care about what she did or didn't do, as long as she continued to look fabulous while she did it. Or close enough to fabulous that he could, with a little digital manipulation, help her along. (So if you were one of the millions of women who *were* driven to the gym by that sandy-colored-miniskirt photo, rest assured that while Isabella looked, in my humble opinion, perfectly presentable in that miniskirt, she did not look quite as *wow* as she did in the famous photo.)

I don't know if Isabella ever realized the help she was getting in this regard. She officially reacted to Joplin's latest photographs with a bored "When will he go away?" sigh, but I often noticed a certain satisfaction in her voice. "Really, you know, he shouldn't shoot me from behind so much," she said during a phone chat not long after a rather attractive shot of her snowshoeing in a cute "mushroom-colored" ski suit that showed off all her assets and sparked one completely inappropriate headline.

"It's just so unnecessary," Isabella said, trying to sound displeased. "It's not like it's hard to get me to turn around. A simple 'Yoo-hoo, miss' will usually do it. I'm quite approachable, you know. That's always been written about me. 'Very approachable.' Ethelbald Candeloro said that in one of the first stories about me. The engagement story, wasn't it?"

I didn't answer, but I was smiling. Apparently, despite her protestations to the contrary, she had missed the fawning attention of her old life while in Africa. At least that was my read on the situation. If an inappropriate but flattering headline could get her this worked up, she must be like the rest of us in our middle age, wondering occasionally if we are lovely, thankful to get a hint that we are.

"I guess I shouldn't complain," she said, not seeming to notice my silence. "It's a nice enough photo—not like that ghastly one they printed of Genia's backside a few months ago. Do you think she works out at all anymore?"

"I don't know," I said.

"Hmmm." She pretended to consider things for a moment. "Still, you'd think if this Joplin fellow is going to make so much money off me, he'd at least flag me down once, just to properly introduce himself."

But I was the only one of the two of us who really got to know Joplin.

It was during that summer visit, which, as I said, was a little awkward from day one. I felt uncomfortable about having Milo around Isabella. And Rafie, too, for that matter. But the prince and princess seemed oblivious to my discomfort and took turns making over Milo in the extravagantly kind but distracted and vague way that childless couples so often display around children.

"So she's walking now," Rafie said, as if this were remarkable for a three-year-old. "Look at her go! So sure on her feet! I'm sure she'll become a football star."

"It's called soccer here, dear," Isabella replied. "And it's a dreadful way to make a living, running around the world in badly tailored shorts. Milo wouldn't stand for that at all. She has quite the sense of style, you know." Isabella addressed that last comment to me, as if I would not have already noticed.

"I saw Milo dressing a doll the other day," she continued. "She put green and pink together in a way that would have knocked Candeloro dead. Simply stunning. And she's bright, too. Have you seen the way she watches television?"

I cringed and glanced at Rafie. I was afraid he would disapprove, despite his own growing interest in televised entertainment.

Isabella didn't notice my reaction. "Yesterday," she went on, "Milo was watching that show—what's it called? *Blue's Clues*? Highly educational." She turned to Rafie to add, "We should get something like that started in Bisbania."

There was a moment of stilted silence, as there always was when Isabella would accidentally suggest a royal pursuit for the couple, apparently having forgotten that Rafie was "dead" and she was no longer a princess.

"Well, of course she's bright," Rafie said, breaking the silence. "How could she not be?"

Another awkward silence. He had surely started to say, "Look at who her parents are." Isn't that what people say?

But Milo's parentage was not a subject any of the three of us wanted to broach as we sat together, each tortured by some guilty knowledge or proud suspicion. Or was it proud knowledge and guilty suspicion? Some of both, I suppose. "Aren't you worried that Milo's not talking enough?" I asked finally, changing the subject. But Rafie gave a dismissive wave and flipped on a game. His lack of interest in Milo's language skills surprised me, given his obsession with speech development and given that the only active parental interest he had taken in his daughter was to insist that she learn the difficult official Bisbanian language, which was useless to anyone not in the nobility of that country.

I thought she should have been speaking more and worried that studying that ugly consonant-heavy language was confusing the child, though the language experts I consulted said that was unlikely. Still, that summer she had coined the word "pleasably" in an apparent effort to use the Bisbanian adverbial form of the English word. It worried me so much that I called the pediatrician—I was, in retrospect, a bit of an anxious mother—but he said she was merely trying to reconcile the grammar rules of two languages and that she would work it out quickly. An assessment that Rafie, with his speech pathology experience, shared when pressed.

Isabella, however, found it highly irritating. Like most modern Bisbanian royals, she had never cared for the old language. I'm sure she was puzzled by Rafie's desire for Milo to learn the language and by my decision to honor that request. She became somewhat cranky about the whole issue. "Can't she speak English?" she asked one day in an irritated way. (Milo had just called out, "Faster, pleasably," as Isabella and I were taking turns pushing the gargantuan stroller around the neighborhood.)

Isabella's question annoyed me, needless to say. But I didn't get to answer, because at that moment the photographer Joplin pulled up. The sight of him filled me with all the aggressive hostility that only motherhood could bring out in a normally unassuming person like myself. I was terrified that he would take and publish a photo of Milo, prompting the gossip columnists to start talking about how much the child recently spotted with the princess resembled the "late" prince.

So, filled with righteous indignation, I marched right up to Joplin and knocked on the window of his sporty little car. "My daughter is only a child," I said when he rolled down his window. "And she doesn't need the likes of you taking her picture." I thumped his camera with my thumb, prompting Isabella to gasp and look off into the distance in an embarrassed way. She had never seen me like this. Besides, she had long ago lost any sensitivity to the indignity of being photographed by strangers.

"Snap the princess at the grocery," I continued with a huff. "That'll suit your purposes well enough."

Joplin stiffened and looked stunned. He had never, ever been accused of being overly zealous. In fact, editors were always saying the photos were not zoomed in enough and that he should work harder to get shots from inside Isabella's home.

Sensing the discomfort of both the princess and the photographer, I regretted starting off on such a confrontational note. But rather than admit my mistake, I launched in further, attempting in some sick way to justify what was an indefensible tone. "Just because you muck around in the scum," I said, "doesn't mean you have to drag children into the muck with you."

Joplin stared. Isabella coughed and let her eyes shift from the distant skyline to her own feet.

I cleared my throat. Paused. I wanted to stop but somehow couldn't. I said, "So back off." And then pitifully added, "Uh, buster."

By this point, I realized that I had gone beyond all hope

of redeeming myself and was relieved when Milo helped me
out of the mess. "Mommy," she called from the stroller,
which I had left parked a few yards off. "Mommy, say
'pleasably.'"

I blushed finally. Isabella cringed. Joplin laughed.

"Well, little lady," he said. "That's a good suggestion.
That just might help her get what she wants."

And then, inexplicably, he asked me if I'd like to go get
a beer, a question I had not heard in a good many years. It
was not an invitation that anyone at the castle ever extended.
(The royal family considered the beverage too German and
preferred to stick with mixed drinks, although beer was
sometimes discreetly served to foreign guests who expected
it.) During my youth in America, the question was common
enough but was usually not posed to married women. So I
had not been asked out in this way since before I married
Geoffrey. And that was arguably a lifetime ago and felt like
longer still.

So I blushed again and stammered that, well, uh, why
not. (The obvious reasons why not—that I had just told the
man off and called him a scum mucker and, perhaps worse,
"buster"—did not immediately leap to mind.)

Isabella and Rafie were enthusiastic babysitters, though
astonished to have the opportunity.

"A date?" Raphael said. He glanced at me, then Isabella.
"With a *commoner*?"

"I don't know if it's a date, exactly—" I began in a feeble manner.

"Mae is a commoner, *too,* dear," Isabella said, interrupt-
ing in a way that made me bristle, although she was only
stating the obvious and I had not known what I was about
to say anyway.

But Isabella did not approve of the date, either.

"I can't imagine why he asked you out," she said, watching me as I looked through one of her smaller closets for a

suitable jacket to borrow. "He's been taking pictures of my backside for months and never even introduced himself."

"You do have a husband," I said in what I thought was a rather pointed way.

"But this Joplin chap doesn't know that," Isabella said, missing my point. "He thinks my husband is dead."

(If you think this is a rather tacky complaint to make to the person whose husband really was dead, then I share your sentiment. But I didn't let it bother me that night, giddy as I was with excitement.)

I did so enjoy myself with Joplin, though he was easily fifteen years my junior. It reminded me, dare I say it, of that wonderful first interview with Geoffrey, the one that was supposed to be about family-owned businesses but ended up being all flirtatious giggles and sly asides. Joplin and I talked and laughed and gazed into each other's eyes a bit. And the thing was that I never had one moment of awkward explanation or discomfort.

Joplin did not ask me how I knew the princess or why I was visiting or how I came to have a daughter or if I'd ever been married before. No, no, no . . . We talked for hours but without ever asking the most fundamental questions of each other.

We talked about the advances in photographic technology and about how bad tattoos look in pictures. We discussed the perils of poor posture. But he also indulged me in conversations about my own interests, allowing me to go on and on about how inaccurate it was for someone, say the author of my most recent review, to describe chick lit as a "failed genre."

"Failed? Failed?" I said, perhaps feeling a bit tipsy from the beer and figuring that after my speechifying at the park, I couldn't scare him off anyway. "It sold more books than that reviewer ever sold, that's for sure." My Americanisms were slipping back in full force. "How many millions must you sell before you're a successful genre!"

Joplin, who was wearing a snug turtleneck that showed off his strong arms rather nicely, grinned and said I was right and, I do believe, called me "babe" a time or two.

For the rest of that Green Bay visit, I took to smiling in what I fancied to be my most engaging way every time I ventured into public with Isabella, in case Joplin happened by with his camera. I confess with some regret that I would meet his eyes, and the two of us would exchange knowing, snide expressions whenever Isabella did something too, well, royal.

For example, we both smirked when she used a hand-kerchief to flip the handle of a public drinking fountain. I put my hand over my mouth and let my eyes laugh meaningfully when she insisted on clutching her purse in her hand, meaning that she could not carry as many groceries as the commoners in her company—me, for example—who would sling their common purses over their common shoulders like common pack mules.

It was cruel. I probably should have been ashamed. But Isabella was on my turf now. All those times she had exchanged glances with Iphigenia or Rafie or, most important, Geoffrey. I suppose I had never forgotten all those days at the castle when I was the amusing sidekick, the pitiful rube. I said Isabella had become my best friend. I claimed all that was behind us. But when Joplin came along, I jumped at the chance to catch the eyes of a man and share a joke at Isabella's expense. I confess I enjoyed it.

As far as I know, the only words that Isabella and her mythmaker, Joplin, ever exchanged were on the night of my second date with him. He picked me up at Isabella's door. (Rafie was, obviously enough, hiding someplace in the recesses of the "cabin," probably with a game on.) I was just about to formally introduce Joplin to the princess when Isabella interrupted.

"Must you always run my photos next to those of Her

Majesty?" she said somewhat abruptly. She did not specifically mention the hair issue, but I knew she had been fretful about being outdone by Iphigenia. The queen's hair was being quietly styled in those days by the finest Parisian beauticians, who had fled to Bisbania when a shaving craze rocked France and nearly bankrupted them. Meanwhile, Isabella was forced to make do with a salon in the Green Bay Mall called "Tresses for Lesses."

"It's not like I'm related to Genia anymore," said Isabella.

The photographer looked a bit amused. "I don't really control where the photos are placed, Your Highness," he said.

"I suppose you don't," Isabella said, sighing in a dramatic way. "But perhaps you could explain to your editors," she persisted. "It's not like we're sisters. We're only former sisters-in-law, and I'm just a commoner again. You shouldn't even call me 'Your Highness.'"

Joplin said, "I'll pass along your concerns." Then he paused—I'm not sure if it was a pause for effect or if he was merely struggling for a better term and failing—before adding, "Your Highness."

Isabella was clearly frustrated. She looked tired and wished us a good night as Milo clung to her leg, pointing in the direction of the indoor pool and crying out, "Pleasably."

As we walked out to the car, Joplin met my eyes, raised one brow, and winked. It melted my heart. I winked back.

I think that is when my post-Geoffrey life truly began, the moment I exchanged winks with a younger man. Isabella and Rafie wanted me to stay as far from Joplin as possible, and I suppose they were right to want that. But at that moment, for the first time in a long, long time, I did not at all care what Isabella and Rafie wanted.

For all our faults, Isabella and I were civilized, refined, soft-spoken, and modest women. But both of us had in the past few weeks lashed out at this rather vacant and dim photographer. We had attacked him without provocation and with very little point. We had ignored the normal protocols and pleasantries and assumed the worst in this guy who was bringing out the worst in us. And I went on a couple of dates with him and drove Isabella mad with envy.

None of this has much to do with Joplin, though I guess we both liked his lanky schoolboy frame and disarming smile. For reasons that someone with a psych degree would be better capable of exploring, Joplin was just the stand-in, the person on whom Isabella and I projected all our unspoken rivalries, worries, and longings. Really, he—as a person— meant nothing to me.

Although I did not realize that at the time, while I spent the rest of the evening and no small part of the early morning with him. Those few hours were a delight that cannot be reproduced in the telling. He complained about what the cold weather does to his camera equipment and compared the ins and outs of photographing stripes, plaid, or polka dots. It sounds boring, put like that. But anything is interesting if you're interested in it.

Joplin's interest was contagious. It was the most stimulating conversation I'd had in a very long time. Then, in the early morning, he talked mostly about the dimple in my left cheek.

I found that conversation more stimulating still.

When I returned to Isabella's house, I went to look in on sleeping Milo and stared at her sweet face and told myself that I was in no position to take up with a much younger American man, a journalist, no less. And that I really must pull myself together. Sternly, I lectured myself. And as I stroked Milo's hair, I was filled with resolve.

I really think that if things had been different, my resolve would have held. But that became a moot point, so to, uh, speak.

Because the next day, in a twist that is fitting for the soap opera that is my life, Joplin was injured in a motorcycle accident, a horrible wreck that stole what had frankly been his already limited way with words and, as is so often the case with head injuries, much of his memory of the events of the previous few weeks.

He never showed any sign of recognizing me again.

Though when he learned to talk again, his first word was "pleasably," according to the volunteer who handled much of his treatment at the Green Bay Clinic of Speech.

The accident did not at all alter his eye for photography and thus caused only a short pause in his career. He later dedicated one of his best-selling photography books, *Princess in Brown Plaid,* to that hardworking volunteer-speech-therapist aide. "To my friend Ralph," the dedication read. "He has not the degree but the heart of a speech pathologist."

Chapter 27

Perhaps now is the right time to tell you what I really think of my daughter's father, the former prince and the wannabe speech pathologist.

Mothers have been known to have rather complicated feelings about the fathers of their children. So maybe you're not surprised that I remain even now conflicted about the prince.

In those last few months in the castle, as Geoffrey and Isabella were spending more and more time hanging out with the bust of Michelangelo and plotting plane crashes, Rafie and I grew closer, too. We sometimes exchanged looks when Isabella punched Geoffrey's arm in a familiar way or when Geoffrey batted his eyes at the princess.

We exchanged a *lot* of looks, particularly during a protracted discussion about what Geoffrey should be wearing when he was found treading water after the crash. Isabella was thumbing through paramilitary catalogs, giggling and carrying on. "Oh, Geoff, you'd look *fantastic* in this," she said, pointing to a futuristic paratrooper ensemble. "I'm sure the tabs would go completely gaga. They'd be waxing on about your heroic self so much, they'd forget all about poor ol' Rafie and his so-called death."

She turned to Raphael then, offered a breezy smile, and said, "No offense, dear."

Raphael returned the smile weakly, then cleared his throat and argued modestly that Geoffrey and he were supposed to be flying off for a day of fishing, not launching an air invasion of France. "We don't want Geoffrey to seem suspiciously *styled*," he said.

"Hmm," Isabella said. "I suppose not. But it is always important to look nice."

She and Geoffrey eventually settled on a khaki-colored cargo-pant outfit that looked suitably rugged in a completely unsuspicious "royal outing to the lodge" way.

Meanwhile, Raphael and I settled into a comfortable companionship, an unspoken alliance. The prince and I never spoke of our mutual discomfort about our spouses' relationship, but that shared irritation gave us a launching point, I believe. The prince started asking me more and more about my writing, and I asked him about the latest advances in the treatment of pathologies of speech. I came to be rather fond of him in those days. I often felt invisible when I was around Isabella and Geoffrey, but when Rafie would arrive, I felt noticed again. "What do you think, Mae?" he'd ask. Just a simple question like that, just the use of my name, would thrill me. I came to love spending time with the prince.

But since then? I've already told you that I sometimes

wonder if he somehow planned for my husband to die. And I've already admitted that he never took an active interest in his daughter. Oh, sure, he gushed and complimented and gave her expensive toys. But he never helped with a single parenting decision, never even acknowledged aloud to me that he was her father until decades had passed and the work was all done.

Obviously, he is not my hero.

But this may surprise you. The single biggest disappointment I have about Rafie involves neither my husband nor my daughter, at least not directly. When I think of Rafie, I just feel profound sadness for his failed professional ambitions.

Everything we went through—Geoffrey's death, Isabella's sacrifices, Iphigenia's woes—and what became of it all? What did Rafie ever accomplish?

He never became a licensed speech pathologist. He did little more than finish a few University of Phoenix online courses that he registered for under the name Ralph Milopadre. And he never pursued any other legitimate profession.

He reportedly was an outstanding success as a volunteer speech therapist aide, taking on Joplin's case especially, but also excitedly reporting to me his progress with a stuttering boy and a lisping girl. Isabella said she had never seen him so passionate about getting up each morning or so eager to apply himself to a field of study.

"You know the way Geoffrey looked when he was tearing a Bisba apart?" Isabella asked me once. "That cute way he'd squint his eyes? And those little crinkles that would appear on his forehead? When Rafie tries to evaluate the communication skills of an autistic child, he looks *just* like that."

But *Princess in Brown Plaid,* with Joplin's kind dedication, marked the end of Rafie's "career." Isabella announced his decision to me casually by phone, and she claimed to view it as the wise and prudent move of a man in hiding.

"That dedication was a wake-up call," she said. "He can't keep working with the public like that."

Her voice had an edge to it that I wasn't used to. She sounded almost bitter. I think she took this personally. Joplin had ruined her husband's life. I think that's the way she saw it.

I suggested the worst was over, that since Raphael had successfully bluffed his way through a relationship with Joplin, the most likely person on earth to expose the prince to the world, then he had nothing to fear from tongue-tied schoolchildren. I pointed out the possibilities of telecommuting, combined with video-image manipulation. Raphael could work with aphasia patients via the Internet while posing as an old woman. "If it's not possible now, it will be any day," I said.

But Isabella just sighed in a resigned way. "You're always so optimistic, Mae."

After the Joplin fiasco, Rafie whiled away the rest of his life reading journal articles on the anatomy of the tongue and throat and writing scholarly papers that he never submitted for publication. Isabella, who edited those documents with touching care and devotion, said they were impressively researched and astonishingly insightful, uncovering, for example, the role accents play in regional sports rivalries or criticizing the lack of speech defects in the world of children's television. "You know those things are one long celebration of diversity," she said, "but there's not a lisp in sight!" She paused and thought for a moment. "Or, I suppose, in earshot."

Isabella was exceptionally proud of one of Rafie's longer essays, which was entitled "Stammering Toward Bethlehem: The Role of Holiday Pageants in Exacerbating Childhood Speaking Disorders."

"It's perfectly ingenious," Isabella would say. "And it just breaks my heart, the way he slaves over these things, knowing he'll never get the glory he deserves, that the world will never see them. It's so . . ." She struggled for the right word and finally settled on one. "It's so unfair."

My own feelings were less generous. What a waste. That's how it always seemed to me. Writing papers no one reads? Writing papers based on his careful viewing of tele-vised sports, Nickelodeon, and the cable-access reruns of local church Christmas pageants? What a stupid waste. I thought Rafie was cowardly. Or at least selfish.

You see, I had bought into the prince's dream. I had believed on that morning when he and Geoffrey climbed into the royal plane that we were doing something noble and rebellious and somehow right. I remember watching Rafie walk onto the runway, his hair blowing handsomely in the wind, his eyes glorious with excitement. I thought he was on his way to doing great things in speech therapy, that he would help stroke victims and head injury survivors and maybe forever end the mispronunciation of the word "nuclear."

In a more general way, I thought we were striking a blow for everyone everywhere who wanted to put one over on the establishment, who wanted to disappoint their fami-lies, who believed they would be better off if they weren't so well off.

After all that, how could Rafie let himself be so easily intimidated? How could he give up on the actual practice of speech pathology? And how could Isabella feel sorry for him for doing so?

I am a reasonable person. Even then I could see why Joplin's dedication gave Rafie and Isabella a moment of pause. I understood there were risks to seizing Rafie's dream. But I thought it was too late to worry about that. I had lost Geoffrey. I didn't want to hear about risk.

I thought Geoffrey had given up his life for something more than Rafie's ability to write unpublished papers about the English language as experienced through television. The only thing more pathetic than Rafie's "work," I thought, was Isabella's tender defense of it and her delusional belief that her husband was a put-upon victim of circumstance rather than an extraordinarily lucky child of fortune.

I suppose I have said too much. I'll go back later and delete most of this, I'm sure. It wouldn't do at all for Milo to read all those hateful words about her now dearly departed father, even if he never did anything to claim his parentage beyond using her name for online speech pathology courses and in volunteer work that he quickly quit. And insisting that she learn the useless language peculiar to her biological family. To Milo, I always try to preserve a happy story, a simple indication that her father had great potential but world events conspired to hold him back.

That was, I guess, Isabella's take on things. And now that I've had a few decades to sleep on it, I can admit that it's true. Mostly true. Arguably true. Not, at least, completely false.

Now I can look back and see that it was a crazy dream. How could he hide from the world and work in the world at the same time? It seemed possible in theory, when we were all sitting around Michelangelo's bust and drinking exotic cider blends. But I guess I can understand now how impossible it seemed to him when he actually stood at the front door with his book bag of speech therapy texts.

Maybe his reluctance wasn't laziness or sloth. Maybe he was just scared. Maybe he was afraid to venture out in the world as an ordinary man, scared to go to school and be graded, scared to take a job and be judged on his merits, scared even to send off his research to a journal and see what happened, scared to no longer be called "Your Highness." He never had Isabella's bravado. Maybe her early days as a princess had toughened her up. She could sign up for a class in flower arranging and not care if her teacher judged her centerpieces as utterly ordinary. She could teach herself to whittle and not be embarrassed by a few nicks on her hands. After you've been publicly called "Dizzy Izzy," after your nose spray has been documented on the front page of newspapers, you are immune to embarrassment.

But Raphael's ego was not as stout. Maybe he feared he could never live up to the lofty goals that Isabella and I had for him, that his papers would not prove to be perfectly ingenious, and that he wouldn't really help anyone at all. Maybe he was frightened of letting Isabella or me down. Or Geoffrey.

It took me a while to see it that way, to feel sympathy for Rafie. But Isabella felt sorry for Rafie right from the beginning. "Poor Rafie," she'd say. "Poor Rafie." She never noticed me roll my eyes and cringe and bristle at her words. "Poor, poor Rafie," Isabella would say. "All he wanted was to hold my hand when I was giving birth to Milo."

Chapter 28

*H*ad I not mentioned that?

I've gone on and on about His Royal Highness the Prince of Gallagher being Milo's biological father. But it occurs to me now that I did not mention the name of her biological mother. It's not something I like to think about. And I have obviously not been in the habit of discussing it.

Isabella gave birth to Milo while we were at Jeb's camp, and so it was I who was there during the princess's labor, holding her hand and mopping her brow and counting her breaths and telling her when to push. It was a frightening time. It was a long, difficult labor, and there was no doctor at the camp and no way to quickly get to a hospital—not that Isabella would consider going anyway.

"No one can know," she would say, sounding as pathetic as the most pitiful pregnant thirteen-year-old. "No one can know."

When I look back on it now, I get so, so angry with Isabella. How dare she put Milo through all that? How dare she risk so much for so many of us?

But in fairness, I'm glad that she didn't simply fly off to Paris and use the best birthing centers in the world and tell everyone that she was pregnant and thus negate the blow to the royal family that we thought we had delivered. For Raphael and Isabella could not escape royal life while raising the heir to the throne, even if the prince was doing it holed up somewhere with a long beard and sunglasses. As long as Isabella was the known mother to the heir, the family's life would be tied to the ups and downs of the royal calendar, with the flurry of activities around the racing season and the quiet that came only after the last day when parliament met.

Isabella said she did not know she was pregnant when we launched the faked plane crash, and if she had known, she would have called off the whole thing. "Obviously," she would say, although it never was at all obvious to me.

Given that Milo was born six months after the crash and weighed nine pounds at birth, I found it hard to believe that Isabella did not know, though she could be awfully absent-minded at times and easily distracted to boot. The timing of Isabella's pregnancy lines up almost exactly with Secrest's departure on her own maternity leave, a fact that to this day fills me with astonishment and wonder. Could it be that Secrest left no one in charge of the royal birth control pill? And that Isabella, unaccustomed to having to look after herself, never noticed? Is it possible that my daughter was conceived simply because of a lack of efficiency among the castle staff?

I never asked. For one thing, in those days I had trouble getting a word in edgewise with Isabella.

"I don't know what to do," she said to me over and over

again on the night I finally guessed that she was pregnant. Despite the meager rations of the camp, she'd been gaining weight, and I had noticed her hair was looking exceptionally full and healthy (hormones).

I hugged her then and reassured her. And I told her we'd figure something out. But she came to me the next day, sounding more confident than ever.

"You'll raise the baby, Mae," she said. "It's the only option that makes sense. We'll use the camp's baptismal records, such as they are."

(Camp record keeping was, as you might imagine, ridiculously minimalist. Jeb was not big on file cabinets.)

"You'll be listed as the mother," she continued. "No formal adoption will be necessary. Rafie and I will pay the bills, of course. Whatever you need. Money's no object." She paused a moment. "And we'd love to babysit now and then." She looked at her feet modestly and added, "If you'll let us."

She then forced a smile and threw up her hands with what I perceived to be feigned bravado. "Voilà!" she said. "Problem solved."

She wiped her right eye discreetly.

Looking back on it, I realize she never even asked me if I was willing.

Why did Isabella do it?

She wanted to protect the child from the rigors of royal life, she said. And she wanted to live in solitude with Rafie and cut her ties to the royal family, something she couldn't do while raising the heir to the throne. It's one thing to hide Raphael from the world, but a child would need to go to school, to ride roller coasters, to keep playdates. Isabella could hide a husband but not a child.

A sacrifice was in order. And later, during one of the endless discussions in which Isabella explained her decision again and again, she even quoted lyrics from the Springsteen song "Spare Parts," in which an unwed mother hocks an engagement ring to support her child. To me, the song's story line seemed to argue for almost exactly the opposite course of action. But I did not point this out.

It was clear that Isabella's mind was made up. And if she had any second thoughts about it as the pregnancy wore on, I think they were quelled by what happened to Geoffrey. I had lost him, thanks to her and Rafie. After that, how could she offer me this child and then change her mind?

She never said that, but she must have thought it. Maybe that was part of what she was thinking that night at the campfire when she talked about penance, about what she deserved.

Conversely, perhaps she did not really feel like she was giving up that much. You could argue that most royal parents have the sort of relationship that Isabella proposed having with her daughter. They provide financial support and occasional babysitting, and that's about it. Isabella perhaps did not know what she would be losing.

Because if she had really understood the enormity of it, if she had any true understanding of what this decision would mean, I think it would have killed her, torn her little heart apart. There would have been a lot more scenes like the one at the elementary school when she got all weepy and leaned on Iphigenia for support. There would have been a few late-night phone calls wondering how the baby was doing. There would have been some obvious regret.

At least there would have been if it had been me in her shoes. But Isabella and I were always made of different stuff.

I have often thought, over the years, about what sort of mother Isabella would have been. She seems to have excelled at everything she attempted, and why would parenting have been any different?

But it *is* different, isn't it?

Before Milo came along, I resented it when people told me that until I was a parent myself, I could not understand the love of a parent for a child, couldn't imagine, for example, how the loss of a child would hurt a parent. I thought that as a reasonable person, I could imagine. But I was a mother for only a few months when I realized that all along, there had been a dimension of the relationship that I had been missing.

I had understood that children, babies especially, are adorable and sweet and innocent and trusting, and that makes it all the worse when harm comes to them. I understood that you expect them to be your legacy and it hits you hard if they're not.

But what I did not understand was the investment—the emotional, physical, and financial investment—that you put into a child. You spend all that time trying to protect this little person. You pick at diaper rash. You do ridiculous coochy-coo dances. You berate yourself for doing something as irresponsible as letting a coin fall from your pocket onto the floor, where a little one might pick it up and decide to taste it. She gets a nasty bump to the head, and you ride in the ambulance and hold her hand and make deals with God. You put so much of yourself into this project, and then to see it cut short by some idiot drunk driver or some incompetent doctor or some stupid, warmongering politician? It prompts a rage that I confess I could not previously imagine.

Those of you who can imagine that sort of rage may also understand the misgivings I have about what I've done here. I have opened up a new world for my beautiful daughter, but I have also exposed her to so much—to photographers with telephoto lenses, to tabloid journalists with sensational appetites, to power-hungry men, to jealous women.

Isabella knows that better than anyone.

"Being a princess," Isabella once said to me, "is like being a bunny caught in one of those inhumane traps. You might survive, but you'll be a bloody mess."

Isabella knows what awaits Milo. That's the reason that she will be so upset at me for telling this story. It has nothing to do with any of the men in our lives. Her irritation with me will be all about what happened to us two women and the daughter we share. All these decades after Isabella, weepy and miserable and pregnant in the desert sun, cried that no one could know, finally everyone will know.

Over the years, as Isabella worried about keeping Milo secret, I have been preoccupied with what is arguably the exact opposite question. While she fretted about who would find out, I wondered about who had known all along.

Did Rafie know? Did he fake his death knowing that he had a child on the way and knowing that child would either have to be raised in hiding or raised away from him?

I'm not sure.

More interesting still is this question: Did Geoffrey know?

I have already allowed that I sometimes fear my husband's motivations for helping Isabella's husband give up royal life were less than noble. I sometimes wonder if he thought Isabella might lose interest in Rafie in that situation, that she might decide that if she was going to take up with a commoner, then it might as well be the good-looking, mechanically inclined one who isn't in hiding all the time.

But I suppose you realize now, there is more to it than that. I think about the night before the crash, when I saw Isabella and Geoffrey talking on the balcony during the investiture ball. I think about the way he moved his hand along the beading at her waist, about the way they were whispering. I wonder if he knew baby Milo was on the way and if that figured into his plans, explaining his willingness to go along with it all.

Did Isabella convince him that she did not want her child born into a line of succession that seemed to make every member—from Lady Carissa to Prince Raphael—miserable? Or was it a worse version? Did Geoffrey see Isabella's ties to the country, the throne, the family, all growing stronger with the birth of a child, making it harder to eventually walk away? Did he think it was his last chance? Did he think she needed to start down the road of walking away from it all before she had a baby that she wanted to give it all to?

But then what did Geoffrey envision would happen to the baby? Did he think that Isabella would raise the child, consulting Springsteen lyrics when it came time to pick a diaper-rash remedy or to select a preschool? Did Geoffrey, who knew Isabella so well, know that she would do what she did, give the child to me to raise? And did he plan to be at my side when she did it?

That is the daydream that pulled me through difficult, lonely days for all those many difficult, lonely years: the idea that Geoffrey thought he and I would be raising Milo in a mountainside apartment in Bisbania's southern working-class suburbs.

I do not know if that wistful daydream could be related even vaguely to the truth. And you can't know, either. I am self-aware enough to understand that anyone reading this story will not know what to make of it. I suspect that at best you are withholding judgment. You are wondering when the DNA tests will be in. You are certainly skeptical.

So, fine. Order the tests and be done with it. There are few things that any of us can know with certainty. But as I said, I was standing there when Isabella pushed and labored and when Milo first appeared in the world. I know perfectly well that Milo is the biological daughter of the Princess of Gallagher, the most famous and most photographed woman in the world. And that alone ought to be enough to secure her place in upstanding Bisbanian society.

But.

But though I promised myself that I would reveal here only the things that would benefit my daughter, I find that once I've come this far, I can't stop my truth telling. So I will tell you the one thing that has always bothered me a little and that worries me still.

Needless to say, I was not there when Milo was conceived, so I have only Isabella's account of who was
involved. I decided long ago to take her at her word, and so
I have to this day proceeded under the assumption that the
young woman I raised is the natural child of His and Her
Royal Highnesses, the Prince and Princess of Gallagher.

When I look at Milo, I see Isabella's posture, her regal
nose, her fine bones, and her figure, which can tend toward
frumpiness but with attention and diligence can achieve a
womanly grace that the naturally thin can never hope for. I
can imagine that I see the prince, too. I see his handsome
ears. (Fortunately for Milo, they work better with a woman's
longer hairstyles.) I think I see his forehead and hear a bit
of his laugh.

But the prince and princess are both fair- and fine-headed.
And Milo has dark thick curls. Sometimes I wonder if she
could have inherited them from the Lady Carissa, the raven
beauty who would be her great-aunt.

And on other days, I wonder if she could have inherited
them from Geoffrey, who I guess would, in that case, be her
father.

Chapter 29

I remember seeing a television interview with a philosopher once. The reporter was doing a story about troubling custody cases, elaborate, outlandish situations, some involving surrogate mothers giving birth to their own aunts.

"Who, then, are the parents?" asked the reporter in an alarmist tone.

But the philosopher said the answer was simple. The parents are the people who come when the baby cries at night.

No one doubts that, really. I certainly don't, having raised a child I did not birth, having known how the simple acts of cleaning dirty bottoms and holding tiny hands while crossing busy streets serve to completely and utterly tie your heart to a child. In this age of genetic manipulation and experimentation, it is amazing that adoption—the oldest form of genetic trickery—still stands as mysterious and powerful. It shows how human will can erase all of science. Adoption is the act that says, "This child is mine. Biology be damned." And it is so.

I'm the one who put my hand on Milo's small chest a thousand times a night to see if she was still breathing. I'm the one who taught her to ride a bike. It was I who agonized about her relationship with that awful guy she dated in high school. I'm the one she called at three A.M. when she had questions about her own child's colic or fever. For all those reasons, I am Milo's mother.

By that definition, she has no father. Which doesn't seem right. Some would say that she must have a father, but it is only a dad she is missing. And that is a linguistic distinction of some merit. But I think that in Milo's case, she is missing both. The uncertainty I've felt about her parentage has colored, as you might guess, my whole life as a mother.

Once this story is published, genetic tests—undoubtedly supervised by the royal courts—are inevitable. I have played out the whole scene in my head. I assume that Queen Iphigenia will be tested for the royal family's DNA, since Raphael is not available. The doctors will come discreetly to the castle for that.

But neither Milo nor Isabella will be afforded such dignity. Milo will surely be rattled by the extraordinary media presence, the crush of the cameras, the stares of the reporters. But for a moment, at least, they will be treating her gently. Milo will be novel and beautiful and mysterious, and they will marvel that she may be queen. So for that one day, at least, the press will be kind.

But poor Isabella. I can imagine the rude questions that will be shouted at her, the violent way the reporters will push up against her as she is escorted into the hospital.

When I imagine this, I always assume she would wear a brown scarf over her hair and hold her eyes in a downcast manner. "Please," she would say, "please let me through."

It's a horrible image.

But what really unnerves me are the test results themselves.

If those tests find that Isabella lied to me and Geoffrey is the father, it would just kill me. I don't know how I would continue. I can't stand to think about it.

Though it does make a certain kind of sense. I'm sure you've thought of that already, realized that it would explain so much if this whole sordid business could have been born, so to speak, of a need to keep the bastard child of an American car mechanic off the throne.

Wouldn't that explain Raphael and Isabella's reactions? What if Isabella gave Milo to me because she thought it would be wrong to ask Raphael to raise Geoffrey's child? What if Raphael kept such an emotional distance from Milo because he feared, or knew, that she was not really his?

For those reasons, I fear the tests might show Geoffrey is Milo's father.

But if the tests show Geoffrey is *not* the father? If the tests prove that Isabella told me the truth and my daughter is the biological child of Rafie and thus the legitimate heir to the throne? That is my entire reason for telling this story, to give my daughter the opportunity to be queen. But if the tests prove Rafie is her father, that, too, will disappoint me, break my heart in a way that is harder to explain. I do not, of course, want to have been betrayed by my husband. But if Geoffrey was Milo's father—as much as I would have hated what it meant all those years ago—I would rather like what it would mean right now. It would mean that I have raised the child of the man I loved. And there would be an honor in that, a privilege I can't deny. Also, simply enough, I would like to know that a part of him still exists in the world.

So I lived a dual fantasy. I came to accept a version of events in which my husband's fidelity to me never faltered, but in which he was the father of the child whom Isabella birthed. Is that so irrational? If I can be Milo's mother without giving her my genetic material, can't Geoffrey somehow be her father?

One night when Milo was old enough to go out alone, I found myself, for the first time in years, at home by myself. I was so lonely, so awfully lonely and sad. And I did something I have never admitted to anyone and that I'm not proud to admit now. I pulled out a box of Geoffrey's personal effects. I got out his journal. I read it.

It was the strangest body of work I could imagine, beautiful and elegant. Geoffrey's humble vocabulary had sometimes masked for me the complexity of his writing, the beauty of his observations. And here he wrote in a lovely and longing way about the beauty of nature and the simple wonder of a finely tuned engine and the poetic mystery that exists in a well-executed hand of poker. He talked about falling in love with Bisbanian horse racing and about the majesty of the Bisbanian skyline.

During the time he kept this journal, he was advising the world's most famous woman on every aspect of life, from fashion to royal politics. But he mentioned none of it. And he didn't mention me. The entire drama of my life centers on my dear husband, who did not see fit to chronicle any of the pertinent details in the lovely journal that he wrote in diligently each night.

Except for one page, one page that makes my heart clutch. On the night before the plane crash, he wrote only a few lines, lines that I have memorized and seared into my soul.

"Been happier these last few months than I'd ever hoped to be," he wrote. "All going to change tomorrow. Don't know how it will go down. Know this: going to live out my life with the best gal in the world. My dear Belle."

Chapter 30

I've always been a little obsessed about names. I tend to go on and on about the issue, chatting for hours about the way people acquire nicknames and drop middle names and combine surnames. People ultimately do choose for themselves what they're called—I think I've mentioned that before—and the choice they make is almost always significant.

In fact, if I think back to the days in the castle when we were putting the finishing touches on the plot to fake Raphael's death, the debate I remember most clearly was over the question "Ralph or Raul?"

The prince thought it should be his choice, and his choice was Ralph. "I must insist," he said. "It is my name."

But Isabella would have none of that nonsense. "Don't be silly, honey," she said. "No one chooses his own name! Besides, I can't fathom calling you Ralph. It sounds positively American." She paused dramatically and finished with a flourish. "I would gag."

Raphael pointed out that sounding American was rather the point.

Isabella sighed in an overly patient, seemingly bored way. "I know," she said. "But it's supposed to sound like modern America. They don't go for generic names anymore. America is quite cosmopolitan now, even in Green Bay. They like style. They like panache. They like mystery. They like Raul."

"Mystery?" Raphael was incredulous. "Isn't it Spanish? What's so mysterious about Spain? It's like France, only with bad shoes."

Isabella ignored him. "Ralph is the sort of name they would give a cow," she said. (The Bisbanian royal family is not fond of cattle, or any other large, thick mammals.) "I might as well start calling myself Bessie. Or Daisy or, or, or . . . Mabel." She spit out that last one with a disgusted snort. But then she looked at me awkwardly and smiled weakly.

"No offense," she whispered. "The name Mae is quite smart, couldn't be less like Mabel. Like a spring day, Mae is." Her brow furrowed as if that did not sound quite right to her. "Or, you know, a whole spring month." She smiled with satisfaction at that and then made a gesture toward the clear sky. "Simply lovely."

Then she glanced at Raphael in a way that I suspect meant: "Exhibit A."

My interest in names got the better of me then. I could keep silent no longer, though it would seem that Rafie's alias was none of my concern. But I had a sister named Elsie, and I'd seen her put up with cow jokes her whole life. This was a pet cause with me.

"Cows aren't really named things like that, you know," I said.

The prince and princess both turned to look at me.

"It's all propaganda from the butter companies," I continued, sounding more authoritative than I felt.

Isabella rolled her eyes and looked off into the distance.

"Cows are named things like Heifer 527, and most bulls aren't named anything at all. It's straight to the butcher block for them."

Isabella cleared her throat and looked at her nails. She wasn't accustomed to commoners talking about butcher blocks. Or arguing with her.

"And besides," I said, "those sorts of wholesome, old-fashioned 'gal' names—'British barmaid names,' they called them—were all the rage for fashionable parents back when we were born."

I wished I hadn't volunteered the British part. Or the bit about barmaids. But it was a trend, dammit. Isabella ought to be able to understand that. I kept blabbering.

"At least hip parents, parents who studied trends and read books like *Beyond Jennifer and Jason*." I feared I was sounding a bit defensive. "It's only in Bisbania's royal circles that people think they have to give their daughters ultra-feminine names with an 'a' at the end."

Isabella stared at me and crossed her arms. She tossed out the next question the way the king's attorney might cross-examine a witness. "What is your sister's name?"

I sat up straight and said the name with as much pride as I could muster.

Isabella nodded in a matter-of-fact way. "And didn't your mother grow up on a dairy farm in Appalachia?"

Now it was my turn to roll my eyes. Tiny Bisbania would fit a hundred times into the distance that separates western Kentucky from Appalachia, but pointing that out would get me nowhere. Isabella thought there was a world of difference between South Main Street and North Main Street, but was skeptical that there could be any difference at all in opposite ends of a long American state.

Frankly, from her perspective, there probably isn't.

Raphael interrupted at this point and steered, so to speak, the conversation back to Isabella and the possibility of being named Mabel. "You can call yourself 'Mrs. O'Leary's bovine,' for all I care," he said. He was exercising a bit more backbone now that Isabella had agreed to his royal escape plan. "I like Ralph, and Ralph it shall be."

But Isabella convinced him—how, I can't imagine—to first seek Geoffrey's advice. "We don't have to take his advice," she told Rafie. "It won't hurt to ask."

It did hurt her case, as it turned out. Her trusted adviser surprised and irritated her by siding with Raphael and going with Ralph.

And yes, I did notice that my husband chose a name for the prince that Isabella said she could not use without gagging.

Still, I had to agree that it was the correct thing to do. Raphael was absolutely right about names. People ought to be able to choose what they are called. Of all the awful things uttered about Isabella over the years, the most unfor-givable, I now believe, was the tabloid insistence on using Izzy, even knowing she despised it.

But no matter how right Geoffrey's advice was, it still seemed strange, coming from him. He was notorious for bestowing nicknames, never asking permission, for exam-ple, before starting to call some nice young woman who showed up in his garage Belle.

Although perhaps this habit of nicknaming was just an unthinking reflex that did not reflect his actual name philos-ophy. After all, he had chosen to change the spelling of his first name and to take his wife's name in marriage. He had some appreciation for the power of deciding for yourself how you will be addressed.

So he sided with Ralph. And I was happy for the prince. I agree with Isabella that it was not exactly the most regal of names. It sounded to me like the name of a slightly over-weight, suburban minivan driver. But I admired the prince for being able to see something solid and decent and true in it. And you know, there is nothing wrong with slightly over-weight, suburban minivan drivers. In fact, they are often quite easy to talk to.

Once I called for Isabella, and "Ralph" answered the phone. He said she was throwing pottery at the time and couldn't talk, so he and I started chatting, and we talked for several hours. It was one of those lovely long conversations you have, carrying the phone about your apartment, watering plants, feeding the cat, painting your nails. I almost forgot that I'd never forgiven him for giving up on speech therapy. And I tried to remember if he had been such a fine conversation-alist when his name was Raphael.

At one point, he mentioned Lady Carissa—Aunt Carrie, he called her—and he talked about how spectacularly fond of her he had always been. I agreed that she was an impres-sive woman.

"I always wondered why she didn't marry that count," I said. "It bothered my friends and me. We couldn't imagine what all the controversy was about."

The prince seemed surprised that I didn't know. "We never told you?" he said. "I suppose we should have. You're practically family, having raised Milo and all."

Then he told me the whole sordid story, the entire pathetic tale, the complete embarrassing saga. I must say it explained a lot, more than I could have imagined. I was so utterly glad that I had asked.

I guess it was an icebreaker of sorts for us. I had been declared practically family, and Rafie opened up to me in a way he never had before. He lowered his voice a little and told me he had been sick lately. He said he was sure he'd be okay, but it had made him look back over his life, and he realized the regrets he had were all about me, about the sacrifice I had made and about the child I had raised. "I also still wish I'd put money on the eighty-to-one long shot that won the Ascot ten years ago," he said. "But never mind that."

He said he wanted me to know that it hadn't been for nothing, that he had lived a life of happiness few people could imagine. "You know Isabella as well as anyone," he said. "You know that she can be vain and headstrong and impossibly dim and unimaginably exasperating. You can imagine what she was like to live with during that pony-print fad."

I chuckled.

"But I've been so happy these past few years," Rafie said. "Snowed in with my princess, frying cheese curds and arguing over whether we put enough garlic in the pasta sauce."

There was a long silence. I didn't know what to say.

Finally, Rafie spoke again. "And spaghetti really is as good as they say."

We both laughed then.

He whispered, "Thank you."

And that was all he said.

Oh, all right. He said one more thing. He hinted at that which I was not going to go into. But I suppose I must.

He said there was something that had always bothered him about Geoffrey, and he said he would like to know the answer before he died. And he was asking the right person, because I knew Geoffrey so well and because I understand that names are almost always significant.

"Why," he asked, "did Geoffrey call you by the same name he used for my wife? Why did he call you both Belle?"

Chapter
31

$\mathscr{I}$ think I've set the story straight now. My husband wasn't a royal mechanic, he was a royal adviser. I wasn't just a mechanic's wife but the secret author of modestly successful lowbrow novels. Isabella was not an effortless icon but a highly managed product of my husband and me. Or mostly my husband. The prince did not really die, at least not when everyone thought he did. And I didn't give birth to the daughter I raised, a girl who was conceived as the legitimate heir to the throne. At least that is what I was told and what I choose to believe on most days.

I choose to believe that she is the biological child of Isabella and Raphael, even though the princess spent way too much time with my husband and even though she allowed him to run his hand along her pregnant waist in a familiar way on what turned out to be the last night of his life. I believe this even though he wrote in his journal about planning to live out his days with Belle. I was able to maintain this belief because my husband called me Belle also, an oddity that completely mystified Raphael and that I understood only in part and don't really like to talk about.

That's pretty much it. Except for Lady Carissa's secret, the one she confessed on the night before her wedding and that Raphael shared with me because I was raising his daughter. It is the final piece of the puzzle, and it explains everything. Almost everything, at least.

Undoubtedly, if Rafie had become king, the truth about Lady Carissa would have been revealed long ago. Despite his many flaws, he was a progressive, fair-minded sort. But she died, as you know, while he was still a prince. Looking back, I wonder if her burial marked the death of all Rafie's kingly ambitions, because the outing of Lady Carissa's disability was the one act he would have relished as king.

Compared to faked deaths and hidden births, this secret is not all that shocking in most circles. But in the particular culture of the Bisbania court, which still conducted all official business in that throaty and consonant-heavy native language of Bisbania, Lady Carissa's secret was too awful to imagine.

The count would not dare risk passing it along to his off-spring, and the queen, Lady Carissa's much older sister, feared it would have prevented her own marriage if the king or his family had learned about it sooner.

But Regina had already married the future king when Lady Carissa began to learn the native language of Bisbania and her tutors discovered what Raphael described as a "lack of fluidity in her speech." I had to consult speech pathology textbooks to find the lay term, and here it is: She stuttered.

Not in English, which she spoke in a lyrical, flawless,

public-radio kind of lilt. But in the ugly, challenging native language of her home country, she could not smoothly say, despite months of desperate practice, even the few words she would have needed to utter aloud at her wedding.

The night before the ceremony, she told her fiancé, with whom she had always spoken English. She had hoped, surely, that the count would strike a blow for progress and insist the wedding be conducted in English. Instead, he broke off the engagement altogether. Which, as I think I noted before, forced embarrassing explanations to five kings and four queens. Or was it the other way around? I can't really remember. It has been such a long time ago.

Little Rafie was so horrified by this story that he vowed to dedicate himself to the study of speech handicaps, a vow that would have—if things had been just a little different— led to a satisfying and successful career.

So that was Lady Carissa's secret. And now I suppose you want to know mine.

Rafie died without knowing. I ended our phone call without answering him. That was my punishment, I suppose. It was the judgment I delivered to him for surviving a plane crash that killed the man I loved. And for, in my mind, wasting the opportunity that death gave him.

But though I like to think of myself as not answering him out of spite, the truth is that I *couldn't* answer him. I did not really know myself why Geoffrey used the same nickname for Isabella and me.

This oddity, this shared nickname, was the one thing that I clung to, the only thing that got me through the journal entry that I found when I shamefully searched through Geoffrey's personal effects. "My dear Belle." He could have meant me. Must have meant me. Surely meant me. That is what I told myself.

But the entire time we lived in the castle, I did not ask Geoffrey why he would choose the same nickname for the two women he spent the most time with. I suppose I was afraid to.

Geoffrey was a man of mystery. I don't think any of us ever understood him, and I can't begin to guess his rationale. Did he call us by the same name because he saw something similar in both of us? Was it a grand and meaningful gesture? Or if it was just a simple, unimaginative, lazy shortening of our names? I guess that is *the* question about Geoffrey. Did the things he said mean anything? Or were we all just reading too much into them? The only difference is that this involves the very fabric of my heart, not the lyrics of "Pink Cadillac."

Oh, and did you catch that? Did you see what I slipped into that last paragraph? You may not realize it, but I've now told you my darkest secret. This is the secret that Ethel Bald knew. She did not know that Raphael was still alive. She did not know that Geoffrey was trying to help him fake his death. She did not know Milo is the heir apparent to the throne. How could she?

She was just a reporter, remember. She did not know the secrets of people's hearts. She knew only the things that she overheard in bathrooms and noticed while scooping up caviar and found by searching public records.

After our encounter in the bathroom that day—the day she got the Green Bay scoop—she worried about the quizzical, suspicious way I had looked at her. She searched immigration records first and then looked into houses bought and cars leased. So by the time I called to tell her that I knew her secret, she already knew mine. It may not seem that shocking in most circles. But it would have destroyed me in the eyes of my snobby Bisbanian friends, the sort of people who dislike cows and believe all girls should have dainty names that end in "a."

"A lazy shortening of our names." That is the line that perhaps you caught.

I don't know why, in a psychological sense, Geoffrey would call me by a nickname that he had previously used for another woman. But I do know in a technical sense why he gave me the nickname Belle.

He called me that because, on the day of my birth, when the nurse asked my parents what I would be called, they recycled a moniker previously given a favorite milk cow. It was not Mae, the name Isabella reluctantly likened to a spring day.

No. The name on my birth certificate is Mabel.

$\mathcal{E}$pilogue

$\mathcal{I}$ suppose you remember the funeral of Isabella's father, the Earl of Cordage. It made quite a splash at the time, marking as it did Isabella's first trip back to Bisbania after accepting the seldom-awarded Nobel Prize of Speech Pathology.

"I hadn't even realized there was a Nobel Prize of Speech Pathology," Ethelbald Candeloro wrote, still gushing as much as ever despite being positively ancient. "But if I had, I would have predicted long ago that Isabella would win it."

Isabella felt terrible about the prize, of course. She had submitted her husband's work to several medical journals as a tribute to him shortly after his death. The real death, I mean. She had always been so proud of what she called

"Rafie's little papers," and she thought the journal editors would be interested. (I think it also assuaged her guilt for having redecorated shortly after Rafie's death, covering forty rooms of green and gold with soothing and tasteful pastels. "It's as if I'm painting right over his memory," she had said in a melancholy way. "But it *does* look so much better.")

The journal editors were indeed interested in the articles, to which Isabella had signed her own name. She had little choice about that, because the work had clearly been done years after the world thought her husband died.

Once published, the articles became the talk of speech pathologists everywhere, and the next thing you knew, she was accepting all sorts of awards, modestly crediting her late husband as her inspiration and creating a mini-sensation by suggesting that singing Springsteen's rat-a-tat early lyrics could be soothing to those suffering from pathologies of oral communication. "There is hardly a situation in life," she said, "that can't be improved by 'The E Street Shuffle.'" No one questioned that Isabella wrote the articles. After all, why couldn't she fit in a little speech pathology training between her Thai classes and welding work?

Isabella called me several times during the Nobel Prize–nomination process, crying from mortification and guilt. But I just laughed and told her to rest easy. I could not think of a more fitting end to the entire ridiculous saga.

At any rate, the Nobel publicity had only just begun to abate when Isabella's father died. She returned to Bisbania for the funeral, wearing an elegant suit of such deep brown that you would swear it was black. (The press called it "brackish.")

Isabella's nephew, the son of Lady Fiona and the heir to his grandfather's minor title, gave a lovely eulogy. He called his grandfather a descendant of heroes and the father of legends.

Isabella had cried at that. And so did Lady Fiona, though I suspect for different reasons entirely.

They had never been close, that family. So few noble families are. Fiona and Isabella palled around enough when they were young, but I suspect Isabella never shared a single secret with the lady—didn't admit that she befriended a mechanic, much less nursed a crush and shared a kiss. And by the time she was off faking deaths and giving away babies, they barely talked at all.

Isabella's mother was a cold, standoffish woman, a commoner who somehow thought that she had married beneath herself by wedding an earl and who thought Isabella had married further down the tree still.

Sometimes when I think about that, I suspect that Isabella's family life explains what she needed from Geoffrey. Maybe he was the brother she never had.

After Fiona's son spoke, Fiona sang a slow and haunting song, and then Isabella slowly walked up to the front of the mourners and said, "I don't know about being the father to legends. But he was a good father to me."

Then she sat back down.

I don't think it was true, judging by how little she spoke of him, how rarely she visited, how infrequently she called. But it was the absolutely right thing to say. I saw Secrest, seated in a back row with her husband and son, nod approvingly.

That was the moment featured on all the websites the next day, and it made people all over the country cry. A lot of people called their parents that night.

This is why we need princesses, you know. We need to know that other people suffer, though they have more money than we do and more servants. We need to see them at funerals, and we need to hear about their divorces. If they gain weight along the way, so much the better.

We need to watch them bear sadness and get their hearts broken, and we need them to dress well while they do it. We need them to always pick the right words.

We need to be able to salute their style.

People might argue about the definitive photo of Isabella. She looked radiant after her wedding, of course, and that is a logical choice. But some argue for the eerie photos of her standing on the stormy beach in those cropped pants. Others remember her shoveling snow or working in the forge. A few mean souls are sure to nominate the "thar she blows" photo. Fair enough. I suppose it is, in its own way, as good a candidate as any.

But I remember one photo that most people paid little attention to. It is a photo from Isabella's father's funeral. She is standing with all her usual poise and polish, and there is a line of mourners waiting to offer condolences. The line is beautiful. All those lovely faces, Bisbanians of all races and classes and ages. And in the front of the line is a slim, raven-haired woman with a regal nose and a snug but conservative black dress.

There is a single tear running down Isabella's face, and Milo is wiping it away.

Why is Isabella crying? That is what I ask myself when I look at that photo. Is she crying for the father she has just lost? Or for the daughter she lost all those years ago?

Dear Milo, when I began writing this book, I told myself that it was the best story I knew, and thus I needed to write it down. I thought it would make a little money, and I hoped it would make Frederick proud. But as I wrote, I realized that I was also settling some old scores. Isabella and Raphael bought my silence over the years, in various ways and at various prices. They gave my husband a job. They gave his death a "purpose." They gave me a baby. I always accepted the deal. But after all this time, it felt good, I confess now, to say to myself, "Actually, I think I'm going to talk."

They would be at my mercy for a change.

It did not take long to see that my actual purpose was, surprisingly, more noble than that. My true motivation was, it turns out, the only legitimate motivation. And it is you, Milo. You should know everything. Take this book and do with it what you will. Do you want to be queen? Then take the DNA test, ship this book to Frederick, and start working on your posture. (You're not a kid anymore, and the crown is heavy—in more ways than one.)

If you are happy with the life you have, then hide this away, save it for your son, and give it to him when you think the time is right. Let him decide if he wants to rule.

I know you the way only a mother knows a child, but I'm not sure what you will decide. Such an agonizing choice for my little girl. I am sorry that I can't make it for you, and yet so glad that it is not mine to make.

In the beginning, I observed that a woman of Isabella's generation, raised in the time that she was raised, could not walk away from an invitation to be queen. A generation later, the question is: Can a woman now?

About the Author

*D*espite fifteen years as a serious journalist, mostly at *The Courier-Journal* (Louisville, Kentucky), and despite a long-standing attempt to pass myself off as an informed citizen, my bookshelves sag with royal biographies. Not those ponderous, important ones about historically significant world leaders. No, no. I prefer the ones that go on and on about the beauty regimens, parenting styles, and in-law battles of people with no actual power—especially a certain ill-fated (but always well-dressed) British princess.

My secret desire was to write such a royal biography, a book that would explain how the mood of a nation, an era, a planet can turn on something as simple as the dietary practices of a young lady who marries "well."

But living in Louisville, I could hardly scare up a suitable princess to share my daily tea, much less one who would choose me as her confidante. So I did the only sensible thing a frustrated royal biographer could do: I made it all up.

I am delighted to say that my make-believe princess loves Bruce Springsteen as much as I do and shares my fondness for lunching with friends and hanging out at the horse track. I did, however, marry better than she did. (My heir, by the way, occasionally humors me with *pretend* tea parties, but only if I promise to discuss Sesame Street characters and types of construction equipment.)

For more information about my teatime habits (and Princess Izzy), please go to www.beverlybartlett.com.

Beverly Bartlett

Beverly Bartlett's Top Five Favorite Bruce Springsteen Songs

- ♥ "Thunder Road"
- ♥ "Land of Hope and Dreams"
- ♥ "If I Should Fall Behind"
- ♥ "Badlands"
- ♥ "Highway 29"